# The Winter Hexagon

## A Novel

Julie Sampson

BookLocker

Trenton, Georgia

# Dedication

In memory of George Sampson —

*"Try writing a steamy novel instead of sports books…"* he *suggested, from the gazebo, more than once.*

"I yelp astronomy like a sun-dog, and paw the constellations like Ursa Major."

— Mark Twain

# Chapter One — Gemini

It all started as I stood on the garden balcony, observing the Boston Harbor skyline, hazy with June humidity. I downed my cold brew coffee — the clink-clink-clink of ice cubes rattled a harsh reminder of the prior night's vodka-tonic overindulgence. Below, chalky dust drifted up from the construction work in the street. The jackhammers pounded in concert with my throbbing temples. I studied the boss lady — an asphalt cowgirl wearing a yellow cowboy-style hardhat. The wide brim shielded her face from the sun's intensity. She marched her steel-toed boots toward two slackers gawking into the hole in the road.

"Chop! Chop!" she hollered, commanding the slackers to pick up their shovels and get back to work.

American flags hung motionless from each building in observance of Flag Day. The construction crew labored in the street, excavating a sinkhole the size of a moon crater. A relentless din of equipment and trucks rumbled up and down the block. Workers in hardhats and yellow vests used long-handled rakes to level the steaming gravel of fresh asphalt. The smell of smoky kerosene overpowered the humidity.

Pedestrians calculated the best direction to avoid the *Men at Work,* according to the orange sign. Shouldn't it be *people at work*? I took a closer look at the asphalt cowgirl corralling the crew to move further up the block. The forty-gallon hat — give or take a few gallons — made her head appear orangutan-oversized atop her broad shoulders and Popeye forearms. She whistled for the rake crew to ride up the block in one of the empty dump trucks. A crewmate offered his gloved hand to pull her up. She cracked a comment, making him laugh. The crew shifted to make room for her.

On the liftgate, a man stuffed his work gloves into his back pocket and leaned against his rake. He wiped a red bandanna across his face, chatting with the man next to him. The workers watched the approaching steamroller that smoothed over the street they'd just patched. I caught a glimpse of yellow-gloved hands — the size of catcher's mitts — appearing from the back of the truck. The hands pushed the shoulders of the man with the bandanna. For a second, I thought the guys were joking around, but the gloved hands shoved the worker so hard his sunglasses jolted from his face. The rake sprung from under his arm, throwing him off balance. He grabbed the side of the truck, but slipped from the chrome trim. The guy next to him lunged for his arm, but it was too late, he went airborne. His hard hat flew from his head as his body dropped into the street.

"Stop!" shouted the man.

The fallen worker face-planted into the black tar, shrieking as his bare hands hit the steaming black aggregate. Workers on the truck yelled, signaling with their rakes at the lumbering drum roller whose operator, in the cab at the rear, was looking backward. The scalded worker frantically attempted to crawl commando style toward the sidewalk. His screaming wails were hideous. Two men jumped from the sidewalk, grabbed his hands, and dragged his dead weight toward the curb. His hips barely cleared the curbside before his legs were steamrolled. The man emitted sounds that humans aren't designed to make — part coyote yip-howl, part screeching bobcat.

The steamroller halted right before the rear roller hit him. Several workers rushed toward the injured man. He was in shock, trembling on the sidewalk. His legs were reduced to flattened blood-stained denim. His mangled work boots looked like squashed recycled soda cans with bloody shoelaces.

The oblivious operator of the double-drum roller stopped and shouted out the window, "What the hell's going on?"

The asphalt cowgirl radioed for medical help. The crew on the truck scattered toward the sidewalk. Within a minute, in the distance, sirens were heard as emergency vehicles penetrated the city traffic.

I couldn't ignore what I had just witnessed. This was no accident. The guy was shoved off the truck. My innate investigative nature kicked into gear. I grabbed my press pass for interning at the *Patriot Lodestar* and raced from my apartment out to the ruckus in the street. I saw that one man bunched up his sweaty shirt to pillow under the victim's head, then knelt beside him to hold his scalded hand.

"We're getting help. Hang in there, Chuck."

Two police cruisers arrived seconds ahead of the ambulance. The EMTs assessed the injuries and loaded him onto a stretcher. The cops pushed back the crowd of horrified onlookers. I should have stepped back with the crowd, disappeared into the day and offered up a prayer for the accident victim. But I didn't. It felt as if I'd stepped in wads of bubblegum gluing my flipflops to the sidewalk. My head told me to leave, but my heart said stay, be a responsible reporter.

"Let's go. Move back," said a police officer.

I flashed the laminated press pass attached to a lanyard that I'd draped around my neck. I told the cop, "I'm a reporter." He looked me up and down, assessed my shorts, flipflops and Martha's Vineyard t-shirt.

"I get it, First Amendment rights, but this seems a bit opportunistic if you ask me," the cop growled.

"It's breaking news. That's what reporters do."

"Fine," the cop said. "Just stay out of the way."

I jotted down all the details of what I had witnessed from my balcony. I approached the shocked crew who mumbled amongst themselves.

"Any idea how he fell off the truck?" I asked.

They shrugged and remained silent. The asphalt cowgirl side-eyed me and asked, "And who are you?"

"Paige Moore. I'm a reporter with the *Patriot Lodestar*. Do you know what happened?"

"This is what you call a classic accident. That's what happened, an unfortunate construction-site accident."

She adjusted her hat and stared down at me. She was a few inches taller than me, but the hat pushed her into the six-foot range. Her straight brown hair was tucked behind her ears, revealing a football shaped raised mole on her right jawline.

"Did he slip? Was there a bump in the road and he lost his balance? Something of that nature?"

"Yeah, put that. There was a bump in the road and he lost his balance," she said, tapping her finger on my notepad.

Another worker stepped forward. "What's this about?"

The asphalt cowgirl said, "She's with the *Lodestar* —"

"There's no story here. He needs privacy, not headlines."

The patch on his work shirt said *McGregor*, so I asked him his first name.

"It's Jake. Why?"

"I need your full name in case I quote you in the article. And yours?" I glanced up at the asphalt cowgirl. There was no name on her shirt.

"You don't need my name cuz I said nothin' quotable."

McGregor returned to the crew. I noticed yellow work gloves tucked in the back pocket of his jeans. I scanned the other workers, they'd all removed their gloves — standard issue with matching hard hats and vests.

"Hold up a minute. Can you tell me the accident victim's name?"

McGregor sighed. "Charles McKim da fourth. Goes by Chuck. Not that you need his name because there's no story here. Look, we're all upset about this —"

"How long have you worked with Chuck?"

"Long time. We've been with the Public Works Department for twenty years."

"Are you friends outside of work?"

"Work is work. Chuck shows up on time, gives an honest day's effort. Reliable."

I flipped to a fresh page. "How old is he? Wife and kids?"

"He's my age, late forties. No wife, no kids. Smart man, if you ask me."

"It's a shame what happened to him," I said, glancing at the stretcher. The EMTs must have medicated him because he momentarily ceased his wailing moans. I moved closer to the ambulance to take one last look before they loaded him into the ambulance. His eyes stared into blank space. His lips quivered as if he were freezing. The bridge of his nose and cheeks were scalded and raw. He turned his head and squinted at my press pass. He stared straight at me as if nothing was wrong and he wanted to invite me out for a beer.

"Come closer," he whispered.

I put my face closer to his.

He mumbled, "You're *Lodestar*?"

I nodded.

"I trust the *Lodestar*. It was Bauhaus. They stole the key to the Winter Hexagon Salon."

"The what?"

"Step aside," said the EMT. They hoisted him inside the ambulance and slammed the doors, so I wrote down his gibberish — probably the last words the poor guy would ever speak.

I pulled out my phone and googled the Winter Hexagon Salon. The only thing that came up were other local hair salons and spas. Then I googled Bauhaus: Brutalist architecture, arts and crafts movement, Walter Gropius design school.

"What did he say?" asked McGregor, who appeared alongside the ambulance with the asphalt cowgirl. He narrowed his eyes on my notepad.

I stepped back. "Gibberish."

"He's been talkin' a ton of nonsense lately —"

"Really? What's he been saying?"

"Early dementia, probably. Asphalt fumes can do that to a guy. I'm sure he's in shock. Did he say anything else?"

"No, why?"

"Just curious," said McGregor. He and the asphalt cowgirl stared back at me until I shoved my notebook in my bag and left the scene. My stomach roiled — stinking hangover — or was I nauseated about what I'd witnessed?

I headed back to my apartment to change my sweaty t-shirt and wash my face. My clothes smelled like asphalt. Inside, a blast of cold air remedied my pounding forehead. I glanced around my apartment: flipflops tossed by the door, half-used sunscreen bottles cluttered the bathroom vanity, empty cans of High Noon overflowed the recycling bin. I figured I should attempt to tidy up for the cleaning lady, so I bundled up the kitchen trash and headed for the garbage shoot.

I was a rising college sophomore, with only two basic responsibilities: one, my internship at the *Patriot Lodestar*, and two, helping Tanya Goforth set up her new coffee shop in Quincy Market. Aside from that, I read *Rolling Stone* online by the rooftop pool most afternoons and met friends in the evenings for concerts and parties.

The glass atria at the newspaper headquarters looked like a fishbowl anchored with a curved receptionist area. A security guard leaned against the wall near a bank of gold elevators. He eyeballed me when I scanned my pass to go up to the newsroom. I wasn't planning on staying long at the office which is why I looked like I rolled off the beach, even though I'd freshened up with a Polo shirt. I was just an intern, a few notches below the editorial assistants and freelance writers, but I was supposed to look professional. I wasn't expected to cover news-breaking events, but I figured reporting on a scoop like what I saw was a smart move considering the internship perks.

I typed in my notes at an empty work station in the back of the congested newsroom. I recalled what the accident victim told me. Pilar Kuhlkoat, the managing editor of the city desk, was known as a crotchety grammarian, slashing hard copy with a red pen like a ninja. Reporters allegedly feared her rants about dangling gerunds, word-choice blunders, and awkward sentence structure. They all cowered behind their computer screens as she summoned reporters to her office.

When the office assistant showed me around on my first day, she mentioned, "You're just an intern, so you should be safe. She intentionally leaves her door open so the verbal thrashings are heard by the entire staff. Take notes on what triggers Hot Throat — that's her nickname around the newsroom."

I was tempted to put on my noise-cancelling ear buds to block the phone conversations and newsroom chatter, but I didn't want to look like an obnoxious Millennial.

A balding middle-aged man occupied the desk across from me. "New hire?"

"Intern," I said.

He kept his eyes on his screen. "What's Hot Throat got you working on?"

I hesitated to answer. There's a long backstory to how I got the internship. I also didn't want anyone to know that I was closely connected to Pilar Kuhlkoat — so connected that I was living in her luxury apartment free for the summer. Last year, as a reward for certain actions, I was promoted into the ranks of the greater Boston Ancient Order of Druids (AOD for short) and Pilar became my AOD mentor, training me in druid rituals.

"Horoscopes," I told him.

He guffawed. "Hey, Eddie, get a load of this."

Eddie sauntered over. "What's up?"

"Hot Throat brought in a new intern for horoscope duty."

"Nothing but the facts," chuckled Eddie. "I thought we took that nonsense off the wire service."

I felt my face burning. "It's one of my interests."

"I'd love to write about what I'm interested in," said the middle-aged man.

"What? Porn?" Eddie cracked up at his own joke. "Good luck with Hot Throat. She scares off most of the interns in the first week."

I said, "Horoscope columns entertain people and spark conversation. You might like it."

"Whatever kiddo. I'm Fred. Go to Eddie if you have any questions. Just one piece of advice: don't get all teary-eyed when Hot Throat rips you a new one. She gets even meaner when she smells blood. You need a thick skin around this newsroom."

"Got it," I said. "Thanks for the advice."

I overheard Hot Throat command a reporter to call the mayor's office for a statement. Hot Throat was barely five-feet tall, and looked shorter by the extra thirty pounds she carried around her hips. She waddled to the Keurig machine and popped a fistful of trail mix into her mouth while she waited for her coffee. Keyboards clattered with a renewed urgency, sounding like heels smacking against marble flooring.

Fred called across the newsroom to her. "I'm waiting for a few call backs to get more quotes. I'll forward the bullet points for what I have so far."

"Get crackin', it's the top story," she said, softening her tone when she saw me. "Paige, would you like some coffee? Come join me in my office."

Fred muttered, "Beware. She starts out nice. Then she bites."

Some of the staff watched me as I approached Hot Throat's domain. On the large wall behind her desk was a collage of framed black-and-white photographs shot by *Lodestar* photographers throughout the years. I eyed the photos of old-time cars parked on Boston streets and the bell-bottomed protesters carrying protest signs of their times.

"Shut the door. Take a seat," she said, chugging her coffee.

I angled the chair in front of her desk as she rolled her desk chair around to join me. I noticed editors and reporters sneaking glimpses into her office.

"The hard deadline is Thursday. Please email your horoscope column to me in advance so I can review it before the copy editors pick it apart. Watch your word count, don't run over or it will get slashed."

"No problem," I said.

"All things considered, I certainly didn't think it would be a problem," she said glancing over her reading glasses. "What's happening in Aries these days?"

I reflected for a moment. "The waning crescent phase of the moon invites deep catharsis and release. The moon is moving into Pisces for a few days, so this is the perfect time to let go of any resentment and control issues. The best way to release is through music and movement, so wear your headphones and take long walks."

She laughed. "*Touché*! I need to let go of my resentment toward my mother-in-law. We're both trying to control my son's birthday celebration and it's like the clash of the Titans. I'll take your advice. My poor husband is stuck in the middle of all the bickering. My husband's a Pisces. What do you have for him?"

"Pisces? A personal goal will be unlocked this week for him. If he has been trying to do a headstand-to-crow balance pose in yoga, for example, then he will unlock that goal. I think a personal accomplishment will connect for him. Also, it's a big family week, so personal time is crucial. He should carve out a sanctuary for himself."

She rolled back behind her desk and jotted a note to herself. "You just gave me an idea to make up for all the stress I've dumped on him lately: yoga sessions at the new studio in town."

Fred appeared by her door and she waved him in. "I just heard about a construction accident near the seaport. One of the workers got crushed by a steamroller. Should I pursue it?"

She nodded. "Get on it. Let me know as soon as you have more details."

I interjected, "I was there. I saw the whole thing."

"Seriously?" asked Fred. "What'd you see?"

"First of all, it was blindingly sunny —"

"Blindingly? I didn't ask for adverbs and a weather report," snapped Fred.

"A man in his late forties fell off the back of an asphalt truck onto steaming black aggregate. He started screaming from the burns, then he tried crawling out of the way of the oncoming steamroller. Some of the workers tried to pull him to the sidewalk, but the front roller crushed his legs before the machine came to a halt. It was gruesome."

"Jeepers Creepers! D.O.A.?" asked Hot Throat.

"Undergoing surgery now," said Fred.

I interjected, "He's been on the job twenty years. A seasoned worker. Reliable, according to one of the men I interviewed."

"You interviewed someone?" Hot Throat's eyes popped.

"I figured while I was there, I should try to get some details. Plus, it didn't look like an accident to me. The way he fell, it seemed like someone pushed him from behind. Anyway, I wrote up my notes."

"Wait. He was shoved?" asked Fred. "Did anyone verify this?"

"Well, no. Not exactly. But that's the way it looked to me. I'm not positive. Like I said, the sun was in my eyes."

I didn't want to make accusations, but I had a strong feeling he was shoved. My instincts told me to trust my gut, always.

Fred pressed, "Did anyone in the crowd see him get pushed?"

"I didn't talk to anyone in the crowd."

"Always talk to the spectators. Always get names," he said.

"Understood."

Hot Throat stood behind her desk. "Did you ask anyone at the scene if they saw what happened?"

"One of his co-workers said they hit a bump in the road and he fell off the back of the truck."

"To begin with, why was he on the back of the truck? It doesn't sound safe," she said.

"It was hot and it seemed like a quicker way to get up the street, I guess."

"Fred, ask around, see if you can find any witnesses," Hot Throat commanded. "Submit your notes to Fred, put me in copy. Fred will take it from here. What's the man's name?"

"Charles McKim. They call him Chuck. I'll send you my notes," I said, heading toward my desk. Fred followed me.

"Were you stoned when you saw this? Hungover? I mean, workers generally don't shove each other off trucks in broad daylight. You seem pretty calm considering you witnessed a human get virtually pancaked."

I smirked at Fred. "Not stoned. Definitely hungover, though."

"I hope you checked spelling on all the names."

"It's all accurate. I'll forward what I have."

Hot Throat summoned me back to her office. She closed the door and paced behind her desk. "Keep this to yourself: Chuck McKim is a Boston AOD. His great grandfather was Charles McKim, the architect who designed the Boston Public Library. This is obviously not information for the article, but I want you to be aware. Whenever there's a hit on a fellow druid, we go on high alert."

"A hit?"

Her forehead was scrunched, making deep wrinkles. I couldn't tell if she was upset because a fellow druid had been badly injured or if she was angry about something else.

"You have a gift for understanding architecture. The way you interpreted Henry Hobson Richardson's architecture to find the ark of the covenant, that was genius-level. Charles McKim mentored with Richardson. Perhaps you should focus on McKim's architecture. Expand your repertoire. It's a shame a McKim descendent was targeted."

"Targeted?"

She waved it off. "Don't mind me, I'm thinking out loud."

"Who would target a McKim?"

"I shouldn't even mention it, but there's an underground operation affiliated with city planning and zoning," she said. "It's mainly construction worker thugs griping about unions and fair wages. Chuck McKim was a longtime construction guy. He probably stepped on the wrong toes."

"The wrong Bauhaus toes?"

Her eyes popped. "What have you heard of Bauhaus?"

"Chuck McKim told me he doesn't trust Bauhaus. But he said he trusts the *Lodestar*. That's probably why he talked to me."

"Interesting." She stroked her chin. "He said that?"

I nodded. "Tell me more about the underground Bauhaus operation."

"My understanding is that it protects Bauhaus style architecture and looks for opportunities to expand its modernistic presence. There's a gross plan to demolish early American architecture to make room for more Bauhaus construction. Bauhaus wants to obliterate Richardson's and McKim's buildings in Boston starting next summer."

"Next summer? They can't do that, can they?"

"Search and destroy is their motto. Rumor has it they'll hoard what treasures they find for their own power and turn the rest to rubble."

"Why would they wipe out Richardson and McKim?"

"To spread the Bauhaus architectural wasteland. Look up Bauhaus. But don't waste a lot of time, you won't be impressed. There's no signs or symbols or Solomon's temple designs. Someone like you will think it tedious."

"You're right, I prefer Richardson Romanesque over modern Bauhaus-style. But, to be fair, I'll look into Bauhaus."

She shook her head. "Stay focused on architects like Richardson and McKim, the elder. You have an extraordinary talent. Look at the symbols and meaning in their work. Maybe you can find more meaning in what Richardson and McKim were designing. I shouldn't have mentioned this Bauhaus business, but I just want you to be aware. I only know about the operation because when *accidents* happen like this, then it becomes suspicious. But we may never prove Bauhaus is behind this."

"Should I go back to the accident scene —"

"Definitely not," she snapped.

"But what if Bauhaus did it? They should be held accountable —"

"Listen, kiddo. They're no-nonsense thugs, especially if they think someone is sticking their nose where it doesn't belong. I have a feeling Chuck McKim set them off. As an AOD he should have known better, as should you. Fred will handle the reporting. Not you."


Back at my apartment, my afternoon nap was interrupted by Melissa, my college friend and Quadster comrade, who pressed the door buzzer so many times it sounded like a fire drill. She'd come straight to my apartment after she finished working at her summer job at Hancock Insurance.

"My job blows big time," she complained as she barged into the kitchen. "I'm just a pretty face at the front desk. Bigly boring. How'd you end up with the cushy life?"

"Cushy? I had to go into the *Lodestar* office today."

"Not dressed like a cabana boy, I hope," she said, taking an inventory of my outfit. She helped herself to a hard lemonade from the fridge. "What are you planning to wear to the stoplight party?"

She'd already informed me that a stoplight party is where guests coordinate their shirt color with their social availability. Green is a go (available), red is a no (in a relationship) and yellow is fair warning (sort of taken, but not really).

"Maybe I'll wear purple. Anyway, I've only gone out with Nolan twice, so there's nothing official. What do you think?"

"Green" she said, never short on advice. "But not Kelly green. More of a jade, that would work well."

"What color are you going with?" I asked.

"Lance is gone all summer, so it's a hard green for me. Exact shade of green not yet determined. I brought three options," she said.

I laughed to myself because she and Lance weren't really dating even when he was around. But in her mind, he was marriage material as a trust-fund baby. Nolan, who was meeting me at the party, was a guy I'd met at a concert, but we were just friends.

I rummaged through the cabinet for a cutting board. Melissa glanced at my block of smoked Gouda and said, "Paigester, you need to up your charcuterie game."

"Charcuterie?"

"Spruce it up with some crackers and grapes. Mixed nuts. You know, a proper nosh."

"I'll get on that."

She wore a mini-skirt and Gucci sandals with a tight teal V-neck that showed her cleavage. I'd planned on shorts and flipflops, but with Melissa joining me, I needed to ramp it up a notch. I decided on a solid black skort and black leather Birkenstocks.

She gawked at my choice. "Don't you have strappy sandals? Those look like Jerusalem cruisers."

"Jerusalem cruisers?" I looked down at my feet, wondering why I let her fashion comments get to me.

"You look like you're rolling deep with the Dirty Dozen."

"The Dirty Dozen?"

"The Apostles. Team Jesus. You can do better." She whipped past me to go investigate my closet. "This apartment is totally Cosmo. Can I move into the second bedroom? Check out this walk-in closet! I'd have it filled in no time."

The apartment was all mine for the summer courtesy of Pilar Kuhlkoat and the *Patriot Lodestar*. The apartment was used by VIPs — which became my distinction after I found the ark of the covenant and joined the AOD. Pilar, a longtime Boston druid, taught me the secret signs and abundant rules.

I first met her toward the end of my freshman year when she came to the North Easton town library where I was working. She chatted privately for an hour with her old friend, the head librarian Ms. Montgomery, before I was summoned to join their meeting. She knew all about how I found the ark of the covenant and was there to recruit me to join higher-ranked Boston druids.

I recalled my first conversation with Pilar; my responses to her questions spun things in a direction that I hadn't expected. She asked me about my infatuation with astrology, early American architect H.H. Richardson, his use of the zodiac signs on Memorial Hall in North Easton. I dazzled her with my understanding of astrology in relation to human affairs. I explained how I used the Solar House System to determine what trends were presenting and how the night sky was interpreted.

Pilar had asked me about her sign, Aries. I answered her like an authority on the night sky: Optimism and boundless energy filled her interactions and she felt flirty and conversational to amuse herself. Mercury, the planet of communication, was in Aries and there was a new moon which meant she had a chance to plant seeds for the future.

Pilar had asked, "I'm offering you a special opportunity. What would you like to do for the *Lodestar*? Name it. The sky's the limit —"

Once she said *the sky's the limit*, it hit me. "Horoscopes."

At first, she stared at me as if she hadn't heard what I'd said. I wondered if I was supposed to take more time, mull it over, then choose something mainstream like sports reporter, cover the Celtics and Bruins.

"Horoscopes! You got it," she said, snapping from her trance. "Listen hon, having your own column is just the beginning of what's coming your way. The internship — for lack of a better word — has more perks than you'll know what to do with."

"Like what?"

"Unlimited car service. An open pass to museums, buildings, libraries, and whatever else you want access to. Tickets to concerts, sporting events, shows. Open-tab dining at *Lodestar*-reviewed restaurants —"

My eyes bugged. "Wow."

"You can stay in the *Lodestar* VIP condo for the summer. Get to know Boston better. You'll love it."

I'd glanced at Ms. Montgomery, hoping she didn't mind that I was moving on from the library internship. She'd cracked a smile. "Go on. You're in good hands with Pilar. But you must stay in touch. I can't wait to see what you do next."

I couldn't wait to see what I'd do next. I studied the art of horoscope writing and memorized the major tone of each house. I accumulated stacks of notebooks with my research. I bought a set of astrological charts that showed each planet in relation to each sign, illuminating how the planets move and when they come in and out of contact. They were color-coded which helped me calculate pressing issues and changes for each sign. I became obsessed with what was stirring in each house.

And there was always something stirring.

I called the *Lodestar* car service for a ride to Peabody Terrace where the stoplight party was hosted by Nolan's friend, a teaching assistant who lived there with his fiancé. We were picked up in a Mercedes SUV with tinted windows and a professional driver. Pilar had boasted about the German engineering and advanced safety features in the *Lodestar* fleet, encouraging me to use the car service whenever I needed it.

Melissa grinned when she saw the Benz idling outside the apartment.

"It's good to have friends in high places," she said, elbowing my ribs. "Is Nolan serious dating material or just one of your boy toys?"

"I wouldn't know what to do with a boy toy."

"Make him a friend with benefits." She winked and elbowed me again.

The city lights reflected on the Charles River as we headed toward the north bank. We pulled up to the Peabody Terrace. The building resembled cinderblocks on steroids. We rode the elevator up to the efficiency apartment. Nolan greeted us at the door in a red shirt. His face dropped.

We each took a beer and Melissa whispered, "He's cute. You should've gone red. Is he good in the bedroom?"

"I wouldn't know."

"You always drag your heels," she sighed. "You should've worn yellow, the way you keep one foot on the brake all the time."

"Do you like the apartment?" Nolan straddled the arm of the gray felt couch. It had square screw-on legs, probably Ikea.

Melissa made a horse sound with her lips. "You should check out Paige's condo overlooking Boston Harbor. Her place is right out of *Architectural Digest*."

"I'd love to see it."

"Trust me, you won't want to leave," Melissa added.

I was distracted by a familiar face in the kitchen. "I'll get us some beer."

"But we just started —"

I beelined for the kitchen toward the tanned stud. I gushed, "Remember me?"

His chiseled jawline eased toward a polite smile. "I wish I could."

"Last year at the tailgate. Hash brownies?"

He chuckled. "If there were hash brownies involved, then you must have met my brother. We look like each other, but I don't bake."

"I didn't realize Axel had a brother. Do you row crew as well?"

"I'm Xavier and no, lacrosse is my game. I'm in Cambridge for the summer working at the lacrosse camp."

"How about Axel? Working a crew camp?" I blurted and thought, slow down, Paige, that was three rapid-fire questions.

"Training every day at the boathouse."

"Is he coming tonight?"

"He's at the BPL. Working on a paper for a summer class he's taking."

"The BPL?"

"Boston Public Library. I have to pick him up soon. Care for a ride?"

"Sure." I followed him toward the door. I glanced at Nolan and Melissa and said, "Be right back."

Xavier revved his Jeep Rubicon. "First time at the Peabody Terrace?"

I squinted at the building. "I've been reading about Brutalist style. Architects like it, but everyone else hates it. It's ugly as far as Harvard buildings go. I could picture it in Soviet Russia."

"True."

At Copley Square Xavier searched for a parking spot, and finally settled on a side street a few blocks up from the library. I followed him through the lobby, noticing the marble floor with inlaid brass designs that included all of the zodiac symbols. I followed him to the Abbey Room where Axel stood close to a beautiful woman with long flowing dark hair and an olive-toned flawless complexion. My heart sunk, seeing them together. Axel stared at me for a moment before a high-wattage grin spread across his face.

"Hey, you! Want a brownie?"

"Is it gluten free?" I joked, excited that he remembered me.

Xavier stood on the other side, the goddess sandwiched between them. I wanted to hip-check her across the room and take her spot.

"This is Thalia," they said in unison.

She giggled. Her delicate hand reached to shake mine, and she said, with an accent, "Nice to meet you."

I thought: one, drop-dead gorgeous; two, sexy accent; and three, I don't stand a chance.

"Did you make any progress?" Xavier asked them.

"I was getting nowhere on my own," Axel admitted. "But with Thalia's art history knowledge I'm actually starting to develop a greater appreciation for Edwin Austin Abbey."

He pointed toward the mural — *The Quest and Achievement of the Holy Grail*. The mural started with the infant Galahad and moved through Galahad's search for the holy grail.

"Galahad wears a red robe in each panel. It symbolizes spiritual purity," Thalia explained. She showed us the last panel where Galahad becomes king of Sarras. "Here's where Galahad achieved his life mission to find the holy grail. The grail is rendered in raised relief — three dimensions."

"Who is this guy?" I asked, pointing to a maimed man.

"That's King Amfortas, the Fisher King. He was the last in a long bloodline of keepers of the holy grail. His groin injury left him handicapped, so all he could do was sit in his boat and fish near his castle, Cordenic. He waited for a noble who could heal him by asking a certain question."

"Do you go to Harvard as well?" I asked.

"I'm an exchange student, but not Harvard. I'm starting at Kew College in the fall."

"Hey, I go to Kew! Where are you from?"

"Delphi, Greece. Look over here," she said, leading me to an expansive mural at the top of the stairs. "It's Apollo and the muses on Mount Parnassus. Delphi is at the foot of Mount Parnassus. That's where I grew up. I'm excited to meet someone from Kew. I don't know a single soul."

"I'll show you around the campus."

"Thalia's our cousin," said Xavier. "What do you say we head back to the stoplight party?"

"First cousin?" A choir of angels resonated in my head, until I recalled Eleanor Roosevelt married her fifth cousin Franklin. But what were the chances of that happening?

On our way out of the library Thalia paused. "I'm infatuated with these Daniel Chester French doors."

There were three sets of bronze doors sculpted with bas-relief figures of women that she said represented music, poetry, knowledge, wisdom, truth and romance. I pointed to the allegorical woman on one door who was holding up a veiled object.

"It's great to see a woman holding the holy grail for once. I don't know why Galahad gets all the credit," I said, guessing that the grail was under the veil.

"I like the way you think, sister," she said, looking closer at the details.

The brothers were already outside waiting for us. I paused to admire H.H. Richardson's Trinity Church across Copley Square with his signature archways and ornamental stone carvings; it was another of his Solomon's temple replications.

"Are you familiar with the architect Richardson?" I asked.

Axel followed my gaze. "Who?"

"Architect, 19th century American. He designed that church. He designed two buildings on Harvard's campus, and he was a member of the Porcellian Club back in his day.

Richardsonian Romanesque — the only American architect to have a style named after him."

"Never heard the name before," said Axel.

"I have a thing for him. His protégé was Charles Follen McKim," I explained and stared above the library entrance where carvings of twin boys held the library seal. I froze for a moment when I realized the twins represented Gemini. When I studied Richardson's architecture, I was infatuated by his use of zodiac signs in the ornamentation. I pondered the possibility that McKim the elder used the zodiac in his architecture just as Richardson had done. It was Richardson's zodiac symbolism that inspired my interest to study the zodiac and constellations. I made a mental note to further explore zodiac symbolism in McKim's architecture, as well as all of Boston's architecture. I decided to start with the Gemini twins because it was June and work my way in monthly order through the whole zodiac.

"McKim designed the library. See those twin boys above the entrance? That's Augustus Saint-Gaudens' work. Both were members of the Beaux-Arts inspired era, as was Richardson."

Thalia paused to study the detail. "You must be an architecture major."

"I'm not, but don't get me going, I could talk all day about it. My dad is an architect so I was exposed to this stuff."

"My mother is a painter."

We stopped in front of the library near a bronze sculpture of a woman with a palette in one hand and an artist's paint brush in the other. She hovered over eight inscribed names: Raphael, Titian, Rembrandt, Velazquez, Phidias, Praxiteles, Michelangelo, and Donatello.

"I could show you loads of buildings that feature a lady in a chair."

"Why a lady in a chair?"

But then the boys beeped the horn and we headed for the Rubicon. Xavier tossed t-shirts to Thalia and Axel — both green. Thalia pulled hers over her tank top while Axel removed his shirt for the switch. I eyeballed his muscular physique and hallelujahs reverberated through my whole body. Axel, in his green shirt: fair game. Sorry, Nolan.

The stoplight party was in full swing with loud chatter rising above the thumping music. Melissa's mouth dropped when she saw me strut in with the three Greek beauties.

"God almighty!" she huffed her beer-breath close to my ear. "Where'd you find these two? The dream bank?"

I introduced Melissa. "Thalia will be joining us at Kew in the fall."

Melissa assessed the competition. It was an awkward moment before Melissa greeted her with a casual, "You should definitely live on my floor."

Nolan returned with four beers, one for himself and the rest for the ladies. The brothers needed to fend for themselves. Melissa couldn't take her eyes from Thalia and when I told her she was from Greece, it seemed to fuel her infatuation.

I felt my phone buzz in my pocket: Hot Throat. I let it go to voicemail, but when it buzzed a few minutes later, I figured I better answer it.

"He wants to see you in person. He's at Mass General," she blasted.

"Who wants to see me?"

"Chuck McKim. The guy in the construction accident. Someone from the hospital called and said he keeps mumbling for the *Lodestar* reporter he spoke to after the accident. Go talk to him."

"What does he want from me?"

"Go find out before he dies," she commanded.

# Chapter Two — Cancer

In the morning, I quickly dressed to head to the hospital. I couldn't go when Pilar called because visiting hours were over and I'd had a few drinks during my reunion with Axel. I rushed to leave, kicking over the kitchen trash can.

"Good God. Why are you up so early?" Melissa peered over the sofa where she had spent the night, her eyes puffy and red-rimmed.

"I have to go to Mass General —"

"Venereal disease? Morning sickness?" Her hair was tossed in a heaped mess as if she'd stood on her head all night.

Before I could answer, Melissa flopped back into the couch and groaned. I explained that I had to interview a patient for the *Lodestar*.

"It's f'n Saturday. Take the day off. We'll go to brunch."

"I'll be back in a few, then we can go."

She yawned. "Why did you make me sleep on the couch? Is the spare bedroom off-limits?"

"You passed out on the couch. I never try to move you after you pass out, because you fight."

She glanced at the sticky coffee table, cluttered with shot glasses, spent limes and an empty tequila bottle. "I'm never getting a job that requires weekend hours."

"Special assignment. I usually have the weekends off," I said. "I got myself tangled up in some extra work."

"Speaking of tangled, you should do something about your hair."

"You should talk!"

"Your hair looks like a Roller Derby helmet and it looks like you slept in that shirt. Wear something more profesh."

She was right, my clothes were wrinkled. I checked my hair in the bathroom mirror; I admit it needed some attention, but Roller Derby helmet-head? I quickly brushed it and pulled it back in a ponytail. I had three wrinkle-free blouses on hangers. I chose the light pink one and swapped my jeans for khakis. I located one penny loafer in the closet, then scrounged under my bed for the other. I wondered if the outfit upgrade was a waste of time because a guy dying in the hospital probably wouldn't care what I was wearing.

"Better?" I asked her while I searched for my keys, finally locating them wedged between the couch cushions. There were dirty dishes and glasses on every flat surface. I felt bad about leaving it all for the cleaning lady — another internship perk — but I was late.

She squinted at me. "It's passable. We need to do a wardrobe makeover."

"Maybe after brunch we can hit Target."

She rolled over and groaned. "Not quite the store I had in mind."

Even though Hot Throat told me not to waste time on Bauhaus, I was curious about it. Bauhaus, which means "construction house" in German, was a design school in Germany from 1919 to 1933. It was founded by Walter Gropius, one of the pioneering masters of modernist architecture. The Nazi regime deemed Gropius and his school as a center for communist intellectualism producing "degenerate art" and forced it to shut down.

Gropius emigrated to the U.S. to escape the Nazis. As the chair of Harvard's Department of Architecture in 1938, Gropius deemed Harvard the unofficial home of Bauhaus, setting the standard for modernistic architecture. Soon the Bauhaus Movement infiltrated tradition-rich Boston with modernist architecture and minimalism.

Gropius inspired his Harvard architect students to pursue the Brutalist style — boxes clad in white stucco with metal-sash windows, clean lines, geometric shapes and mass production, a complete contrast to more ornamentation-oriented architects like Richardson and McKim.

I pondered how traditional Boston could be so deeply influenced by an avant-garde school of art. How did Gropius get to be the head of Harvard's architect program? How did Bauhaus control the standard — simplistic, cost-effective, zero style? Who approved the Bauhaus simplicity that stood in extreme contrast to the Boston Public Library or Trinity Church?

When I checked in at the hospital security desk, I was informed that Chuck McKim was in intensive care. Visitations were for immediate family only. The security person checked my license and asked, "How are you related?"

"I'm his niece," I lied.

I waited outside his room for the nurse to draw back the curtain. She told me, "He already had visitors this morning. He needs to rest. He's on a lot of pain meds."

"He asked for me specifically. I'll make it brief." This was true — I didn't want to bother this catastrophically injured man any longer than it took. Plus, I had a major hangover. I wanted to make an honest attempt to see why he called the *Lodestar*, then get out.

"Please do," said the nurse. She adjusted the IV in his arm and side-eyed me before leaving the room.

I cleared my throat a few times and feigned a cough. His heavy eyelids drooped over his bloodshot eyes and we stared at each other. "I'm the *Lodestar* reporter. We spoke after the accident."

His mouth started to move, but no sounds emerged. His arms and what was left of his legs were covered in bandages. He had burn marks on the side of his face, ear and nose. I leaned in, caught a whiff of halitosis that smelled like he was rotting from the inside out. He drifted back to morphine la-la land and muttered, "Bauhaus."

The word hung in the air like a helium-filled balloon lingering after the party had ended.

"You said you don't trust Bauhaus. Why is that?"

"McKim's secret —" Chuck groaned and managed to say, "They want it."

"What secret?"

His weak voice barely released the words: "The key to the salon."

"What salon?"

His eyes rolled upward. I thought he was gone, but then he said, "The Winter Hexagon Salon…for six great architects. But never Gropius or Bauhaus."

"What's McKim's secret?"

He struggled to say, "Hunt…G…the key…the salon…stop Bauhaus."

Chuck's eyes closed and his shallow breathing halted. The medical dashboard near his bed blipped numbers as if the New York Stock Exchange was crashing, then flatlined.

A broad-shouldered nurse rushed into the room. A lanyard with her name badge — Nurse Brenda Shepherd — dangled in the patient's face when she checked for a pulse. She hit a button calling for help. Then she lunged across the bed and drilled her meaty sausage-sized pointer-finger into my shoulder. "Step out!"

I couldn't get out of there fast enough. I almost collided with the doctor and another nurse who flew down the corridor. I tried to watch from the hallway, but the curtains were drawn around the bed. I saw their white clogs shuffling around his bed. I heard the doctor order for the defibrillator, calling out, "Clear!"

The bedside hustle continued for ten minutes before they declared McKim was dead. Nurse Brenda unhooked the equipment that had flashed his final vitals, then rolled it out of the room. An orderly wheeled in a gurney with a black body bag set to take McKim to the morgue. The precision timing by the staff made the dying business seem as simple as stocking shelves. I felt sick about what happened to him — the misery of his last day on earth — and that the McKim family secret had died with him. The nurse parked the medical equipment in the corridor and marched her white clogs toward me.

"I'm sorry for your loss," she said, stepping in front of me to block my view into the room. "What did he say?"

I figured nurse Brenda wouldn't care about Bauhaus or McKim family secrets. I shrugged and said, "Gibberish."

She disappeared down the hallway with her cart. I passed the nurses' station on my way to the elevator and saw a rugged man gesturing with his thick hands while he spoke in a boisterous tone. He was jovial, cracking jokes by the nurses' station. I noticed it was Chuck's co-worker, Jake McGregor, chatting with nurse Brenda. And that's when I noticed nurse Brenda had a football-shaped mole along her jawline just like the asphalt cowgirl. It had to be the same woman nurse and construction supervisor. I figured she had two jobs to support her family, maybe she was a single mom. She appeared at ease chatting with McGregor — odd considering a patient had just died on her shift. McGregor looked cleaned-up in a button-downed cotton shirt and jeans. They stopped talking when they saw me push the elevator button. In four swift strides, McGregor arrived by my side.

"It's a shame. I was too late to say goodbye to my buddy. Did he say anything to you?" asked McGregor.

"He was pretty out of it." I recalled that Chuck told me not to trust Bauhaus, and Hot Throat had mentioned that the underground Bauhaus operation comprised construction worker thugs. I wasn't sure if McGregor was Chuck's friend or a Bauhaus thug, so I said, "I'm sorry about your buddy."

McGregor stepped into the elevator with me. "It's a shame. I've known him for a long time. He was close to retirement. Are you sure he didn't say anything?"

"He was doped on morphine."

"The nurse was the one who called the newspaper. He kept asking to talk to the reporter. He couldn't have been that out of it if he remembered —"

"It's pretty common, actually. It's called terminal lucidity. But the nurse would know better than me —"

"The nurse said she saw you talking to him. He had to say something," insisted McGregor. "It'd help me a lot to know what he was thinking."

I shrugged. "I was trying to wake him. Unfortunately, I was too late."

The elevator stopped at ground level. McGregor said, "And I was too late to say goodbye."

Outside the hospital, I called Melissa. "Brunch and Bloody Mary's? Quincy Market?"

"Too late. I'm getting a mani-pedi. Then I'm going for a Thai massage. I have a massive knot in my neck from crashing on your couch."

I power-sighed. "Aren't you hungry?"

"I raided your fridge. Let's meet up at the Barking Crab later, say around sevenish? Watch the fireworks together?"

I agreed, despite feeling annoyed by the brunch blowoff. I made my way through the Faneuil Hall tourists to check on the renovation at Goforth's Daily Grind. I'd worked for the owner, Tanya Goforth, last year when she opened her coffee shop in North Easton. Now she was branching out into the city. I opened the door to controlled chaos. Tanya flipped through the checklists on her clipboard.

"Looking great," I called to her.

"Hey kiddo, I didn't expect to see you today."

"I had something to cover for the *Lodestar*. Need any help?"

We moved toward a quiet corner. "You're just the person I want to see, actually. I'm thinking of decorating with a black and white theme to tie in the tile floor."

"Classic."

"I need some objects of interest for our window display. Black and white décor. Vintage. You're clever with that stuff. Go hunting." She slipped four Ben Franklins into my hand.

"Objects of interest? Like what?" I analyzed the empty wall space and front window.

"Up to you. We need a cool vibe. Something like we did at the North Easton shop with the old library books hanging from the ceiling. Whimsical. Off-beat."

"I'll give it my best shot." I stuffed the cash in my pocket.

"Get receipts. Bookkeeping — like laundry — is endless." Tanya directed one of the contractors to install an extra outlet inside the kitchen. She glanced back at me. "How's things?"

"Fine," I said, realizing she was studying me with a raised eyebrow.

I met Tanya during the fall semester of my freshman year when she hired me to work at Goforth's Daily Grind. It took me awhile to get used to her New Age vibe. She always sensed if I was stressed or suffering *third-eye blockage*. She introduced me to meditation and taught me her recipes for coffee blends. She lent me the "Peace Train" — her Volkswagen hippie van — to take the Quadsters and my boyfriend Stoph glamping in Wyoming. She was my lifesaver after the road trip ended tragically. She seemed to know when I had flashbacks or struggled with the auto-replay nightmare that ran through my head like a hologram: the blast through the pyramid tunnel, the last time I saw Stoph, the helicopter crash...

Tanya wasn't just my boss, but she became my voice of reason. She helped me release the trauma so I wouldn't end up trapped in a negative loop of past events.

She said, "You've met someone new, haven't you?"

"Maybe." My face reddened. "Nothing official."

"But you'd like it to be —"

"If the stars align."

"Ah, the universe delivers," she said, squeezing my shoulder.


I called Axel's cousin, Thalia, to enlist her artist's eye and schemed that maybe Axel would be around as well. I meandered through Government Center to catch a ride on the red line. I passed Boston City Hall that many consider the ugliest building in the world because it resembled an upside-down wedding cake. It was hideous, no doubt about it, but I bet if I looked hard enough, I'd find even more Bauhaus-hideous buildings in Boston. Adjacent to City Hall was the Gropius-designed JFK building with two giant drab blocks, resembling a prison. No wonder Gropius was rejected by this mysterious salon — his work was downright offensive. There was nothing of beauty, no ornamentation, no gargoyles or graceful archways, no interesting stone texture — just concrete blocks.

I met Thalia in Harvard Square *sans* cousin, who was rowing, she explained. I told her about the coffee shop and Tanya Goforth.

"A healthy coffee-monger?"

"Exactly."

Already, I decided: I wanted a sexy lady-friend with a James Bond accent. She had a cool saunter with her backpack slung over one shoulder and a 35mm camera on the other. We wandered through Cambridge and peered in the window of an antique junk haven. We went inside to poke around.

Thalia gushed over a sky-blue tin robot toy with coiled-wire hair. A man behind the cash register said, "That's a covetable lithographed tin variety. It's only forty bucks but it could be easily flipped on the internet for five times that."

I wondered, if it could be easily sold for a higher profit, why he didn't sell it online? We browsed around the store checking out the World's Fair memorabilia, China dish sets, Duncan Phyfe chairs, pottery.

"Ooooohhh, Maria Martinez iconic black ware," said Thalia.

I eyeballed the price tag on a vase and whispered, "A small fortune."

Then I saw it, jammed on a cluttered shelf toward the back of the store. "Bingo!"

"That's a 1932 Royal typewriter," said the store owner, sneaking up behind us. "Still works. New ribbons, too. Go ahead, give her a whirl."

Clack, clack, clack. I admired the keys and metal return bar. I pushed down the chunky keys: *I must have this.*

"How much?"

"I can let her go for two hundred."

"That's too steep for my budget. I need it for a display in a new coffee shop in Quincy Market. Would you consider leasing it for a month or two? Or maybe do a product placement?"

"Product placement?"

"Well, instead of leaving this beauty collecting dust on a back shelf, we could polish it up, showcase it and if someone wants to buy it, we can broker the deal for you on consignment. Then when it sells, we can display another antique."

His face brightened. "Great idea. But what if I never hear from you again?"

"Do we look like con artists?" asked Thalia.

"Well…"

"I'll give you a note from the shop. Goforth's Daily Grind."

He hoisted the hefty Royal from the shelf and lugged it to the front of the store. He slid in a fresh piece of paper and typed: *Leon, proprietor of The Victorian Rose at Harvard Square. Royal typewriter, $300.*

"If it sells, you keep twenty percent. That's the standard consignment rate in the trade."

"Awesome. You won't be disappointed," I said and we shook hands.

I hauled the typewriter — it must have weighed twenty pounds — toward a cement park bench. Thalia caressed the keys. "It's hard to believe people used to write this way."

"Now we need to develop the typewriter theme. Something black and white."

Thalia squinted at the Royal. "I can photograph the typewriter in unusual places. I brought my Nikon."

"Brilliant."

She removed the lens cap and positioned the typewriter on the end of the bench. "The rule of thirds — don't focus the main attraction in the center of the photograph."

The afternoon light diffused through the oak branches. Thalia shot from different angles. She switched to a macro lens to zoom in on the keys. "Let's move it around the city. Then we can frame our favorite prints to display with your typewriter. Gingbo?"

I smiled, making a mental note to learn some Greek slang. "Gingbo. Where to next?"

She pointed across the street. "The café table in front of the window. Quick, let's grab it before someone else does."

We hustled over and plunked the Royal on the wrought-iron, marble-topped bistro table. Thalia shot pictures from a side angle, careful not to put herself in the reflection of the window. She told me to move back because my shadow was creeping into the frame. The weathered wood trim around the window enhanced the vintage vibe.

A waitress stopped at our table. "Menus?"

"Just a coffee," I said. "Black."

"Make it two, please. Mine with cream."

When the waitress returned with our order, Thalia asked her to take a picture of us. The waitress backpedaled to get us and the typewriter in the frame.

I asked her, "*Gingbo*? Is it Greek slang?"

"Greek? No. Isn't that what you said in the store when you found this treasure?"

"Bingo, not *Gingbo*!"

She stifled her cackle with her napkin. "I'm a little dyslexic," she explained.

We finished the coffee and traipsed around Cambridge with the typewriter, photographing it on the hood of a taxi, at the bottom of a playground slide, and one centered in the road with cars driving toward it. I suggested we pass the Harvard Graduate Center so I could introduce Thalia to the work of Walter Gropius.

"I can't stand the Bauhaus style. Maybe your artistic eye sees something that I don't. I'll try to be open-minded," I said.

Thalia feigned a gagging sound. "This looks more like a housing project than a graduate school. We're definitely not taking any photos here."

"It's a shame that Gropius influenced so many postwar-era American architects. Even the heavy hitters — I.M. Pei, Philip Johnson, Henry Cobb, Hugh Stubbins, Paul Randolph — they all fell under his spell. We have a country polluted with concrete behemoths."

"You'll have to show me what you're talking about," said Thalia.

"I'm meeting Melissa at the Barking Crab tonight. Lobster rolls and craft beer. Care to join us?"

Thalia adjusted her hair behind her ears and sighed. "I sense that Melissa doesn't exactly fancy me."

I could understand how Thalia picked up on that vibe. When I was first getting to know Melissa, I thought the same thing. It was almost as if she didn't want to like me, like she had no room in her life for someone like me — a person who couldn't care less about fashion, social status or wealth. Then, out of nowhere, Melissa would do something nice, like lend me her car, and I would feel like we were best friends. But it wouldn't take long before she insulted my clothes or hairstyle. Melissa is a good friend, but it takes time and patience to get used to her. I remember complaining about her to Tanya Goforth last year. She advised me that Melissa's idea of me is not my responsibility to live up to. The advice helped.

"It takes time for her to warm up. Besides, we'll be together."

When a garbage truck pulled up at a light, Thalia asked if she could take a quick photo of the trash collector holding the Royal. He jumped off the back, pretended to throw in the Royal, and pulled the lever so the compacter activated like a giant claw. He hammed it up for the photo, flexing his biceps. Thalia fired away. Then he sat on the liftgate with the typewriter on his lap, with his elbows resting on top. The driver of the garbage truck beeped, so he handed back the Royal and they rumbled away.

"That was a kickass idea," I said. "Call it *One Man's Junk...*"

Thalia cackled. "That's so corny. I didn't expect him to roll with it like that."

By the time we stopped at my apartment to drop off the typewriter, my arms were spent. I plunked the Royal on the kitchen counter, grabbed two Coronas and flopped onto the sofa.

"Great apartment," she said, joining me on the couch.

"Come hang out anytime," I said, wanting to add *and bring your hot cousin.*


In the evening, we strolled the Harborwalk from my apartment to the Barking Crab. It was a hot night, but the breeze that drifted off the water kept us cool. We stopped to check out a pair of four-hundred-feet high residential towers. When I researched the Bauhaus influence on Boston, these Harbor Towers, designed by Henry Cobb of I.M. Pei & Partners in 1971, landed on my must-see check list.

"These concrete towers — they look like fat zippers on a winter coat," I said. "They built them to spruce up Boston's waterfront when it was rampant with litter and parking lots."

"The area is so beautiful. Hard to imagine it was ever dumpy looking," she said.

"The towers turned this area around. But they clash with the rest of historic Boston. My favorite view of the skyline is from the courthouse, but these towers come close to ruining it."

"They do seem out of place," she said.

I paused to analyze the John Joseph Moakley United States courthouse designed by Henry Cobb in 1999. "Check out the curve in that building. That was probably designed to give maximum water views from the inside."

"Would you be interested in going to some galleries or museums with me sometime?"

"I'd love to," I said, deciding to let Thalia in on my search for zodiac signs in Boston. "I don't know you that well, but I feel like I can trust you with my wild ideas."

"One hundred percent," she said, smiling reassuringly.

"I'm sort of on a mission. I'm looking for the zodiac signs in architecture — like when I showed you the Gemini twins at the library. Now I'm searching for a symbol that represents the Cancer sign."

"Is that why we're going to the Barking Crab?"

I laughed. "You're going to be good at this!"

"Why zodiac signs?"

I wanted to tell her about my infatuation with Richardson and how it led to my discovery of his building Solomon's temple according to biblical dimensions from the Book of Kings. I was obsessed with Richardson's use of the zodiac symbols and I suspected there was more to the zodiac regarding early American architecture. I couldn't tell her about my finding the ark of the covenant and giving it to the North Easton druids for protection — I was sworn to secrecy. I took a vow with the AOD that I knew breaking would mean I'd sever my ties to the *Lodestar* and all its perks. Oversharing any details could lead to ex-communication from the AOD...or worse.

I realized that my being a druid was off-the-charts weird, something that could scare off Thalia and her cousins and most sane individuals. How could I share that I belonged to a secretive group dedicated to protecting religious relics and preserving ancient rites?

"I think it's fascinating how the zodiac gets used in architecture," I said, settling on a simple explanation.

"I bet we can find the zodiac in art as well. I'll start looking for the signs."

"Perfect. But there's something else," I said, deciding to share what happened with Chuck McKim. "The mission I mentioned. There's a key that goes to a place called the Winter Hexagon Salon. I need to find the key and the salon."

"I get my hair highlighted at Castleman's salon —"

"Not the kind of salon I'm talking about," I said. "It's some type of a secret meeting place. For six architects and artists. But let's keep this between us."

She hooked her pinky onto mine. "I swear. I won't say a word to anyone."

There was a long line outside the restaurant — no surprise, considering it was the Fourth of July. Melissa called to say she was running late because she needed an emergency blowout after the masseuse rubbed oil through her hair.

"It's criminal. I look like I haven't shampooed in a month. Go ahead and grab a table. I'll be along ASAP," she said, knowing the Barking Crab was going to be a mob scene.

Thalia took a call from Xavier. She put aside the phone to ask if her cousins could join us.

I gulped, trying not to sound too excited.

"Sure. We'll get the table," I said, chuckling to myself about the *would I mind if Axel joined* part.

We entered under the red and yellow striped awning. I asked for a table for five, mentioning that I was with the *Lodestar*. She checked my press pass and entered my name on her tablet. She said it would be a few minutes for the table to open up.

When the guys arrived ten minutes later, I noticed the hostess ogled them, which most likely contributed to our scoring a waterside table. The restaurant was packed and the service seemed slow.

"We should order straightaway," I suggested, hoping we wouldn't miss any of the fireworks if the food order took too long.

Thalia told her cousins, "We lugged a vintage typewriter around Cambridge for a photo shoot today. It was insanely heavy."

"A typewriter?" asked Xavier.

"I work at a coffee shop. My boss asked me to decorate the front window display."

Axel scratched his head. "What do typewriters have to do with coffee?"

"Nothing. It's a black and white theme. Thalia, I was thinking we should photoshop the letters to rearrange the keys to spell out Goforth's Daily Grind."

Thalia nodded. "Cool idea."

Melissa showed up just as the waitress delivered our food. She looked a thousand times better than when I left her on the couch whining about her stiff neck. She looked at the outfit I was still wearing from that morning and rolled her eyes.

"I ordered for you," I said as she dropped her Coach bag.

She pushed her plate back into the middle of the table. "The mayo in the lobster roll will annihilate my complexion. And do you know how many booty-blasters my trainer will make me do to offset the beer? Puhleeze, Paige, you should know me better by now," she said, signaling the waitress for a salad — hold the croutons — and Skinny Girl margarita.

Thalia grinned. "Paige, let's split the extra lobster roll. Another round of beer?"

Melissa sent back her margarita. "I didn't order it with salt on the rim. Ugh, water retention! I'll blow up like a blimp."

White paper tablecloths served as a giant doodle pad. A plastic cup with colored pencils and crayons stood between the mustard and ketchup. Thalia sketched a caricature of Melissa with a margarita primed in her fist and her nose up in the air. She exaggerated Melissa's coifed hair to be three times larger than her head. She added an oversized Gucci bag with matching shoes for the finishing touches.

Melissa cracked a half smile and snapped a picture of the drawing. "I'm posting that as my new Instagram profile."

I carefully stowed away the drawing to save it before the waitress cleared our table and handed Axel the bill. I said, "Can you sign your art please?"

Thalia scrolled her initials. "Could be worth a fortune someday."

I snatched the bill from Axel and signaled the waitress. "The *Patriot Lodestar* has a tab here."

"I'm aware," she said. "But it's for V.I.P. personnel."

I pulled out my V.I.P. pass and handed it to the waitress. She read it, stared, and said, "Sorry. We usually get the *Lodestar* old-timers for Wednesday lunch. Glad to see there's a new VIP in the newspaper business."

A minute later, a robust middle-aged man in a grease-stained chef's jacket and sweaty bandana doo-rag covering his bald head made fast strides toward our table. The waitress trailed him with a tray of draft beer. The chef reached out his sweaty hand to shake mine.

"Paige Moore! What a pleasure it is to have you dining with us. Was everything to your liking? Please enjoy a round on us. You can keep the Barking Crab pint glasses as well. It's a small token of my appreciation for you dining with us. Let me know if there's anything else you'd like to try, on or off the menu."

"The lobster rolls were terrific, thank you. I know it's a busy night. I don't want to tie up the table."

"Relax. Stay as long as you like," he said. "Next time let me know when you're coming. I can do a chef's tasting for you and your friends off the menu."

"Wow. Thank you," I said.

When the chef left, Axel asked, "What the hell just happened?"

Melissa said, "It pays to hang out with the Paigester."

"How about we finish our beer and go back to my place to watch the fireworks from my balcony?" I suggested. "We'll need to pick up some beer and snacks."

Thalia clinked her glass to mine. "Great idea."

The brothers nodded and Axel said, "We're game."

Melissa downed the rest of her margarita and winked at Axel. She gave him her pint that she hadn't touched. "I claim the spare bedroom. I'm done sleeping on couches."

On our way out of the restaurant, Melissa suddenly started hopping on one foot. At first, I thought she was doing one of her crazy dance moves, but then I saw the blood gushing from her toe. She'd stepped on a crab shell that a waiter had dropped. Thalia grabbed some napkins to press against the cut.

"Do you have a Band-Aid?" I asked the waiter and pointed at the floor. "My friend stepped on that crab shell that you dropped."

"My bad! I'll get the first aid kit," said the waiter, hustling into the kitchen. He returned in a flash, followed by a worker from the kitchen crew.

"Do you want to fill out an accident report?" he asked, eyeing Melissa's toe.

"Of course not," she said, peeling the wrapper off a third bandage.

He leaned closer to me and said, "You might be on the *Lodestar* list, but we know who you are. Accidents tend to happen around those who withhold important information. Why don't you give it up?"

"Give up what?" I asked, feigning a blank expression.

"Listen, Moore. We know McKim told you something. Stop playing innocent with us. You have no idea what you've stumbled into."

"I have no clue what you're talking about."

"Have it your way, but if you don't wanna play, you're gonna pay," he grumbled, storming off toward the kitchen.

"Geez, what's his problem?" asked Melissa. "I'm the one that should be disgruntled."

"Let's roll. Can you walk or should we call a car?"

"I'm okay to walk."

I looked over my shoulders feeling paranoid. I couldn't help but feel as though I was being watched by Bauhaus every time I went out. This was starting to feel creepy. It would be easy enough to tell them what McKim had said, but there was no way I was going to help them on their crusade to obliterate early American architecture. Thalia wedged herself between the brothers, making them laugh while Melissa and I trailed behind them on the stroll back.

"How could you tolerate being with her all day?" Melissa whispered.

"What, you don't like her?"

"She's too weird for me. Like, why did she draw a picture of me? There are a million other things to draw. Why me?"

"Maybe she thinks you're an interesting subject. Maybe she's trying to impress you. Give her a chance."

"I'll cut her some slack, but only on account of her hot cousins."

We ducked into Gus' corner bodega for beer, chips, and hot dogs. Melissa plunked a box of Trojans on the counter and we all looked at her.

"Here's hoping," she said, glancing at Xavier.

Up at my condo, Axel sunk into the overstuffed couch. "So, what am I missing? I thought you were a run of the mill — well, exceedingly pretty — Kew College sophomore. Who the hell are you, anyway?"

"Long story," I said, opening a beer for him.

"I've got time," he said, sliding closer.

At that moment, Melissa appeared with two shot glasses and a bottle of tequila. "Don't say I never did anything for you."

"I'd never —"

Melissa poured a shot for Axel and one for herself, clinking glasses with him. She downed the shot, leaving with the bottle for her next shot victim.

Axel beckoned me close and lowered his voice. "I really appreciate you taking Thalia around today. I think she's a little homesick and she doesn't know anyone other than me and Xavier."

"We had a blast. I think she's great. Come check out the balcony."

Thalia brought the Royal out to the balcony, balanced it on the corner ledge, and photographed it with the sunset in the background.

"I'll shoot more when the fireworks start," she said.

Melissa busted out to the balcony. "Couldn't find any limes, Paigester."

"We wiped out the supply last night."

She brushed against Xavier's backside, so he straightened upright. She slid her arm on the railing behind him and pressed into his side. "Did I mention the spare bedroom is mine tonight? It's got a queen-sized bed."

"So I heard."

Melissa, already tipsy from the tequila, had him cornered. She leaned in and rubbed up against his shoulder. She slurred, "I'm not a friend with benefits. I'm a friend with drawbacks."

The wall blocked him from stepping away from her. I shot a narrow-eyed look of annoyance toward Melissa, then went into the kitchen.

Thalia brought in some of the empty beer bottles. "Everything okay?"

I rifled through the refrigerator. "Double-checking on limes."

"Looks like you bit into a lime."

"Melissa," I explained, smoothing the folds from the caricature of Melissa and stuck it to the refrigerator with a Cape Cod magnet. "She gets on my nerves sometimes."

"I can tell," said Thalia, sliding the magnet to cover the face.

When the fireworks erupted, Thalia staged the typewriter and set the self-timer for a group shot. Melissa barged past me to be near Xavier in the photo, tripping over his foot. He caught her elbow to steady her. She pressed her body into his and hugged him.

"We should stop meeting like this," she said, cackling.

"Gladly," said Xavier.

"You don't like the perfect looking model type?" she said, batting her lashes.

"Oh, it has nothing to do with how you look," he said.

"Is my charming personality too much for you?"

"It's not that either."

"Are you a boob man? I'm not big enough for you?"

"I'm definitely not a boob man," he said, rolling his eyes.

"Then what's the issue?" She staggered backwards. "Are you gay?"

Thalia guffawed. "Gingbo!"

The brothers laughed and toasted with their beer cans.

"Learn English," she sneered, staggering from the balcony and slamming the bathroom door where she proceeded to emit high-pitched retching sounds.

I tapped on the door. "You okay in there?"

"Cleaning lady's gonna have to deal with the Tijuana taco salad splattered on the wall," she said, dabbing her mouth with a hand towel. She pushed past me, passing out on the bed she'd claimed earlier.

I grabbed a bottle of cleaner and paper towels from under the sink, swabbed the dripping puke, and got rid of the evidence in a plastic trash bag that I took down to the trash shoot.

"I guess she was over-served," I said, re-joining the others on the balcony.

Axel shrugged, "It happens to the best of us."

Just as the grand finale erupted, my phone rang. It was Hot Throat, so I answered it.

"I hope you're watching the fireworks from the balcony," she said.

"Best view in Boston."

"Did you go to the hospital today?"

"Yes. Early this morning —"

"Anything to report?"

I hesitated to answer, not wanting to slur my words in front of my boss. It had been a long day and my thinking was fuzzy. "Actually, he died."

"What? Did you say he died?" she bellowed.

"His vitals crapped out mid-sentence and he, ugh, died."

"Paige Moore! If you're going to be a reporter, you better learn to report. A death is news."

"Yes, I see that now."

"My office. Noon tomorrow." She hung up.

I made a mental note to never answer Hot Throat's call after I've had a few drinks.


In the morning, I brought coffee and bagels to review the photos with Thalia. She lived in a small spare bedroom in her cousin's Cambridge apartment. She had an easel propped in the corner near the window with a half-finished watercolor of the weeping cherry tree outside her window.

"Never mind that," she said. "Check out these pictures. I stayed up all night cropping and printing."

I was blown away. Thalia was a pro. She made the Royal look like Marilyn Monroe. We looked through the images, first in color, then transformed into black and white. She'd photoshopped the closeup of the keys to spell Goforth's Daily Grind like I had suggested.

"Gingbo!" I exclaimed.

She grinned. "I'm thinking we go big frame with the one that says Goforth's and put it in the front window with the typewriter displayed on a pedestal. Then on the walls, we hang five in frames."

"How soon can we get this turned around? With matting and framing?"

"Not long. We can buy stock gallery frames at the art supply store if you'd like. Then shoot over to the coffee shop and set it up."

"On one condition: sign your work. I think you're the next Annie Leibovitz. Someone will buy a framed print."

"Fine, but only because you want me to."


At the Daily Grind, I was relieved that Tanya wasn't there yet because I wanted to surprise her. We borrowed a hammer and measuring tape from one of the construction workers and mapped out the wall arrangement.

I put the finishing touches in the window just as Tanya arrived. Her mouth dropped open; she was speechless.

"Do you like it?" I asked her.

"I don't like it," she said. "I love it."

I high-fived Thalia. "Tanya, this is my friend Thalia, the photographer."

"What do I owe you? Name it," gushed Tanya.

"It was my pleasure. Paige gets all the credit. She found the typewriter. But there is one thing, if I may ask —"

"Of course."

"I could use a job. If there's a position available —"

"You're hired! I always need another artistic barista. I'll put you and Paige on the same shift. You obviously work well together."

And just like that, our barista dream team was made.


I dressed for a visit to the newsroom: a tucked-in, pink-striped oxford shirt, pressed khaki pants and light brown penny loafers. Hot Throat was waiting for me in her office.

"Sit," she said and pushed a chair toward me. "I confirmed with the nurse in charge. Chuck McKim died. It's a great loss to the AOD. With no descendants, the McKim legacy is done. What did he tell you?"

"Nothing we can use in an article, that's for sure," I said. She crossed her arms, waiting for me to continue. "He said something about a missing key."

"Go on." She stared with an intensity that I worried was a prelude to a verbal thrashing, typically reserved for interns.

"He said the key goes to a salon called the Winter Hexagon."

"Where is this alleged salon?"

"It's McKim's secret. He told me to hunt for it. He also said it's not for Bauhaus."

"Interesting." She jotted a note, folded it and slipped it in her pocket. "He shared more with you in five minutes than he did in all his years of being a druid. Not to speak negatively about the dead, but between us, he was a strange man."

"How so?"

"Secretive. Paranoid, if you ask me. He didn't trust anyone. It's odd he trusted you, a complete stranger."

"Probably because he knew he was close to his death. He didn't want the McKim secret to die with him."

"What do you make of it?"

"I'm not sure yet."

"See if you can figure out what the Winter Hexagon Salon is all about. Use your architecture detective skills, like you did with the ark. Bauhaus hated McKim's architecture. It was too —"

"*Ecole Beaux-Arts*? Too fanciful?" I suggested. "McKim mentored under Richardson. If Richardson hid the ark, I wonder what else his protégé architects were up to?"

"There you go, already piecing things together. Let's make a deal. If you figure out McKim's secret — the Winter Hexagon Salon —I'll arrange for an all-expenses paid year abroad for your junior year. How's that sound? You can go to Italy —"

"Really?"

"Yes, really. Just keep me in the loop. I can help with all my connections, if you need something. Deal?"

"Deal," I said, already imagining my daily espresso on a balcony with a view of the Tiber River.

# Chapter Three — Leo

Jill roped me and the other three Quadsters into volunteering at the annual Kew College alumni golf outing held at the renowned-for-crooked-investors' Bushfoot Country Club on Cape Cod. Jill had a cushy summer position as the alumni director's assistant where she got paid to water the office plants, take dictation, but mostly leave after lunch every day to work on her tan. We would work as beer-cart girls and schmooze the affluent Kew alumni.

"It'll be a blast," guaranteed Jill.

Pilar gave me the keys to the *Lodestar* cottage on the Cape for the weekend. The Quadsters — Melissa, Jill, Sheila and me — planned to hit the beach as soon as the golf outing ended. I invited Thalia so she could get to know the Kew gang. I stayed overnight with her in Cambridge and we got picked up by the *Lodestar* car service on Thursday morning to go spend an extra day at the beach. Axel hauled our cooler to the SUV. He'd stocked it with beer, hard lemonade and ouzo, which he called a Greek treat that he wanted us to experience.

He eased the cooler into the trunk. "Any chance there's room at the cottage for me and Xavier?"

My brain spiraled. There was plenty of room in my massive bed with a view of the ocean, I wanted to blurt, but I held my tongue. "I thought you had a family obligation."

"My Aunt Pasha got sick, so the family party is postponed. We're free this weekend."

I made him suffer in silence for a few seconds. The look of expectancy on his face was just too good.

"Well," I finally said. "What are you waiting for? The driver's not going to sit there all day."

"I have a crew workout later. I need to track down Xavier and let him know the plan. We'll come out tomorrow. Is that cool?"

Cool was not even close to the right word. "I'll text the address. The weather is supposed to be great. See you there."

"Can't wait," he said, flashing a smile.


I had the driver stop in Plymouth so I could show Thalia Plymouth Rock and the National Monument to the Forefathers, formerly known as the Pilgrim Monument, built in 1889.

"This is where the Pilgrims landed? It's much smaller than I expected."

I agreed with her and led the way to the monument, an 81-foot granite statue built to honor the Mayflower passengers. The 36-foot figure on top of the monument was called Faith. Surrounding Faith's sides were four smaller figures: Morality, Law, Education and Liberty. There were four reliefs interpreting scenes from Pilgrim history. I mentioned that Faith was holding an open Bible and pointing to the heavens.

"Nice detail," said Thalia, circling the monument to study it from various angles. Morality was personified as a woman holding a tablet of the Ten Commandments in her left hand and the scroll of Revelation in her right. Liberty was a shirtless warrior. "I understand the depiction of religious freedom in the monument, but I'm perplexed by Liberty. Why a warrior with a dead lion slung over his shoulder?"

"The paw on his shoulder is a cool detail. The dead lion — it's Leo. I guess I've arrived on Leo in the zodiac now. Remember. We're on a mission. We need to take note of the zodiac signs that we encounter."

Thalia laughed. "I'm used to my artist friends being weird, but you are *out* there, Paige. But don't worry, I'm all in."

"Thanks. We're definitely in Leo. It's right here in plain sight."

Thalia smiled. "Go on."

I explained that Liberty represented Hercules with his lion skin. "The twelve labors of Hercules were associated with the zodiac. When Hercules killed the Nemean lion, he was battling Leo."

"One of my Greek heroes! I'll search for him in art," she said. "Is it my imagination or does Faith resemble the Statue of Liberty?"

"I think they're first cousins," I said, laughing. "Let's roll. There's a cottage, beer and waves calling us."

Thalia and I gabbed in the back seat all the way to the cottage — a sprawling beach house, as it turned out. Long rows of purple and blue hydrangeas lined the curved driveway. The front porch wrapped around to the back of the house, leading to a short flight of steps that descended to the sand. A firepit, surrounded by navy blue Adirondack chairs, was stocked with wood and dried sticks pruned from the lush landscape. Inside the cottage, the granite-topped kitchen island expanded into a great room that had floor-to-ceiling windows with water views. Thalia unpacked the cooler.

"The fridge is already stocked! Burgers, hot dogs, coleslaw, shrimp, potato salad — the works. And loads of beer and wine, too," Thalia announced.

I was staring out the window at the waves, thinking about boogie boarding. "Let's go for a swim. It's a perfect ten out there."

I sorted through my duffle bag to discover that I had brought a purple top and orange bikini bottoms, a total mismatch. If I had known Axel was joining us, I would have bought the sexy bathing suit that caught my eye in TJ Maxx. Normally, the only one who would notice and comment about my fashion faux-pas would be Melissa. I slathered SPF-50 from head to toe. Then I rummaged through the pile of boards and found the two newest looking ones, with Velcro wrist straps and aerodynamic edges.

"Want some sunscreen?"

Thalia extended her bronze arms toward the sun. "I'm Greek. I drink up the rays."

"Lucky you," I muttered, thinking I'd kill for skin like hers, or at least maim.

I grabbed my board and paddled into the surf. A wave swelled, then curled over my head, propelling me back to the shore.

"Bravo!" shouted Thalia.

She paddled out to join me. We boogie-boarded for an hour. After, we rode bikes into town for dinner. Pilar had reserved a table for us at the Sailor Moon Surf & Turf. It had an upscale menu and, more importantly, an open tab covered by the *Lodestar*. We both ordered medium-rare filet mignon and broiled Maine lobster tails with grilled corn on the cob. Surf and turf, I explained.

"Are we pushing it if we order a bottle of wine?" asked Thalia.

"Of course not."

I wasn't familiar with wine lists, so I deferred to her. "Pick one. Go crazy."

She ordered a California cabernet called Editorial and when the sommelier presented the bottle, it had a vintage typewriter on the label. He had a silver tastevin draped around his neck like gangster bling. He poured a splash of the wine into the tastevin and sipped it to ensure it was flawless.

"This will not fatigue your palates," he announced. I couldn't imagine a day when my palate would experience fatigue. "The nose presents with blackberry jam, vanilla and hints of chocolate."

"It's our sign," I said, after he left. "You nailed the coffee shop art gallery. Tanya is not easy to impress, I might add. It's a bit exhausting sometimes."

"I hope she's not an energy vampire," she said.

"Nah, she's cool, you'll see." We clinked our glasses and I toasted, "To vampires."

I met the other Quadsters at the country club in the morning. We were handed white tight-fitting Kew College women's sleeveless golf shirts with matching white visors. The alumni director gave us our assignments.

"As beer-cart girls, you will cater to Kew's highest donors. Your job is to maintain a respectable distance from the foursomes, but be on hand to provide whatever they want throughout the day. You need to circle in your golf carts and the golfers will signal you if they want something. Do not interrupt their golf games. There are coolers in each cart stocked with water, soda, beer and lemonade. Cigars, lighters, Scotch, snacks and emergency first aid kits are on the back seats. If they want something not on your cart, then come back to the clubhouse and retrieve it. Be polite and charming."

"May I have one of the baseball hats like the guys are wearing?" I asked. "I'd prefer full sun protection."

"No, visors for the ladies, baseball caps for the guys. Besides, you look cute."

I glanced at Melissa who'd already coifed her hair around the open-topped visor. She pulled my visor lower and yanked my ponytail off to one side. "Adorbs," she said.

"My scalp will fry out there," I complained.

"Don't even think about spraying your head with sunscreen. It'll make your hair look greasy," said Melissa. "You need to rub the zinc from your nose. You're not a lifeguard."

On our way to the golf carts, I passed the crowded check-in table where Kew swag bags were handed out to the registrants. I swiped one of the men's bags and stashed it in my golf cart. I descended upon the group of Kew alum from the class of 1988: a divorce lawyer, a robotics entrepreneur, an investment banker, and an orthopedic surgeon.

I turned on the college charm. "Gentlemen, you're looking dapper today. Refreshment? Beverage? Or am I in your way?"

"No, no, please, get in our way!" flirted Leonard the lawyer who didn't realize I could see his eyes through his sunglasses as he ogled my chest. The other men chuckled and took practice swings. They asked for four beers.

"What's your major?" asked Leonard.

"English."

"You want to be a teacher?"

"I'm leaning toward journalism. I have an internship at the *Patriot Lodestar*."

Leonard cracked open his can that exploded and drenched my shirt collar.

"Oh shit, sorry," he said and pulled a handkerchief from his pocket to swipe my neck.

"Ah, no worries," I said, heading back to my cart.

I overheard the gentlemen bantering as I grabbed the wheel: "With a rack like that you should've aimed for the front. When's the last time we saw a wet t-shirt contest?"

"Spring break senior year," joked the surgeon.

I sifted through the swag bag of golf pencils, score cards, a men's medium-sized Kew golf shirt and a baseball hat. I jogged behind a pine tree and swapped shirts. The sleeves reached my elbows so I rolled them up. I used the elastic tie from my ponytail to gather the lengthy shirt hem in a side knot. I tossed the visor on the seat and adjusted the snapback on the baseball cap to fit my head.

Leo, as his friends called him, took a few practice swings, then came over to my cart. He pressed a $50 bill into my hand and muttered, "For the dry cleaning. Oh, and don't stray too far."

"Thanks," I replied but he already headed back to tee off. His shot sliced hard to the right and landed in the woods.

I shadowed the parade of endless foursomes. Most started with beer but veered deep into Scotch and cigars by noon. On the tenth hole Leo stepped behind a tree to relieve his bladder and then waved his hat for my cart.

"Sweetie, what do you have for lunch? Any hot dogs?"

I slid back the lid on the snack cooler and said, "Protein bars, sandwiches and mixed nuts."

"I'm in the mood for a hot dog. Can you get a half-dozen for the guys? Mustard, ketchup, relish on the side. Buttered rolls."

I zipped up to Jill in my cart. She was a few holes behind me, taking videos of the golfers for the college website. She hit the pause button.

"Not exactly *Happy Gilmore* material," she said, "but it'll work. How's it going?"

"Duffers. Slowest game in the history of athletics. If you can call it athletics."

A shrill cackle rose over the hill as Melissa zig-zagged her cart off the path. She raised her beer as she flew past us and shrieked, "Potty break!"

Her passenger bellowed, "Don't make me laugh, I'll pee my pants."

Jill went slack-jawed. "She's partying with the octogenarians. I hope this doesn't turn into *Caddyshack*."

"She's just hamming it up," I reassured Jill and headed to the clubhouse for hot dogs.

Upon my return, I unzipped the insulated food tote for the guys to help themselves to the boiled hot dogs wrapped in tinfoil. Leo devoured two hot dogs and asked, "Do you play?"

"Only if you count miniature golf."

Leo held out his nine-iron. "Go ahead. Take this shot for me. Couldn't be any worse than how I'm hitting today."

I took two practice swings and then went for it. I softened my knees and kept my head in the drive. Thwack, the ball sailed low and straight, hit the ground and trickled onto the edge of the green. The gentlemen howled with approval.

Leo pulled a putter from his bag. "Finish it off."

I stepped on the green and two-putted. I handed him his putter and thanked him for letting me play.

"A few lessons and you could be a pro," he said.

I wanted to tell him I once dreamed of being an Olympic soccer player. I'd played on travel teams ever since fifth grade. I'd quit two years ago due to a concussion in high school. I had not considered replacing soccer with another sport, but taking those strokes had stirred my competitive embers.

"More beer?"

They all took a can. The day dragged on. Old men shouted at me across the fairways, waving their caps, and some chanted *beer-girl-beer-girl-beer-girl*. At the 18th hole, Leo handed me a tip from his group which I stuffed into my pocket, a hundred-dollar bill. I zipped my cart around to the back of the clubhouse, finding Melissa and Jill.

"It's about time. Where's Sheila?" asked Jill.

"I haven't seen her all day. Why?"

"She's doing *closest to the pin* awards. She's handing out sleeves of golf balls and cigars as prizes," said Jill.

Melissa said, "Hop in. Let's go find her. She needs to pick up the pace. I'm dying to get to the cottage."

"Just wait till you see it." I snagged the last beer from my cooler and guzzled it while she sped across the course. She flew down the hill without so much as tapping the brake. A cart of red-faced geriatrics headed toward us.

"Sons of pitches!" she shrieked.

"Are you crazy? Slow down!"

She roared with laughter and barreled ahead, forcing the other cart off the path. She flew around the bend and the cart tipped to the right, nearly clipped an oak tree, then bounced hard to the left. She corrected the cart back to the path and somehow managed to accelerate even faster. We sped around the corner just as a groundskeeper appeared in our path in a landscaper's Bobcat.

"What the fuck?"

Melissa jammed the brakes. The cart tipped, sending me airborne. I braced for the fall with my left arm and rolled in time to see Melissa plant the front end of the cart into a sand trap, the back end jutting out like a lawn dart.

Melissa emerged from the sand trap with her face full of blood. She dropped to her knees and wailed, "My nose! Oh my God, my nose!"

I clutched my wrist against my body, rocking to soothe the pain.

A golfer ran down the slope. "I'm a doctor."

Melissa cupped her hand under her nose. "Oh my God, my nose!"

The doctor checked Melissa's nose. He grabbed a towel from the cart to control the bleeding. My wrist had already ballooned by the time he got to me.

"That looks broken to me. You need an x-ray," he said. "And her nose should be checked as well. I can take you to the ER and arrange to have you both seen by specialists. Come on."

The groundskeepers speculated how to proceed with removing the embedded golf cart. The operator moved the Bobcat to the edge of the sand trap. He hopped out of his wheelhouse, removed his Panama hat and wiped the sweat from his head with a handkerchief. The workers huddled and murmured, inspecting the deep runway tire marks across the green.

"You sure know how to make a mess out of things," said Bobcat. He had thick black caterpillar eyebrows; the right one arched half an inch higher than the left. He swiped the sweat from his forehead and adjusted his hat with black fabric trim that I noticed had an interesting label shaped like an abstract design of man's profile.

"The brakes malfunctioned," said Melissa, her voice muffled by the towel pressed against her nose.

He stared hard at me. "Which Bushfoot member are you affiliated with?"

"We're with the Kew College tournament. I don't know any members."

"Yeah, okay. Then why are you on the radar?"

"What radar?"

"One of the Bushfoot members — a major city real estate developer — told me to keep an eye on you."

"Seriously?"

"Do I look like I'm joking?"

"He must have me confused with someone else."

When he hopped back into his wheelhouse, he pointed his two fingers at his eyes and then pointed them at me. His crew roped the backend of the mangled cart to the Bobcat. He slowly guided it from the sand.

We left with the doctor. I sat in the back of his car wondering why I didn't think to ask Bobcat the name of the real estate developer.

The doctor checked on Melissa while I waited for a radiologist to review my x-rays. I overheard the doctor tell Melissa, "It's not broken, but you might end up with a bump on the bridge of your nose. Let's see how it heals."

"But a nose job would totally cure that, right?"

"If it comes to that, but it should heal without any issues. Keep icing it. Re-check it in a week."

The radiologist brought me into his office with three wide computer screens on his desk. He pulled up the images to show me the crack in my wrist bone. "It's a clean fracture. You will be in a cast for six weeks, then physical therapy to regain the range of motion."

Melissa and I left the hospital with the doctor who brought us there. He drove us back to the beach house. He gave us his business card and we thanked him. He said, "Take it easy and don't drink alcohol if you decide to use the painkillers. But try not to use them, they're addictive."

As he drove away, Melissa grumbled, "I'm totally suing the country club. The brakes didn't work."

"Seriously? You were out of control. Were you drinking all day?"

"Not *all* day. It was probably the gummy bear."

"Wait, you had an edible?"

"One of the old guys gave it to me. His foursome — they totally loved me — was hilarious. They were all stoned." She stopped to check her reflection in the front porch window. "Crap. Do I have black eyes already?"

"Not yet," I said. "And you're not suing anyone. Between the beer and edibles, they'll easily prove you were the one at fault."

"There's some truth to that."

"Do you know how screwed I am? Six weeks with this stupid cast and then rehab. All because you —"

"I'm sorry, Paigester, but look at the bright side. You can still hold a vibrator with your good hand. It doesn't disfigure your appearance like my broken nose. This is truly tragic. Do you know how many people have told me I have a Bella Hadid nose?"

I ignored her and went to the back porch where Thalia, Jill and Sheila were drinking strawberry daiquiris. Melissa followed me out.

"Brake failure," she said. She shot me a look. "Daiquiri, please."

Sheila revved the blender and poured us both an icy pink drink. Jill handed us golf shirts embroidered with *Bushfoot Country Club.* "Compliments of the club director," she said.

"It's the least he could do." Melissa sipped her daiquiri and smacked her lips. "What took you so long? This all happened because we were heading back out to rescue you."

Sheila said, "An octogenarian foursome. They did more farting than golfing. What was I supposed to do?"

Melissa shrugged. "Give prizes to everyone and take off. Duh."

"I felt bad for them."

Thalia offered to grill chicken skewers and make a salad. "My cousins should be here soon," she added.

Melissa's eyes bugged from behind the ice pack. "Wait. What? Axel and Xavier are coming? I thought this was a girls' weekend. I'm in no condition to be around boys. Who invited them?"

"I did," I said.

I followed Thalia and Sheila into the kitchen to show them the barbecue tools.

"Is it painful?" asked Sheila.

"Extremely." I heard car doors and headed for the front porch. "Welcome."

Axel eyed my sling and cast. "What now?"

I shrugged it off. "Minor golf cart debacle."

Thalia bounced down the porch steps to greet her cousins with hugs and Euro-style kisses on both cheeks.

"That sucks," said Xavier.

Axel handed me a tray covered in tinfoil. "Maybe this will take the edge off."

"Let me guess. Your special brownies?"

He grinned. "Freshly baked today."

Axel slid a brownie off the tray and broke it in half to share with me. We went out back where Melissa wore a wide-brimmed hat pulled low to cover her nose. She smacked the outdoor speaker because her playlist wouldn't synch with it.

"I'm totally mortified to be seen like this," whined Melissa. "It will take an iceberg to get the swelling under control. Do I look like an absolute freak?"

"The bridge of your nose has a small red bump, but it's not like Nada Sargin in *The Woman with a Broken Nose*," Jill reassured her.

"You should switch your major to film studies," said Melissa. "It'd be an easy A for you."

"I looked into it, but it's writing intensive," said Jill.

"Screw that," said Melissa. "You're not wired like Paige."

I went to help Thalia with the grill. "What can I do besides stand here and supervise?"

"Nothing. It's almost done. How are you going to type your column with one hand?"

I hadn't thought about it. "I'll write long hand and ask someone to type it. Or I'll hunt and peck with one hand."

Thalia lowered the heat and flipped the chicken skewers. "You can join me when I visit the art museums. You don't need two arms for that."

"Actually, I'd love to get your take on the library murals."

"Happy to show them all to you," she said and called to the others, "Food's ready."

After dinner we munched the hash brownies. Xavier and Axel lit the firepit and we sat around listening to music and drinking beer. I had some fresh ideas for my next horoscope column, so I jotted notes on a yellow pad with my good hand.

"Are you journaling?" asked Thalia.

"Horoscope column. I'm feeling inspired by the sky," I said.

"Bullshit. Admit it, Paigester, you're inspired by the brownies," said Melissa, pressing a cold beer against her nose.

"Guilty! But, seriously, soul-changing moments happen according to planetary movement."

"Oh shit, she's night-sky stoned. It's like *A High and Awful Price: Lessons Learned from the Camp Fire,*" said Jill.

"It's so sexy when you talk Rotten Tomatoes," said Melissa.

I gazed at the stars and pointed toward a popular asterism — Vega, Altair and Deneb —the summer triangle. "The brightest stars in the constellation of Lyra, Aquila and Cygnus. Cygnus, the swan, also known as the Northern Cross."

"Is this astronomy or astrology?" asked Xavier.

"Astronomy is science and astrology is funky creative," I said, explaining that astrologers use astronomical calculations for the positions of celestial bodies within the zodiac which is centered along the ecliptic. The sun's apparent circular yearly path against the background of fixed stars are those of the twelve zodiac constellations; they're all construed by the ancients to be mythical heroes, heroines and creatures except for Libra.

"Paigester, your science lecture is killing the party vibe," said Melissa, exchanging eyerolls with Jill.

I said, "I can't help it if I play connect the dots with celestial events and human affairs."

Xavier studied the sky for a minute. "What else do you see?"

"Well, I don't want to geek out too much, but there's the teapot of Sagittarius, Ophiuchus and Scorpio all under Aquila, the eagle."

Axel asked, "I know Sagittarius and Scorpio. But who's Ophiuchus?"

I pointed out the snake formation. "The serpent holder, the Alice Cooper of Greek mythology."

"It looks more like a martini glass to me. Personally, I can't see how Aquila looks anything like an eagle and Lyra looks more like rhombus than a lyre," said Axel. "I'm Capricorn. What's happening in my sign?"

I pondered Capricorn: detail-oriented, intelligent, hard-working, and fully in control of their destiny. Or so they think. Capricorns get what they set their minds on, making no excuses on the journey. As with all the signs, there are some less-positive traits, and Capricorns are stubborn because they know what they want, setting high expectations for others. I was most familiar with Capricorn because it was my sign, too.

I flipped through my notes and read: "Capricorns need to realize it takes a lot of energy to hold on to what is not meant to be. Let go. Be free. Perhaps you've been feeling trapped, as if you don't have enough breathing room. Freedom is the boat waiting to be rowed through choppy water."

"Ooooh, that's good," Axel said, laughing.

"What's so funny?"

"The brownies make everything funny. But honestly, you're spot on. I've been frustrated with the direction of my summer training. My summer coach is a dick. I was thinking of switching things up." He reached out his hand to pull me up. "C'mon, let's go down to the water."

"I hate to break it to you, but you're not actually a Capricorn. The earth wobbles, like a top as its rotation slows down, called precession, so the position of the stars relative to the earth change over time. If you were born over two thousand years ago, you would be a Capricorn. But when you were born, the sun was in Sagittarius. Technically, if you believe the position of the stars on the day of your birth affect your daily life, then you are a Sagittarius."

"When you write your horoscopes, do you go by the corrected dates?" asked Axel.

"Nope. I thought about it, but that would probably upset my readers. My boss thinks she's Aries, but I hate to notify her, the sun was in Pisces when she was born."

The tide was out. Axel and I approached the calm surf. "Thalia and I rode the waves yesterday. They were powerful," I said.

"Good thing you got to do that before —"

I lifted my casted arm. "Yeah, it blows."

"Are you pissed at Melissa?"

"Not really. I'm used to her insanity. It's part of the package. I'm sure she feels bad about it —"

And that's when he leaned in and kissed me.

"Oh, wow. Didn't see that coming."

"Sorry. Couldn't resist. Been waiting to do that since —"

"Since last year's tailgate." I kissed him back, longer this time. "Me too."

"Really? I came to the coffee shop to visit you, but you—"

"Ah, yeah, well — there was Stoph."

"Yeah. I still can't believe it. Our team is setting up an Ultimate Frisbee tournament in his honor."

"That's a cool tribute, but I don't want to talk about Stoph right now."

We watched the moonlight shimmering on the ocean. I kissed him again, amping it up. My heart pounded as he pressed against me, turning my back against the sand. He slid on top of me. A smile crept across his face.

"Is this okay?" he whispered.

I scrambled to say something beach-sexy: *Lately, sex on the beach is all I seem to think about*; *let's do it while the seagulls sleep*; *whoa, that's some driftwood…*but blame it on the brownies, I abandoned all sexy thoughts, deferring to humor: "As long as you don't have crabs —"

He collapsed forward in a fit of laughter. I didn't exactly derail the moment; things just took a minor detour.

When we returned to the cottage, Axel stoked the bonfire with driftwood. Thalia emerged with S'mores fixings and a bottle of ouzo tucked under her arm. We both took shots of ouzo and searched for marshmallow-roasting sticks.

"I think Axel fancies you."

"I fancy him," I giggled. "I hope that doesn't creep you out."

"Not at all. My cousin and a stargazer, go figure."

I found a multi-pronged stick to roast five marshmallows at once. We passed around shots of the anise-flavored aperitif. The gabbing ceased when two guys — thick glasses, Michigan hoodies, sagging cargo shorts — crashed our bonfire.

"Great fire," said the shorter guy. "Mind if we join?"

"Depends. Which Michigan do you go to?" Melissa eyeballed them.

"University," he said.

"You pass. Plenty of S'mores," she said, gesturing with a hand wave for them to help themselves. "Cold ones in the cooler, too."

They loaded marshmallows on their sticks and took large swigs of ouzo and raided the cooler for summer ales.

"Do you have a summer house nearby?" Melissa blew out her flaming marshmallow.

"Three houses down from here. We could smell the bonfire. Seth's visiting for the weekend," said Marty, the taller dude.

Melissa scooched next to Marty. "What's your dad do? Investment banking?"

"He's a teacher."

"How does a teacher afford one of these beach houses?" Her words slurred together; beach houses sounded like *bitchusses*.

"My mom makes the bank."

"Doing what?"

Marty sandwiched a charred marshmallow between two graham crackers, squishing it together with a chocolate square tucked inside. "She's a producer for Netflix. She got in early, when they offered stock options."

"Let's take a stroll. Show me your place so I know where I'm having breakfast."

He chuckled. "The fam's not here this weekend, in case that matters. Mom's filming on location in California."

"Even better," she said, tugging on his arm to get up.

They left, but Seth stayed with us. Jill sat next to him, claiming Melissa's leftovers.

"Do you come here often?" he asked.

"Not often enough," said Jill.

Sheila cranked her music, then propelled herself around the beach to the beat. Seth watched her for a few minutes, downed the rest of his Corona and joined her. He shifted his feet as if he were heal tapping the corners of an imaginary box drawn in the sand. His ramrod upper torso stiffened with minimal arm motions.

Sheila took his hands, guiding him outside his box. "Relax, it's sand dancing."

"I thought I was relaxed."

She giggled. "Your shoulders are up next to your ears. Lower them and swing your arms, like this."

He flung his arms overhead, but it looked like his feet were stuck in mud. Jill joined them, imitating his moves. She called to the others, "C'mon guys. It's like Elvis in *Blue Hawaii*!"

As we staggered toward them, my head spun like a pinwheel.

"One-two, three-four, five-six. You should feel like a can of cold beer on a hot night that just popped open. Try to mirror me. Free flow."

My ouzo-inspired dancing resembled quicksand rescue efforts — me flailing in the sand, Axel yanking me up by my good arm, me flopping around — until Axel steered me inside the cottage.

The next morning, I recovered in the kitchen with a bowl of cheerios and hot coffee. I heard coughing in the living room — Seth was crashed on the couch and by the foul smell of things, he'd emitted beer farts the whole night. I opened the kitchen windows and lit a candle.

Melissa filled a plastic sandwich bag with ice. "Did you brew a fresh Goforth blend?"

"It's Newman's Organic. Want some?"

She pressed the ice pack on her nose. "Definitely."

"What's the story with Marty?"

"Nice house. Waste of time."

"How come?"

"Gay. Does the bump look larger today? Check from the side."

I stepped around to view all the angles. It was purple and swollen. "A tad bigger."

She pressed the ice on the bridge of her nose.

"How do you know?"

She cackled. "I tried to make out with him at his house — makes this place look like a shack — and he ran away. My nose isn't so bad that it would repel men, right?"

"Right. But why did he invite you back to his house?"

"He didn't exactly invite me. I just assumed he'd be into me. He was being polite, I guess."

"Ah." I fixed her coffee with cream and sugar.

"He invited us to Provincetown. It's Bear Week."

"What's Bear Week?"

"Bear Week is large hairy gay men on full display. It'll be a blast."

It didn't take long before Melissa rallied everyone for the P-Town excursion, as if she were chaperoning a middle school trip to the zoo. It was pushing 95-degrees when we parked and penetrated the carnival crowd. Sweat rolled down my back pooling in the waistband of my shorts. My casted arm itched like an ant colony. The Bushfoot golf hat trapped the heat inside my head so that my brain parboiled.

"You okay?" asked Axel.

"It's hotter than a fat lady's crotch! We should've stayed at the beach," I whined like a ten-year old.

Jill said, "This reminds me of BearCity, the film with Joe Conti searching for the perfect man."

"Never saw it," said Axel.

Marty strutted into the crowd with Xavier trailing behind him. Xavier's gait transitioned from his usual bouncy jock strut to hip-swinging, similar to Marty. I wondered if Xavier was being comical, imitating the carnival vibe or if he was just getting into the swing of things.

A parade of potbellied, middle-aged men — loaded with orangutan hair on their backs and chests — sashayed past us in Speedos, their sweaty Sasquatch chest hair clumped together like used Brillo pads. When patriotic fife music came on the speakers, the crowd erupted. Seth and Marty cheered. That's when I started to dry heave by the curb.

"Do gay men repulse you?" Marty snapped.

"Get her water. She's dehydrated," Axel said.

I chugged the lukewarm water, but in truth I wasn't dehydrated or homophobic. I suffered from trichophobia — a fear of hair. As a child, I was sent for cognitive behavioral therapy after a traumatic bathtub episode where a long strand of loose hair entangled my fingers. I reacted like a blind seal in the tub and almost drowned. Then there was the time in kindergarten when there was a long brown strand imbedded in Play-Doh and I puked on the floor. The therapist opted for exposure therapy, plucking a strand of her curly hair and placing it on the table in front of me. She coached me through my thoughts and feelings, then made me hold it. I was a quick study, making sure I was completely cured in one session — *look at me holding your hair, it's a miracle* — never to return to exposure therapy again. It still seemed odd that torturing a patient with what they suffered from could be a cure.

But all the counseling in the world couldn't get me through Bear Week. I tried to talk myself down: *Just get to the end of the street. Focus on the ground. Don't look at the ...armpits.*

A man in cutoff denim shorts and a wife-beater stared at me. His shoulders and forearms were coated in thick fur. He had a tattoo near his right shoulder — a man's profile drawn in right angles. He slid his sunglasses toward the end of his nose and stared at me with narrowed eyes.

I looked the other way, but he took quick strides toward me and bumped his shoulder into mine, leaving his sweaty slime on my skin. I was knocked off balance, tripping on the curb. My casted arm slammed against the sidewalk.

"Ow!" I cried in pain, shuddering from brushing against his hairy body.

"We know McKim told you the secret. Now you tell us, or else," he growled.

"Or else what?"

"How many bones do we need to break before you give it up?"

"What the fuck is wrong with you guys? He didn't tell me anything!"

Axel stepped in, grabbing the thug's hairy arm and twisted it behind his back. "What's your problem, dick head?"

"Fuck off, Ken doll!" shouted the thug, slipping out of Axel's grip. He shoved Axel and ran off, disappearing into the crowd. Axel didn't chase him. He helped me up, asking if I was okay.

I swallowed hard, but couldn't stop my gut from backing up, and I hurled Cheerios all over the sidewalk. My head pounded. I spiked the Bushfoot hat into a nearby trash can, thinking it made me too easy to spot in the crowd. The Bobcat operator had the same pin on his Panama hat that matched the tattoo on the thug's shoulder. A symbol, one I needed to figure out.

"Let's get out of here."

# Chapter Four — Virgo

On Monday morning I met Thalia in Copley Square for coffee. We sat on a bench waiting for the public library to open, admiring the rows of arched windows. We'd planned to spend the day exploring the city for zodiac signs in architecture and art. I was deep in thought about the Winter Hexagon Salon, trying to decipher where such a place might be located. So far, my Google searches for Winter Hexagon, Bauhaus, and early American architecture proved unproductive. I searched the *Lodestar* archives for reporting on unusual Bauhaus activity, locating not one article. Now that Pilar had promised a year in Rome, I was motivated to pursue every angle I could think of to find the key to the Winter Hexagon Salon.

"That's *Ecole des Beaux-Arts* influence on Charles McKim — classic Renaissance style. McKim called the library the *Palace for the People*," I mentioned. "After we see the murals, we can go to Trinity Church. Richardson's finest work is there."

When the doors opened, we headed through the main entrance where I pointed out the white marble floor inlaid with zodiac symbols. My mind flashed to Memorial Hall in North Easton where Richardson used the zodiac in the carved stone on the tower frieze. I had often wondered about its significance, and here again all the astrological signs were inlaid across the entrance hall.

The staircase split into two sections, each guarded by an enormous marble lion. I recalled my research on Solomon's temple and Richardson's use of carved lions on the entryway steps. I wondered if McKim was building his version of Solomon's temple just as Richardson had done.

Thalia pointed out a series of murals called *The Muses of Inspiration* by Pierre Puvis de Chavannes. "This is Chavannes' only work on display outside of France. He was too old to travel to Boston, so McKim sent him the dimensions to make a scale model of the staircase for him to work from. The murals were shipped to Boston and installed here."

One of the Chavannes' murals caught my eye.

"That's Prometheus chained to a rock surrounded by sea nymphs," explained Thalia. "Prometheus stole fire from the gods and gave it to humans. For that offense, the gods gave him a particularly gruesome punishment. Everyday an eagle eats his liver. Every night it grows back. The eagle returns the next day to do it all over again."

I focused on the eagle, which swooped in readiness to attack. "That's a strange story."

"Greek mythology? Not strange to me!"

"Strange as in sadistic. What's so special about fire anyway?"

Thalia led me up to the Abbey room where the library workers were setting up tables covered in white linen with centerpieces filled with autumnal-toned roses and baby's breath.

"This room is gorgeous. I'd like to be a guest at the party," I said.

Thalia asked one of the workers: "Can we look around? We won't get in the way."

"Don't stay too long or we might put you to work," joked the man arranging the chairs.

The Abbey room featured a mural depicting Galahad's search for the holy grail. Abbey included Galahad, Lancelot, King Arthur and the Round Table, castles, spells, dark knights, maidens, and a bride named Blanchefleur. Galahad was pictured kneeling before a white angel carrying the holy grail on Solomon's ship.

"All this detail, just to tell the story of Galahad finding the holy grail," I said.

"It took Abbey eleven years to complete the work. He painted a lot of Shakespeare scenes as well," explained Thalia. "Sometimes I wonder if there are secrets hidden in the murals."

"Let me know what you come up with. Remember to look for zodiac signs," I said.

We studied the painted panels for a few more minutes, but the workers were a distraction. Thalia said, "This room is great, but the highlight of the library is the John Singer Sargent murals on the third floor. The entire hall is the triumph of religion, from paganism to Christianity. I'm a little obsessed with it."

On the third floor we studied the Sargent murals: *Handmaid of the Lord* and *Madonna of Sorrows*, both paintings featuring the Virgin Mary.

"Mary could represent Virgo — a virgin, unwedded girl, a maiden. So now I think we're in Virgo," I said. Mary, the lady in the chair in the other mural, was surrounded by four living creatures: a lion, man, eagle and bull. "It's interesting. Those four were mentioned in the Book of Revelation. They carried Ezekiel to heaven. They were also ornamentation on King Solomon's temple. It's interesting how they're labeled as Matthew, Mark, Luke and John, the evangelists."

Thalia thought for a moment. "Is it safe to say that they're related to the zodiac? Perhaps they represent the two equinoxes and two solstices in Leo, Aquarius, Scorpio and Taurus."

"That's out of order. Aquarius doesn't really match because the man isn't pouring water. Also, there's no eagle in the zodiac."

"Okay, but I deserve partial credit for the idea," she said, moving on to look at the murals of Moloch and Astarte at the opposite end of the hall. "Did you notice that Astarte is standing on the crescent moon, which is the same crescent moon that the *Madonna of Sorrows* stood on?"

After further review, I noticed that Sargent had painted the symbols of the zodiac ring between Moloch and Astarte. I said,

"Okay new thought: Mary could represent a later version of Astarte, the same character."

In the background behind Astarte, I noticed another depiction of Prometheus suffering an eagle's attack. I made a mental note to watch for Prometheus in other works. There had to be some significance to it and a possible connection to the zodiac and the night sky.

A woman with a clipboard who'd been organizing the staff in the Abbey room passed us for the third time. I sensed that she was eavesdropping. I didn't want to rush the Sargent mural visit, but I felt annoyed by her presence. I suggested we head to Trinity Church to get some fresh air. "Is it me or was that lady following us?"

"What lady?"

"The one with the clipboard. She was in the Abbey room and followed us to the Sargent murals."

"I didn't really notice her."

"Seriously? I think she thought we were scheming an art heist," I said, picking up the pace toward Trinity Church.

"You're not scheming an art heist, are you?" she asked. "Maybe that's what the Winter Hexagon Salon is — a room full of stolen art."

I stopped outside Trinity Church, thinking Thalia might be on to something. "Maybe the salon was a place to protect masterpieces from getting into the wrong hands. McKim told me he didn't trust Bauhaus. Maybe McKim hid art from Bauhaus —"

"What art would they hide? There are masterpieces displayed in the library, the museums, the churches. Did he say anything about Rembrandt? Michelangelo?"

"No. It's like a scavenger hunt without knowing the prize."

"Can you imagine if we found Rembrandt's *A Lady and Gentleman in Black*? It was stolen in the Gardner Museum heist in 1990. That would be epic!"

Not as epic as finding the ark of the covenant, I thought. I was convinced that the McKim secret was something passed down from Richardson, leading him to replicate Solomon's temple when he designed the library. The zodiac signs imbedded in the library foyer floor were not a random placement. *Hunt for the key, find the Winter Hexagon Salon —* there's something more to this, maybe something as big as the ark of the covenant. But what?

"Now you get to pick one thing from Richardson's church design and I'll try to explain it."

Thalia meandered the outside perimeter for five minutes before she paused in front of a stone carving. "Okay. This."

I grinned because it was an easy one. "That's St. John the Evangelist. Legend has it that St. John went to Ephesus in Turkey where he was given a cup with poisoned wine. He blessed the wine and then pulled a snake from the cup, making it safe to drink."

"I'll drink to that," said Thalia. "Is St. John the patron saint of wine?"

The eagle carvings above St. John reminded me that Sargent's mural associated the eagle with St. John. I noticed the façade was covered with images of the four creatures. This was not a coincidence and I wanted to figure out its significance.

"Jesus was the one who turned water into wine —"

"Good one," she laughed. "I've been meaning to ask you a question."

"What?"

"I was wondering if you wanted to room together this semester?"

The idea had not occurred to me. I was set up with the biggest suite on campus courtesy of the Kew College president, a fellow North Easton druid. I quickly warmed to the idea of sharing it. "One condition."

"Name it."

"We collaborate on our dorm style and make it so kickass that it blows away Melissa and Jill's room. You should have seen them last year. They were the queens of the campus. Their room was like a Pinterest page with everything all matchy-matchy. We need to dominate the Battle of the Dorm Decor."

"Deal," she said.

Next stop, the Christian Science Center to check out the mapparium — a three-story, stained-glass globe. When we passed Reflection Hall, I mentioned that it looked out of place. "It's like a Bauhaus spaceship."

Thalia shielded the sun from her eyes. "Ready for liftoff?"

I shared a few Bauhaus details: Gropius' most accomplished student was I.M. Pei. The Christian Science Center was designed by Araldo Cassuto, a Gropius-Pei groupie. We gazed into the reflection pool that mirrored the vast complex of Brutalist buildings — dull when compared to the Italian Renaissance style of the Christian Science Church. I wondered if this compound could be Bauhaus headquarters.

"The original church has a globe mapparium. Let's check it out," I said.

At the crowded ticket line, I flashed my *Lodestar* ID. The security guard glanced at my ID and studied my face for a moment. Then he looked Thalia up and down before letting us pass. He mumbled into his headset, "*Lodestar's* in the house, plus one."

I wondered why it would matter that a *Lodestar* staffer was visiting the mapparium. Who was he telling? He glanced again at me with suspicion. He turned his back and said, "Paige Moore. They're heading in now."

We watched the mapparium three-dimensional presentation enhanced with orchestra music and LED lights. I noticed a security guard in the corner of the room, staring at us.

He was shaped like a wine barrel with his thick arms folded across his chest. When the presentation ended, we headed out.

"Right this way, ladies." He gestured with his hand for us to go through a side door.

"Isn't this the exit?" I pointed to the neon sign above his head.

"This way please."

He blocked the door and directed us to exit through the side. I followed Thalia down a dimly lit hallway that snaked behind the globe room. Thalia startled when she walked right into another barrel-chested security guard.

"Sorry. I didn't see you," she said.

"Follow me." He took us to a bare white room with only an oversized rectangular clock on the wall and a one-drawer black desk and white resin chairs. "Take a seat."

"What's going on?" I asked.

He pointed to the chair. His bulging biceps left us no choice, so we sat like obedient poodles and silently waited. Five minutes later, we heard thunderous heels clack in the hallway. A swirl of pungent gardenia perfume arrived ahead of a woman who slammed her leather portfolio onto the desk. She stood about six-feet in her heels. She positioned her hands on her hips, her splayed elbows widened her dense frame. She unbuttoned the chalk-striped black blazer that looked fresh off-the-rack from Brooks Brothers and slung it lopsided across the back of the chair. Sweat rings orbited the armpits of her light blue silk blouse. She dropped into the chair with a thud. Her long legs stretched toward us exposing her sockless tree-trunk ankles and practical black pumps.

"I recognize you," I said.

"If it isn't Ms. Paige Moore from the *Patriot Lodestar*." She snapped open her briefcase and pulled out a file. She clicked her retractable ballpoint pen three times. "Tell me how you knew Chuck McKim?"

"Who are you?"

We locked eyes. She interlocked her fingers and cracked her knuckles. "I'm asking the questions. How did you know Chuck McKim?"

"I didn't know him."

She grimaced as if she'd chomped into a dill pickle. "Do you often visit dying patients in the hospital that you don't know and tell the staff you're a family relation?"

I glanced at her cheek and saw the football-shaped mole. She was the asphalt cowgirl nurse — Brenda Shepherd. But what was she doing here?

"You were his nurse when he died, right?"

"You signed in as his niece. Were you related to him?"

"No."

She launched a power sigh that revealed she'd eaten tuna fish for lunch. "Then why did you lie?"

"Do you work for the Christian Science Center or the hospital? We didn't do anything wrong and we are under no obligation to speak to you."

"This isn't about me. This is about what you're up to," she growled. "We'll let you go as soon as you reveal what McKim told you in the hospital. He said something to you at the accident site that made you want to see him before he died. What was it?"

"Gibberish, that's all."

"Jake McGregor says McKim told you *something*. Let's talk about that." She popped her eyes, as if she'd proposed a great solution to a problem.

I regretted taking the hospital elevator with McGregor. Now I knew what McKim meant when he said not to trust Bauhaus. I feigned cooperation. "Look Brenda. You people keep threatening me. I've already told you ten times, it was nonsense. What do you expect? The guy's legs were flattened like pancakes."

"There's something you're not saying."

"Why would I withhold information?" I asked. "I have no idea who you are. Why are you so crazed about having this anyway?"

She pushed away from the desk with her hands locked behind her head. Her eyes scanned the ceiling as if she were looking for cobwebs in the recessed lights.

"It looks like you're not going to make this easy," she said, shoving the file back in the briefcase and snapped it shut. "Last chance."

"I've told you everything I know."

"We're done here," she huffed. "For now. Show them out." Her heavy heels smacked down the corridor with a gardenia wake trailing her.

Outside, Thalia asked, "What the hell was all that about?"

"I'm not sure, but it confirms what I already knew. That construction accident was no accident. McKim must have known something and I'm going to figure out what."


The Quadsters planned a Labor Day shindig at my apartment, our last chance to let loose before we moved back to campus to start the new semester: pre-game by the rooftop pool, dinner, concert at the Sinclair.

"Four tickets?" Jill called to confirm.

"Make it seven. I'll call the *Lodestar* to add the extra three," I said.

"Who else is joining us?"

"Thalia and her cousins," I said.

Jill groaned. "Does Melissa know about this? She was adamant: strictly a Quadster weekend, she said. She's still self-conscious about her —"

"Nose? Give me a break. You can't even tell there's anything wrong with it. She's such a drama queen. Try having a ten-pound cast!"

"I'll pick up seven tickets. But you should tell Melissa, so she's not socially sabotaged again."

"Socially sabotaged?"

"Like when the brothers showed up at the beach house. It was like that movie, *Psycho Beach Party*."

"Get the tickets. I'll deal with Queenie."

I left a message for Melissa updating her on the plan. She arrived at the apartment early to claim the extra bedroom. "I was getting my nails done when you phoned," she said. "What's the deal with the extras?"

"Technically, Thalia isn't an *extra*. We're rooming together so you better get used to her."

"Since when are you rooming together? I thought you had a palatial dorm suite all to yourself."

"It's big enough for four. I figured it'd be cool to have a roomie."

Melissa sauntered into the kitchen in her Frankies Bikinis LA-inspired terrycloth coverup. The bright colors on the dress looked like a bowl of rainbow sherbet. "Which one are you claiming? Or are you still deciding?"

"Huh?"

"The cousins, which one is yours? I'm giving you the courtesy of choosing before I make my moves on the other one. I need an end-of-summer fling."

I dumped a can of frozen coconut mix into the blender and added rum. "Axel, I guess."

"You guess? You had the whole summer to stake your claim. Why the delay?"

"Keeping my options open?"

She sipped and added more rum to the blender. "For the record, I'm gunning for the X-Man tonight. Xavier is the better-looking one anyway. His ass in jeans is GQ material."

"I'd rather not think about his ass."

Jill and Sheila arrived, and we headed to the pool. Melissa updated them that Thalia was going to room with me, followed by an eyeroll exchange with Jill.

Sheila sat on the pool's edge dangling her feet in the water. "What will we call ourselves now? Thalia makes five."

I said, "Let's leave it as Quadsters. Quintsters is too close to spinsters."

Melissa chimed in, "The Quadsters and the Greek Geek."

"Greek goddess is more like it," said Sheila.

We got dressed for the concert. I wore faded jeans, flip flops and a floral cotton top that passed Melissa's side-eye without comment.

"Tucked in or out?" asked Melissa about her vintage Rolling Stones *World Tour 81-82* t-shirt.

"In," said Jill. "Shows off your skinny waistline."

We met the three Greeks at the outdoor patio at the Sinclair music venue in Cambridge. They ordered pitchers of Sinclair's signature sangria.

"Interested in appetizers?" The waitress jotted down our order of nachos, chicken wings and fish tacos.

"Do you guys room together?" asked Jill.

Axel laughed. "No, we'd kill each other."

Thalia nodded. "They're competitive about everything. It would be a disaster."

"Plus, we play different sports. We need to give each other space when we're in-season," said Xavier.

"Yeah, he parties his ass off in the fall, while I'm crushing the workouts for the regattas."

Xavier said, "When aren't you crushing the workouts?"

We quickly emptied the pitchers of sangria. When the waitress returned with the appetizers, Sheila ordered more drinks. "Can we get a round of Love Your Friends, Die Laughing?"

"What's in it?" asked Thalia.

The waitress said, "Ketel One, Citroen, lime and lots of bubbles. What band are you seeing tonight?"

Jill collected the menus and passed them to her. "Gasoline Kisses. I saw them last year and there's no way I was going to miss them. I love the lead guitarist. He jams like a vacuum sucking up chaos."

"I'm not familiar with Gasoline Kisses. They're opening for Frat Mouse, right? One of the best bands to play here," said the waitress.

We ordered burgers and disco fries. Melissa and Jill went for salad and grilled chicken. We moved onto beer, so I chose Clown Shoes Bubble Farm just because of the name. When the waitress returned with the bill for me to sign off on the *Lodestar* tab, she suggested we visit the rest room before the concert so as not to lose our place on the floor once the concert started. We went inside early to claim our real estate close to the stage.

"Spread out a little, girls. I'm gonna need room to work my moves," said Sheila.

The venue was packed and minutes before the music started, two rugged six-foot-something guys in denim jackets and baseball hats worked their way up to the front and stood in front of us. The jackets had matching patchwork as if they were roadies or part of a street gang. It took me a minute to decipher the design: the abstract profile of a man's head I'd been noticing lately.

I tapped one guy's shoulder and asked, "Hey, what's that symbol? I keep seeing it all over town. What does it mean?"

"Get lost." He barely turned his head.

"That's not right. We got here early to claim our space. You can't just stand in front of us."

He sneered, "Yo, it's general admission. You don't *claim a space*. There's plenty of room over there."

Axel stepped forward to compromise. "The ladies were here first. They can't see over you. If they move closer to the stage, you can stand behind them."

They blew him off. Then the crowd erupted as the band took the stage. The lead vocalist shouted, "How ya'll doin' tonight? We're Gasoline Kisses. We're super stoked to be back in Boston!"

The guitars wailed. The space invaders ignored Axel and cheered with the crowd. They swigged their beers and bopped their heads to the beat. Axel's face tightened and the veins in his neck flared.

"Let it go. It's not worth it," I told him.

We bunched closer. Sheila busted out her dance moves, whipping her head and thrusting her hips in synch with the beat. Her gyrations were contagious as the Quadsters and the

Greeks mimicked her moves. The lead guitarist dropped to his knees by the edge of the stage to grind out the refrain. He reached out toward Sheila and pulled her onto the stage like a ragdoll. The drummer pounded out the start of the next song with an up-tempo marching cadence. Sheila strutted across the stage, Mick Jagger-style. The audience erupted, including the two losers who stood in front of us. The lead guitarist jumped in Sheila's path and made sounds like a jet taking off. She whipped her hair around as if being electrocuted. It was tough to determine who the crowd appreciated more, Sheila or Gasoline Kisses.

"Factory settings defied right there!" The lead singer shouted and pointed to Sheila. "Cambridge, we love you!"

We reached out to help Sheila down from the stage. She gushed, "Oh my God, that was a blast!"

Everyone cheered and called out for them to play their most popular songs: "Gazebo Wine Time" and "Gear Head."

The lead singer shouted, "Does anyone know where we can crash tonight? Hotels in Boston cost more than we're making on this whole damn tour!"

The drummer started pounding out the next song. Melissa whipped out a pen and a crumpled Target receipt from her crossbody Gucci purse and jotted down a note. She handed it to Sheila. "Give this to the hottie guitarist."

"What did the note say?" asked Axel as Sheila bolted to deliver the note.

"Paige's address. They can crash with us tonight."

"What?" I surveyed the band: one, dreadlocks; two, sweaty grunge; and three, total west coast stoners. I protested, "We don't know anything about these guys!"

"Just think, if they hit it big, we can say we knew them when they were no-names," said Melissa.

"What if they go Keith Moon and trash the place?"

"Relax, Paigester. They won't. And even if they did, your *Lodestar* connections will take care of it."

I tried to convince myself they wouldn't show: what rock and roll band asks the audience for lodging arrangements?

Gasoline Kisses pounded out an encore and exited the stage. The crowd screamed for more, so they raced back onstage and bellowed, "You rock, Boston! Thank you, Paige Moore for hosting us tonight. This one's for you!"

I exhaled. "I'm fucked."

They cranked out a cover version of Vampire Weekends' "Ladies of Cambridge" and the fans erupted.

A Sinclair staffer approached us after their encore and said, "Which one of you is Paige Moore? Kurt wants to talk to you."

"Who's Kurt?" I asked.

"Gasoline Kisses' lead singer."

I grabbed Axel's hand. "Help me out of this shit show."

We followed the staffer backstage to a room that reeked like a men's locker room. Gasoline Kisses swigged beer and passed a joint.

They quieted when they saw me.

"I'm Paige," I said.

Kurt said, "Yo, Paige. You sure this is cool? There's like six of us?"

All eyes settled on me.

"Plenty of room for all," I said.

"Awesome. We're ready to bust a move, if you are."

My mind raced, failing to find a way out of it. "No problem. There's a parking garage so just tell the guy at the gate my apartment number."

Axel sucked up to them. "In the mood for steak? We'll fire up the grill when you get there."

We pushed back through the crowd. I shouted over the din of Frat Mouse. "We have to roll. They're ready to move in with us. Now we're feeding them, too, thanks to Axel."

The denim jacket bros butted in. "Is it true? Are you really hosting Gasoline Kisses?"

Axel stared hard at them. "What if we are?"

"Can we come? That sounds like a blast."

"Fuck off," Axel responded. He took my hand as we bolted out of the Sinclair. "Can you believe those losers?"

"Total dicks."

We moved in a pack. Jill started imitating Sheila's dance and we all joined in, creating a drunken uproar along the Harborwalk.

"We need to divide and conquer," said Axel. "I'll pick up the steaks, Xavier you get beer and tequila, and you ladies go straight to the apartment."

Everyone seemed to think this was the best plan ever devised, except for me. What if they do lines of cocaine on the coffee table? What if their dreadlocks clog the shower drain? What if they expect groupie sex on the couches?

"What's wrong?" asked Thalia.

"I'm not sure about this plan."

She lowered her voice, "What's the worst that could happen?"

"They trash my apartment like Keith Moon wannabees."

"I don't think they're wannabees. They really rocked it."

"You think so? 'Gazebo Wine Time' was —" I began, then felt my shirt get yanked from behind. The forceful tug spun me around; I thought someone was joking with me at first. Then a man, who resembled the barrel-chested security guard at the mapparium, released my shirt. He pointed his jagged-nailed forefinger into my face.

"A message from Brenda Shepherd," he said, lowering his shoulder into mine, knocking me back several steps. His two-day old beard appeared an inch from my face. A cigarette-and-beer stench came off his Red Sox t-shirt. "Next time, I'll hit you for real."

Thalia kicked his leg. "Back off, asshole!"

He stiff-armed Thalia and shoved me in the chest. I went flying backward and found myself suddenly in the air. The eight-foot drop seemed to last forever. The lights from the Boston skyline blurred into a streak that disappeared when I plunged into the water. A minute later, I saw someone dive in next to me; Axel's head rose from the water. "Paige!"

My arms flailed. I choked on the water I'd swallowed. He flipped me onto my back, cupping his hand under my chin. He swam around twenty yards, pulling me to safety. "It's shallow here. Put your feet down."

The Quadsters looked down at us. Jill shouted, "Should we call the cops?"

"I'm okay." I twisted the hem of my shirt to wring out some of the water.

"Maybe we should," said Axel, brushing his hand across my dripping bangs.

"What good would it do? We can't identify the guy —"

"Fine. Let's get out of here," he said, pulling me by the arm. We climbed the ladder back up to the sidewalk where the Quadsters met us.

His shoes squished while I tiptoed carefully in bare feet.

"My flip flops. They fell off in the harbor." My legs trembled. I fought back the tears.

"Take my shoes," he insisted.

I felt like a little kid playing dress up with grownups shoes. Axel's soaked boat shoes flopped off my heels as we shuffled back to the Quadsters. He put his arm across my shoulders, holding me close to his side.

"Are you sure you're okay?" asked Jill.

"I'm fine. Let's get out of here," I said.

Back at my apartment, I headed for the shower. But what I wanted to do was put on dry clothes and go to bed, preferably with Axel snuggled by my side.

"When the band arrives, keep things under control. I don't want the cops showing up here. Got it?"

"Cops? What are you so paranoid about?" asked Jill. She plucked a bottle of Grey Goose from the freezer and lined up shot glasses on the kitchen counter.

"I just got attacked. Sorry if I seem paranoid."

"Make hers a double," said Melissa.

My insides burned: one, if Melissa was pushed into the harbor, it would be on the evening news; two, she invited the band to stay at my place; and three, my cast was soaked and probably going to fall apart.

"What the fuck? Why didn't you invite them back to your piece of shit apartment? These aren't exactly the type of guys you'd bring home to your parents."

"Chill out, Paigester."

The buzzer sounded. Melissa darted across the kitchen to tell the doorman to admit our guests. "If one of these guys turns out to be Mick Jagger, I'll bring him home to meet my parents. Okay, Paigester?"

"I highly doubt Gasoline Kisses is grooming the next Rolling Stones."

Melissa whipped the door open to greet the band. "Hi guys. Beer? Vodka? What would you like?"

Kurt strutted in followed by his lady friend, Lydia, the tambourine player. Nova, the drummer, grabbed a beer and said, "Awesome pad."

The bass guitarist, Carl, grunted, "Is it craft beer?"

"He's a Portland beer snob," explained Kurt. "Trust me, we'll take whatever you've got."

Melissa rifled through the beer selection. "How about Fat Tire? Is that crafty enough?"

"Only if you have one with me," said Carl.

I eyed Melissa, who'd announced at the Sinclair that she was gluten free for three months and *wouldn't dream of poisoning her system ever again*. She popped open two Fat Tires and said, "Deal. Let me show you around."

"Whose place is this?" he asked.

Melissa batted her eyes at Carl. "Paige and I lived here all summer. It's a cute apartment. We're heading back to college in a few days."

"Damn, you're jailbait," Carl chuckled. "We all graduated two years ago. We met at Reed College and started the band freshman year. Been working gigs ever since. We love the Sinclair."

"You'll top the Billboards in no time," gushed Melissa.

The doorman buzzed to say the bass player was heading up the elevator. He emerged with a wheeled container stuffed with worn pillows and sleeping bags that reeked of skunky, burnt-rope smoke. Kurt and Lydia made themselves comfortable on the balcony, chain smoking and chugging beer. Axel and Xavier emerged with grocery bags and more beer.

Axel hugged me. "Are you okay?"

"Thanks for rescuing me."

"Ten years of swimming lessons. Glad they came in handy."

We headed to a common area by the pool with picnic table dining spaces, oversized grills, and big-screen tvs. We set up the feast and pre-heated the grill. Gasoline Kisses ditched their shirts and ripped jeans and dove into the pool in their boxer-briefs.

"Sweaty underwear in the pool? Call Hazmat," I confided to Thalia.

Melissa launched a bikini-clad cannonball near Xavier.

"Total wedgie," she said, throwing her arms around Xavier.

Axel tossed the steaks and chicken on the grill. I peeled the lids off the store-bought macaroni and potato salads. "Will you stay over? I feel kinda weird having these strangers in my place."

"Of course. I was counting on it to tell you the truth. Even before Gasoline Kisses showed up." His smile instantly eased my anxiety.

When the band sat down to eat, I felt relieved that I couldn't see their soggy boxer shorts under the picnic table. Kurt raised his beer. "A toast to our hosts. No matter where we're playing, we'll hook you up with complimentary tickets. Guaranteed for life."

"You had me at hookup," cackled Melissa. "But what if the band breaks up? Do we get complimentary tickets to your future bands as well?"

"We'll never break up," said Kurt.

The band was exhausted and decided to return to the apartment to spread out their sleeping bags. Xavier distanced himself from Melissa and hung out in the corner of the balcony, smoking a joint with Carl. They chatted alone for an hour, then headed to the spare bedroom.

"It's official," hissed Melissa. "In the pool, I figured he was gay."

I glanced at Axel. He nodded. "Not many people know, though. He's quiet about it. Not fully out yet. I'm glad he's opening up. He must feel comfortable around you guys."

I wondered where Melissa was going to sleep now that they stole her bedroom, but I enjoyed the fact that she'd have to rough it. She deserved to sleep on the floor with the band.

Lydia exited the bathroom in my plush terrycloth bathrobe with a towel wrapped on her head. Kurt followed her with a towel around his waist.

"Love the mint-cucumber shampoo," said Lydia. "Whose razor's in there? Hope you don't mind we borrowed it. I could practically braid the hair in my armpits it's been that long since we had a proper shower."

"Good to know," I choked and made a mental note to ditch the razor.

Axel and I followed Kurt and Lydia onto the balcony. They lit a joint and passed it around. Lydia started singing reggae style, "Pass the Dutchie pon the left-hand side..."

"I'm gonna work you in as a lead singer one of these days," Kurt joked. I wondered if he was going to sit around free balling in the bath towel all night.

Melissa clutched the railing and staggered across the balcony. She doubled over and got sick in the geraniums. She swigged from a water bottle and spit into the potted plants, then dried her face with the hem of her t-shirt.

"It's the gluten. I swore it off all summer. Now my head feels like I'm stuck on an elevator."

I couldn't resist asking, "Are you sure it's the gluten? Not the vodka shots?"

"Don't be a douchebag, Paigester."

I took Axel's hand, leading him to my room. "I owe you for rescuing me."

"If you insist," he said, flopping onto the bed.

"I insist."


My Kew connections allowed us to move into the dorm a day ahead of the rest of the students. Axel and Xavier hauled my stuff from the apartment. I carried what I could, but I was limited with my broken arm.

I had the best living quarters on campus: two spacious separate bedrooms attached to a common room, a private bathroom, and a kitchenette with a full-sized refrigerator. Floor-to-ceiling windows revealed a swaying lakeside Weeping Willow. Pilar had upgraded her den, so she gave me the smart tv, two velvet plum-colored loveseats, accent pillows, and floor lamps with fringe that matched the furniture. It looked fresh out of a designer showroom.

"This is more like a luxury condo than a dorm room," said Axel. "I can see where I'll be hanging out."

"If you play your cards right," I said with a wink.

I felt excited about the new semester. I tucked my clothes into the dresser as Xavier carried in the last load. He put the old beanbag chair in my bedroom.

"That's been collecting dust, plus it screams freshman year. Let's ditch it," I said. The real reason: The beanbag reminded me of Stoph, who'd gifted it to me.

"Housewarming present!" Thalia maneuvered a rectangular frame through the door — her black and white photograph of us laughing at the café with the Royal typewriter between us at the bistro table.

"Love it! How about we hang it above the couch?"

"I made this for us, too." She photoshopped the typewriter keys rearranged to spell *Gingbo!* in a smaller print.

"We'll tell people it's Greek slang for orgasm."

Xavier said, "You two are going to be trouble."

I handed Thalia a gift bag. She ripped through the tissue paper and held up the vintage tin robot that I'd bought for her from the antique dealer.

"I can't believe you remembered this," she gushed.

"He gave me a deal," I said.

Xavier and Axel went outside to get the silver-trimmed black shipping case that was for Gasoline Kisses' instruments, decorated with stickers from every west coast city. There were cracked decals from pubs, nightclubs and coffee houses, mostly from Portland, San Francisco and LA. The band had brought it to the apartment after the concert and forgotten it.

Xavier shrugged. "Carl gave me his number. I left six messages. But he's blowing me off. I thought things were cool between us —"

"They're probably busy with the next gig," said Axel.

"It's the perfect coffee table," I suggested. I flipped open the latches on the case and took out the guitar. "Does anyone play?"

"I can play a few basic chords. Nothing too flashy." Axel took the guitar and plucked on the strings.

A brown paper bag was wedged on the bottom of the case. Inside the bag was a manual coffee grinder, rolling papers, a lighter and a wad of enormous marijuana buds. I dumped the stash onto the case.

"This will make a ton of brownies."

Axel followed me into my bedroom to help stack my books on the shelves above my desk. At the bottom of a box, he found the *Fresh Eggs* farmstand sign that I hung over my bed freshman year.

"I guess this should go in the kitchen," he said and took it to hang near the cabinets.

I had ordered pizza from Kewtie Pies and heard the delivery person knock on the door.

"Interesting body ink. What does it mean?" I pointed to his bicep. It looked like an Etch-a-Sketch rendering of a man — the same abstract profile of a man's head that was patched on the backs of the denim jackets at the concert. It was a thin white circle inside a solid black square. The eye was a small white square with a right angle drawn on top. A white line inside the circle stretched top-to-bottom with slight indentations to form a nose, mouth, chin and neck.

He snorted. "I thought it looked cool. It beat getting my ex-girlfriend's name."

"I've seen that symbol before —"

"It'll be etched on your forehead if you don't tell us what McKim said," he hissed. "Don't think we're screwing around."

"McKim didn't tell me anything. Who sent you here?"

"Look, I'm just following orders. If I were you, I'd cooperate."

"If I knew something, then I'd cooperate. Who gave you orders?"

"All I know is you must've done something to get on the radar —"

"What radar?"

"He told you something significant."

"He was probably going to, but he died. Or should I say, he was murdered?"

"Watch your language, missy," he said, dropping the pizza box. "You're playing with fire."

Then he disappeared down the hallway.

# *Chapter Five — Libra*

I was reading one of my astrology guidebooks when Thalia tapped on my bedroom door.

"I need a tampon. Where do you keep yours?" she whispered.

"Under the bathroom sink," I said, dog-earring the page.

"I looked there. Didn't see any."

I rummaged through my closet, finding a dented, half-filled box wedged between the pile of sneakers and dirty laundry. "Guess I'm running low. Let's go to the store. We could use some snacks, too."

I sucked in my bloated gut to button my jeans. A zit the size of an eraser head protruded from my chin. I wasn't due to get my period for another week, but I felt a wave of cramps roiling.

"That's weird," I said as we headed to the store. "I feel like my cycle is kicking in, but it's early."

"Better early than late. Axel would have a stroke and I'm not talking about crew —"

I snapped, "Just for the record, we haven't. And, if I'm ever late, you'd better be more concerned for me than him —"

"We better buy extra tampons. You're never this crabby."

"And chocolate. Lots of it."

Inside the store, I tried to separate two stuck shopping carts and smashed my pinky on my good hand. I cursed and shoved the cojoined carts back into the row. Thalia pulled one out from the next row.

"We're syncing. That happens, you know."

"You must give off power-pheromones," I said, dropping a supersized box of tampons into the cart. In the snack aisle we chose Pringles, Oreos, and brownie mix. "Are you thinking what I'm thinking?"

Thalia laughed. "Sure, why not? Let's make one batch for us and one to bring to the crew party. The weed will go stale anyway."

We polished off the can of Pringles on the walk back to campus. I asked, "Do you know how to bake hash brownies?"

"Let's just follow the directions and add the extra ingredient to the batter. It can't be too complicated."

I Googled a recipe. "Did you ever hear of decarboxylation?"

"Decarba-what?"

"The herb needs to be heated to activate its psychoactive agents. We have to bake it for thirty minutes before we add it to the mix," I said, turning the oven to pre-heat. I opened the guitar coffin to get Gasoline Kisses' stash. I ground up some of the cannabis and spread it evenly on a pan before sliding it onto the oven rack.

"I wonder why we haven't heard from the band about their missing guitar? You'd think they'd want it back," I said.

Thalia dumped the brownie mix, oil and eggs in a bowl and stirred it until the batter was smooth.

There was pounding on the door. Melissa shoved her way past me. "Jesus, it reeks all the way down the hallway!"

"Oh shit, I didn't think about the smell. Quick, light some incense." I whipped the hash out of the oven to mix into the batter.

Melissa cackled. "I'm getting out of here. I've done enough community service. Turn on the shower, you need to mist this place. Open the windows and block the crack in the door with towels after I leave. Call me when the first batch is ready."

We opened every window and lit incense sticks. I put a fan backward in the window to blow the stench outside. Thalia started giggling as she licked the spatula.

"What's so funny?"

"I think I'm getting high from the smell."

I wasn't laughing, just sweating from the panic of getting caught with weed on campus. "These better come out good after all this commotion."

"We'll have to hide them now that Melissa knows. Although, they're not gluten free. Maybe she should abstain."

I laughed. "Two words that never go together: Melissa and abstain."

After the brownies cooled, we wrapped them in tinfoil and hid them inside the guitar coffin, just in case campus security should show up.

"The last thing we need is a drug raid this early in the semester," said Thalia.

I wondered if drug raids would be any less problematical later in the semester.


I promised Tanya I would promote her coffee at the Head of the Charles regatta. So I rented a bright white, pimped-out repurposed UPS truck to use as a coffee-sales mobile. It came equipped with a chrome trim cutout in the side wall for a pop-up window and drop-down service counter.

I filled the portable vats with special roasts named for the event: Row to Go, the Regatta Roast, and the Charles River Chaga.

"Grab one of those and follow me," I called over to Tanya.

"Do you think you need all those cups and lids? It seems like you're being a bit ambitious," she said, carrying a vat out to the truck. She whistled her approval when she saw the Goforth magnetic signs on the side doors.

I hopped in the driver's seat and started the engine. The vendor permit was taped to the windshield. "I'll call you with an update."

Tanya flashed a peace sign. "As soon as I have the morning crew settled, I'll come over to help out."

I arrived in Cambridge well ahead of the rowers and spectators. I angled the food truck at the top of the hill, parking close to the main entrance by the boathouse overlooking the Charles River and a pedestrian bridge. I opened the windows to air out the stagnant *eau d'old hot dog water* aroma from the food truck.

The sunrise spread a burnt-sienna glow across the river, then brightened to an orange shimmering radiance. It was a fleeting moment of serenity before the mob swarmed Cambridge. I propped a portable Goforth Daily Grind sign on the grass.

"Good morning!" I beamed at my first customer, who was wearing jumbo-lensed Jackie Onassis sunglasses.

"A large Row to Go, sugar and cream," she ordered. "Evelyn, stay next to Mommy."

"Mommy, I want a soda."

"Sorry, I only have coffee."

Evelyn whined, "But I want a soda."

"Evelyn, honey, the lady said they only sell coffee."

She emphasized *only* as if it were criminal. I wanted to tell little Evelyn that soda has tons of sugar and it was too early in the morning for soda, but then, what did I care if Evelyn's teeth rotted out of her head? I had mentioned to Tanya that we should sell water and soft drinks, but she'd bristled at the thought of the plastic waste products and sugar-laden drinks.

Evelyn's mom slid three singles across the counter, leaving no tip in the jar or even a thank-you as she strutted away with her daughter in tow.

It wasn't long before the customer line snaked around the truck and down the hill. The early arrivals placed their orders while figuring out where to claim their team tents and chairs along the riverside. The rowers flowed in and out of the boathouse in team colors as varied as a Crayola crayon deluxe box.

I wore a special event Goforth's Daily Grind red hoodie with oars crisscrossed across the chest and bold *Coffee Crew* lettering. I chuckled to myself as I thought back to when Tanya started her healthcentric coffee business last year in an old shipping container behind the town library in North Easton. It had received a rocky reception, thanks to Ms. Montgomery, the head librarian, who disapproved of the hunk of junk plunked in her library garden. It amused me to learn later that Ms. Montgomery and Pilar Kuhlkoat were druids in *cahoots* — their word, not mine.

It was still early when I called Thalia for backup. "I'm slammed. This is a *brew d'etat.*"

"Seriously?" she asked, groggy-voiced. "Didn't you just get started?"

"It's nuts. The line is a killer. Get here as soon as you can. Bring more cups and lids."

"I thought you were going to pack a million —"

"Trust me. It's insane. I'll run out by noon."

I served coffee like I was fighting a five-alarm fire.

From the back of the line, I heard: "Grind it, baby!"

I turned to see the Quadsters, ready to patrol the boathouse scene for brains, biceps and buns — not necessarily in that order. When they reached the front of the line, I handed them complimentary coffee.

"See any hot prospects?" I asked.

"Butt loads," said Melissa, flashing a grin.

"Don't you mean boatloads?"

"You catch my drift." Melissa sported a preppy collar-popped, red-white-and-blue rugby shirt with an embroidered Polo Yacht Challenge centered on the chest.

"You realize this is a rowing event, not yachting, right?"

"Can't blame a girl for setting the bar high," she said. "When can you blow this clambake? We'll pre-game in the dorm while we get ready for the crew party."

"I'm here all day. I'll catch up with you at the dorm."

"Cool beans," said Sheila, zipping her cheetah-print fur coat up to her chin. "Is there dancing under any of those tents over there?"

"No clue," I said. "It's my first regatta."

"Mine too," said Jill. "It reminds me of Nicholas Cage in *The Boy in Blue*."

A man's voice boomed from the back of the line. "Ladies, can we keep the line moving, please?"

Melissa flipped her hair from her shoulder. "C'mon girls, there's men in Spandex dying to meet us."

It took Thalia an hour to arrive with a trash bag stuffed with sleeves of recyclable lids and cups. I tossed a matching red hoodie to her and she stepped into the truck to help me.

"Goforth was miffed you didn't call her with an update. You haven't answered her calls. Don't be surprised if she shows up soon to inspect your sales operation."

I glanced at my phone to see seven missed calls from Tanya. "Crap. I've been slammed."

"Got any music on this truck?"

I pointed toward a portable speaker, but I was distracted by a text message from Axel. He wanted me to meet him in the boathouse. "I need to pee. Can you handle this scene for a few?"

"Gingbo!" Thalia put on Rainbow Kitten Surprise and got to work.

Wall-to-wall rowers and coaches awaited their races near the boathouse. I found Axel stretching his hamstrings by the water fountain.

"Good luck today," I said and hugged him.

His mouth was tight, his forehead wrinkled. "It has nothing to do with luck. At this point, the proof is in the training. It's time to let it fly."

"Okay, then. Let it fly."

He cracked a half smile. "How's the coffee business?"

"Booming. I should get back. I abandoned Thalia."

"Say hi to Tay-Tay for me. You're coming to the crew party, right?"

"Tay-Tay?" I laughed.

"I couldn't say Thalia when I was little. It came out as Tay-Tay."

"That's cute. We'll be there."

I hustled back to the coffee truck. Thalia rolled her eyes and gestured toward the back of the truck. Tanya showed up and was sorting through the cash register, organizing the bills so the heads faced in the same direction. "We're making a killing here," she said.

I couldn't help a smile. "I told you selling coffee at the regatta would be a solid move."

"It's good to see you happy again. Does it have anything to do with that young man at the boathouse?"

"You don't miss a thing," I said, knowing she wasn't being nosey, that she cared about my wellbeing. In return, I'd do anything to help her, including selling coffee at the regatta instead of Spandex-ogling with the Quadsters.

She closed the register drawer. "A new boy will help you move on from the trauma. A new love, that is."

I shrugged. "Your blends are perfect for today's event."

"Fine, change the subject."


Late in the afternoon, a municipal truck pulled up alongside the coffee truck. The driver hopped out and grunted, "You need to move this sardine tin."

"I have a permit to park for the day," I said, pointing to the windshield.

"This is where the memorial bench for Coach Redgrave is being installed. You need to get out of the way for the delivery truck and crane to get in here."

"Seriously? The bench installation should've been done before the regatta."

"There were production delays, not that it's any of your business. Ceremony's tonight, after the races. Can't have a dedication without the bench. Move it."

"Where do you suggest I go?"

He smirked. "That's a loaded question."

"I'm not moving. This is a prime spot. You'll need to work around me," I said.

He muttered, "Bitch."

"What did you say?"

"My crew has a job to do. Stay at your own risk."

Thalia and I looked up and down the street at the other vendors selling hot dogs, oversized pretzels and ice cream. Every parking spot was taken. The sidewalks were jammed with pedestrian traffic. If we moved, we'd be done for the day.

"Screw him."

"No thanks," joked Thalia.

A flatbed lumbered down the road hauling a 12-foot-long marble bench. A second truck with a crane clambered behind it. The drivers got out to talk to the boss, glaring at the coffee truck.

"A memorial bench is a stupid idea," said Thalia.

"Why do you say that?"

"I don't know about you, but when I die, the last thing I want is for people to park their asses on my memorial."

The boss returned to the front of the truck. "Last chance to move, lady."

I poured a large coffee as a peace offering. "The permit allows us to be here until 5 p.m. You'll have to wait until then."

He swatted the cup. It flew out of my hand and dumped on the grass.

"Okay people, move back. Coffee break's over. Starbucks is right up the street." He corralled the crowd with his long-outstretched arms. Our customers backed away, but stayed to watch the workers.

He signaled for his crew to proceed. The crane operator revved his engine and swung the dangling claw toward our truck, grazing the roof. He lowered the claw and swung it back so it dragged deeper into the roof. It felt like an earthquake. Cups, lids and coffee spilled all over the floor. The claw swung into the side wall, smashing through the window. Thalia and I shrieked as we jumped out the back of the truck and raced toward the crowd.

The crane hovered above the roof, opening its mouth like a raging T-Rex. The claw's death grip lifted the truck's body off the ground. The coffee truck hovered, then see-sawed like scales of justice weighing in on who had the right to occupy this spot. The Goforth sign slid from the door, landing face down on the grass. The coffee vats dumped over, releasing a brown stream that trickled out like a weak shower.

I grabbed my phone from my pocket and panic-dialed Captain Biff, my go-to police contact and first druid mentor.

"Now what?" he said. Captain Biff sighed after I explained the jam. "Stay there. Don't say another word to the construction crew. I'll send one of my guys."

"How will I recognize it's your guy?"

"A police cruiser and cop in uniform should give you a clue."

The crane swung the coffee truck toward the road and lowered it perpendicular on the opposite side of the street so it blocked traffic. Horns beeped.

The workers hustled over to help ease the hefty marble bench to its spot on the hill. A few onlookers cheered about the bench. The boss removed his cap and took a bow, hamming it up for the crowd. The patrons who wanted coffee booed him.

Daily Grind napkins and cups littered the area around the bench. I followed Captain Biff's instructions and said nothing to the boss. I stared hard at his face, finding his ruddy complexion and puffy eyes familiar. I wondered why I kept having these odd encounters with construction workers. He headed for his truck. Thalia said she'd pick up the trash then she was going to meet Axel's parents and the other relatives at the team tent.

"You might want to move your truck. It's blocking traffic," snapped the boss, slamming his truck door. He floored it down the street, passing the approaching cop car.

It took four turns before the coffee truck ignition engaged. I was about to shift into drive when the cop approached the driver's side window.

"You're blocking the road," he barked.

"I'm trying!"

"Move this out of the way. Pull into the parking lot near the boathouse," he ordered.

The truck jolted into drive. A screeching sound emitted from the engine or the muffler, probably both. I felt as if the tires might spring off if I increased the speed. I bounced into the parking lot and killed the engine. The cop pulled up behind me. Pedestrians gawked at us.

"What happened?"

I told him, noticing his olive complexion and soft brown eyes. He seemed young, maybe in his late twenties, and he looked muscular in his uniform.

"I had a permit for the day," I protested.

"What did the individual you called *the boss* look like?"

"Around 6-foot-1, 200 pounds, baseball hat, green windbreaker zippered up to his neck. Bushy eyebrows."

"That sounds like most of the city workers. You didn't get his name?" The cop circled the truck, noting the damage.

I shook my head. "A supervisor might know who was responsible for delivering the bench —"

"I'm sure that detail will go missing," he mumbled.

"What should I do about the damage to the rental?" It was dented in on the sides where the claw gripped its teeth. The interior white walls were splattered with coffee stains. Shattered glass covered the floor.

The cop handed me a paper. "Submit the accident report to the rental place. They'll file a claim with their insurance company."

"Am I liable for the damages?"

He turned to leave. "Tell them to contact the captain if there's any questions."

"Is this truck safe to drive? It felt wobbly when I pulled in the parking lot."

"I'll call a tow truck," he offered.

"Perfect," I said and asked him for a ride back to the coffee shop in Quincy Market. "I've got a lot of cash —"

"Best to play it safe. Hop in," he said.

I took the portable cash register from the truck and slid into the front seat of the patrol car. A woman's voice crackled with orders from dispatch on the police radio. He turned down the volume.

"We sold a ton of coffee before that jerk showed up."

He sprayed wiper fluid on bird droppings, smearing a milky streak across the windshield. He repeated the spray-wipe sequence until the glass cleared. "What's so special about your coffee?"

I gave him the healthcentric sales pitch how ill-sourced coffee is often contaminated with mold and pesticides. "Plus, our stuff tastes ten times better than Starbucks and Dunkin' Donuts."

"I love Dunkin'," he said, wheeling through Faneuil Hall. We went into Goforth's and I deposited the cash with Tanya. I insisted he sample the various blends before he chose on the dark roast.

"On the house." I secured the lid on his takeout cup.

Tanya eyed the officer as she slid a piece of paper across the counter toward me. "This was left in the typewriter. What the hell does it mean?"

The note was typed on the back of a coffee menu:

*PM Our patience is growing thin!*

*Tell us what you know…or else! BS*

"Did you see who typed this?" I asked.

"Nope. Lots of customers check out the typewriter. I can't even guess who left that."

The cop slurped his coffee. "Whose initials are PM and BS?"

"I'm Paige Moore. I don't know about BS."

"The note says tell us what you know. Why would you know something?" he asked, putting air quotes around *know something*.

I glanced at the cop's nametag near his badge. "Tanya this is Officer Delgado. He gave me a ride after we had a little incident with the coffee truck."

"An incident? Is everyone okay? Where's Thalia?"

"She went to visit with some of her relatives at the regatta," I said, gesturing toward the cash box. "We did well."

She tucked the box under her arm. "What happened?"

I explained the encounter with the crane operator and the damage to the truck. Tanya massaged her forehead with her thumb. "Next time just move out of the way, Paige."

"But we had the permit. We had the right to that spot. I wasn't moving!"

"Officer Delgado, it's been a pleasure," she said, leaving with the cash box.

I topped off his coffee. "Do you think I was wrong?"

"I'm more concerned about this," said Delgado, tapping the typed note. "Any idea who wrote it?"

I shrugged. "No."

"Has anyone at school been acting odd?"

"No more than usual."

Delgado gulped his coffee. "I'm no detective. You should contact Captain Biff about this. We don't take threats lightly."

"Got it."

"You need to figure out who is BS so you know who you're dealing with."

Back at the dorm, I could hear the music thumping all the way down the hallway. The Quadsters were pre-gaming with a dance-off on the guitar coffin coffee table. They chanted my name when they saw me and handed me a Budweiser.

I looked around the room. "Where's Thalia?"

"Still hanging with the fam at the regatta," said Jill.

"How'd you guys get in here?"

"C'mon Paige, move those hips." Sheila hopped down and bumped her hip into mine. "The door was open. We figured you wanted us to get the party started in your place."

"The door was open?" I bolted for my bedroom. The windows were wide open, my closet looked like it had been turned upside down, and the desk drawers were dumped onto the floor. My laptop was gone.

Jill followed me into my room. "What happened in here?"

"Didn't you guys notice this mess?"

"We didn't trash your room, Paige!"

"I got robbed. Someone stole my laptop!"

Melissa peered into my room, then went to Thalia's room. Her windows were open and all the drawers were dumped onto the floor. Her laptop was gone and the tin robot lay broken in pieces on the floor.

"This is a mess," said Melissa, picking up the robot pieces. "I would stroke if someone stole my laptop. It has all my contacts, social media passwords, the works."

I looked out and saw that my book crates were flung out the window. My books lay strewn across the lawn like confetti.

"We'll go pick up your books," said Sheila.

"What kind of a thief throws shit out the windows? Weren't they afraid of getting caught?" I asked.

Melissa said, "You should call Officer Bestie. Get the place dusted for fingerprints like they do on CSI."

"Officer Bestie? You mean Captain Biff?"

"Mmmm, no. Not the Biffster. I was thinking your new bestie, the hottie cop we saw you with at the regatta."

"Delgado. I didn't get his number."

Melissa smacked her forehead. "How many times do I have to tell you? Always get the digits."

"I'll call Captain Biff. But first I need a big favor."

"Name it."

I grabbed the tinfoil-wrapped brownies and the brown bag of Gasoline Kisses' pot stash. "Hide this someplace."

She opened the bag and took a deep inhale. "They're not bringing bomb-sniffing German shepherds, are they? They'd track this scent right to my closet."

I froze when she mentioned German shepherds.

"What's wrong?"

"Brenda Shepherd. That's BS," I mumbled.


By the time Captain Biff and Delgado arrived, I'd already re-organized my bookcase. They visually swept the rooms floor-to-ceiling.

"The main disturbances are in the bedrooms. The intruders were targeting your computers and notebooks. Anything else missing?" asked Captain Biff.

"The kitchen and sitting area look fine. Just the bedrooms got trashed. They chucked some of our stuff out the windows. Don't know how that went unnoticed by the whole dorm."

"We'll ask around. Somebody probably saw something."

I started thinking about possible suspects. The men who delivered the bench? The Kewtie Pies delivery guy? BS? Brenda Shepherd was agitated that I visited McKim in the hospital.

"Do you know Brenda Shepherd?"

Captain Biff spun around. "Brenda Shepherd?"

"The other day my friend and I went to the Christian Science Center mapparium. When we were leaving, the security guard forced us into a private meeting room where Brenda Shepherd interrogated me."

"What did she want?"

"She wanted to know why I visited Chuck McKim in the hospital before he died. She was the nurse tending to him. Then she was at the mapparium. Do you know her?"

"She's a goon. Low-level Bauhaus troublemaker." He sighed. "Bauhaus is onto you, Paige. I bet they broke in here and now they have your computer. Did you keep anything important on it? Anything that would indicate you're with the Boston AOD?"

"Nothing. I keep all druid things in my head, just as you instructed."

"No notebooks or literature about the AOD? Nothing you've been independently researching?"

I shook my head and glanced around my room. My horoscope guide poster was gone. The stack of notebooks with my horoscope insights and research were missing as well.

"Crap! They took my notebooks that I use for my *Lodestar* horoscope writing."

"Anything significant in those notes pertaining to our druid mission?"

"No."

"Go to the Apple store and ask for Steve at the Genius Bar. He'll set up you and your roommate with new MacBooks. Get whatever you need. Tell him to charge my account."

"Thanks."

"I'll arrange for better security on the dorm, so you don't need to worry. I doubt they'll come back."

"I've been noticing a symbol," I said, explaining the profile of the man's face on the denim jackets and pizza delivery man's tattoo. I sketched it on scrap paper.

He stroked his chin. "It's a symbol for Bauhaus solidarity. It's similar to putting a Marine or Army bumper sticker to show allegiance for military service."

"Is Bauhaus an official organization? Can anyone join?"

He shook his head. "Bauhaus is secretive and selective. It's like a gang. It has a lot of minions who do the dirty work for the top echelon. Someone connected you with McKim and they must think that you have something. If you've noticed the symbol, then you're definitely under their surveillance."

I told him about the golf cart accident, getting shoved into the harbor, and the attack on the coffee truck. "All these things can't be random. What do you think they're up to?"

Captain Biff sent Delgado out of the room. He sat on the guitar coffin as I folded into the plum loveseat. "There's been tension between the AOD and Bauhaus for a long time."

"Did Bauhaus ever come after you?"

"They're smart enough not to tangle with cops," he said, clutching a fresh toothpick in the corner of his mouth.

"So what's the real issue?"

"Power hungry, control freaks. The architectural differences are the tip of the iceberg."

"Druids such as Richardson and McKim preserved the biblical elements of architecture while Bauhaus obliterated cityscapes with its brutalist cement block structures. Do you think Bauhaus wants to keep people boxed in?"

"That's one way to look at it," he said. "Go on."

I explained to Captain Biff my understanding that Bauhaus architecture was designed with its idea of perfect worker housing that resembled compounds. Bauhaus wanted workers divided into boxes, working in cubicles. Skyscrapers were nothing more than stretched boxes typically covered in glass. When Gropius took over the Harvard architecture program, the teaching of architecture transformed overnight. Students were taught to design in the compound style. The Bauhaus approach to architecture spread rapidly and in no time the American greats such as Richardson were overshadowed by concrete, steel and glass boxes.

Captain Biff nodded. "Correct. Bauhaus was extremely anti-bourgeois. Have you figured out why?"

I reflected on my discoveries with Richardson's architecture that I used to find the ark of the covenant. I needed to set aside my distaste for modernistic architecture in order to understand it. "I have no idea what Bauhaus designs mean. It's ironic that it was anti-bourgeois but, in the process, Bauhaus became bougie themselves. It stuck ugly buildings in every available space. The skyscrapers are like a middle finger to the world."

I recalled something I had read about how World War I destroyed human imagination. It was a time when Bauhaus focused on machines, mass production and work. Gropius took over Harvard's architecture program and redirected some of the most talented architects of that time away from the druids. American cities suffered the consequences aesthetically and the Bauhaus style never proved it increased worker productivity.

"Do you want to know what I think?"

"I'm listening."

"I think there was a secret group of elite architects and artists called the Winter Hexagon Salon. I figure the salon originated in the 1880s when Hunt and Richardson were in their prime. McKim was a Harvard and *Beaux-Arts* grad who trained as a draftsman at Richardson's firm when he was completing Trinity Church. The architects surrounded themselves with the best artists and sculptors of their time, such as Sargent and Daniel Chester French. I wonder who else they included, maybe even Mark Twain, the best American writer of that time. The Winter Hexagon Salon was no doubt a private think tank."

"I'd like to have been a fly on the wall," said Captain Biff.

"I think Gropius had major anger issues because when he came to the U.S., he got rejected by the architectural power players who ruled the Winter Hexagon Salon. Somehow, he found out there was a secret group of six elite architects and artists who'd met in a hidden location that served as their headquarters. He'd already been driven out of Germany and he faced rejection again."

I explained my theory that McKim had designed significant gates on Harvard's campus and he must have been appointed the gatekeeper of the salon after Richardson and Hunt died. He was the last one to hold the only key to the salon and Gropius stole the key.

I said, "The problem was that Gropius didn't know the location of the secret salon and he never figured it out. That was the beginning of the war between Bauhaus and the druid architects. Bauhaus wants to find the salon and take its secrets for their own uses. Bauhaus doesn't want the secrets of the early American architects to be revealed. Bauhaus wants total domination."

Captain Biff pulled a fresh toothpick from his shirt pocket and started chomping on it while he mulled. "Chuck McKim told you to find the key and find the salon. In all my years with the druids, this is the first time I've ever heard about the Winter Hexagon Salon. Any ideas where this so-called salon is located?"

"Not yet, but I'm working on it."

"Keep exploring those ideas," he said before he took a call from the precinct in the kitchen, providing one-word responses to the caller. He opened the cabinets and refrigerator, searching for any clues from the break-in, I assumed. But then he found a package of Oreos and popped one in his mouth. I was relieved the hash brownies were out of the apartment.

"Want some milk?"

"I'd love some coffee, but I don't trust those Goforth mushroom concoctions." He opened the oven door, and when the light didn't turn on, he grimaced. "You need a new oven bulb. Call me if anything comes up."

"Just one more thing —"

"What?" Captain Biff propped his foot on the guitar coffin and re-tied his loose shoelace.

"At the hospital I signed in as McKim's niece. They must think I'm a McKim —"

"And now they're trying to scare the family secrets out of you."

"Exactly."


Pilar told me to join the Marsh Writers Collaborative at Boston University. My *Lodestar* horoscopes were gaining popularity, but Hot Throat said my writing wasn't "up to *Lodestar* standards."

She smiled when she pitched her suggestion, then slipped in a Hot Throat zinger: "It behooves you to collaborate more with university intellectuals and less with those Kew College debauchers you call friends."

I stuffed my new laptop — courtesy of Captain Biff's Genius Bar contact — in my backpack and called *Lodestar* car service to drive me to Marsh Chapel to attend the workshop. The SUV crawled through the crowded streets.

"I hope you won't be late. The traffic is brutal," said the driver, glancing back at me. His bald head shined like a bowling ball.

"It should be fine. I left early so I'd have time to check out the architecture."

"Are you studying to be an architect?" His eyes flashed in the rearview mirror when he spoke to me, so it felt more personal instead of talking to the back of his head.

"No. I'm an English major, but I like early American architecture."

"Do you have a favorite building?"

"Anything but Bauhaus," I said.

He turned his shoulders to face me. "Seriously?"

"I struggle with Bauhaus style, or lack thereof. It's not attractive."

He smiled, turning his attention back to the traffic. "It's everywhere. You'd better get used to it."

"That's true," I said. "Aren't you the same driver that took me to the beach?"

"I drove you and your friend. We stopped in Plymouth first. Did you have fun?"

"It was a blast. What's not to love at the Cape?"

"You're lucky to get all the *Lodestar* VIP perks," he said, handing me a business card. "My name's Logan. Take my direct number. Call me anytime for a ride. I'll take you and your friends wherever you want to go, no questions asked."

"Awesome. Thanks, Logan. I'm Paige."

"Pleasure to meet you again," he said, driving past the Boston University Law School.

I stared at the grotesque Brutalist tower with its concrete façade. I wondered about the wisdom of putting classrooms and community spaces into boring boxes in front of the river. The law school was built directly behind Marsh Chapel and was designed by Josep Lluis Sert, who took over the Harvard Graduate School of Design after Gropius retired in 1952. Sert was the same architect who designed Peabody Terrace. Just looking at the hideous law school building made me curious how Harvard and Boston University had eschewed sane architecture and had allowed the Brutalist school to impose its Bauhaus monstrosities on the Boston skyline.

"I'll let you off here. Text me if you want a ride back to your campus."

"Will do, thanks Logan."

"Take care."

I poked around the Gothic Revival chapel. One of the architects was Ralph Adams Cram, who also designed the Cathedral of St. John the Divine in New York City. The chapel dimensions were 102-feet-by-34-feet — the equivalent cubit measurements for Solomon's temple as written in the Bible. The main entrance of Marsh Chapel had two arched doorways with a large arched stained-glass window above the doors. There was a row of stone detailing between two spires with one of the stones featuring the scales of justice.

"Now I found Libra," I said to myself, noticing that one stained-glass window had the scales of justice in it. One of the windows depicted a palace entryway with the Star of David that had *Solomon's Temple* written alongside it. I was captivated by another window with an effeminate St. John the Evangelist sitting next to Jesus and the holy grail at the Last Supper. St. John had a quill in one hand and a scroll in his other.

I moved along to wood-carved renderings of Jesus and the four evangelists who each held a book with their appointed symbols on the cover — the same symbols of the bull, the lion, the eagle and the man that I saw in Sargent's murals in the Boston Public Library. I made a mental note to watch for the recurrence of these signs in other architecture. Then it occurred to me that Cram might have been a member of the Winter Hexagon because of his use of Solomon's temple.

I found the meeting room and introduced myself to the man filling out the name tags. He jotted my name in all caps, but misspelled my name as *Page*. I didn't correct him because I thought Page seemed like a better spelling for a budding writer.

There were about twenty students at the meeting and the teacher started us with a writing prompt: *Take fifteen minutes to write a fifty-three-word flash fiction short story about something ripening.*

I considered bananas, but then I thought, no, that's what everyone was thinking and who wants to read about rotting fruit? I jotted down my idea, tweaked it, counted the words, crossed out the excess, swapped out weak words, and dropped my pen when he said to stop.

"Who wants to share?" he asked, gazing around the room.

A woman with a paisley silk scarf and reading glasses raised her hand. She seemed so confident, reading her fifty-three words about strawberries. The group raved about the imagery of the cascading mound of whipped cream that topped the shortcake. I thought it sounded like a Betty Crocker recipe, but I kept my thoughts to myself.

"You're new to the group, Paige. We'd love to hear what you came up with," said the teacher.

I sat up straight. "I've never done flash fiction before, but here it goes: *The defender tripped the striker. The referee whistled a penalty shot. I sweated in goal, waiting, shifting my weight from side to side. The shooter stared right corner. Coach shouted, 'Focus!' Sweat ripened the armpits of my shirt with a chicken soup stench. Bam! I sprawled low left — smothered the shot — game saved.*"

"That's different," said Lara, still basking in the appreciation for her strawberry shortcake recipe. "But is *bam* a word?"

"Isn't it?"

"I'd say grotesque," Lara pronounced. "Chicken soup stench? Don't most athletes use deodorant?"

My face turned redder than her famous strawberries. Another critic said, "I wonder if the coach could say something more original than *focus*?"

Another said, "It was fine but it had absolutely nothing to do with the prompt. So, I'd give it an F."

"Well, we're really not assigning grades," said the teacher.

"Still," said the critic.

My mind raged: one, I wrote this in fifteen minutes; two, it was more original than fruit; and three, sometimes armpits do smell like chicken soup.

The teacher said, "Did anyone else think of sports when they heard the prompt?"

"I wrote about a mouse in a trap," said the woman sitting next to Lara.

Lara clapped. "Do share!"

I slumped in my chair.

# Chapter Six — Scorpio

When I returned from the Marsh Writer's Collaborative, I took a power nap, showered and met Melissa who'd packed the brownies in a canvas Rive Gauche Saint Laurent bag. "Don't worry, it's a knockoff. I picked it up on Canal Street," she said.

We went to Axel's teammate's off-campus house in Cambridge for the post-regatta party. Melissa wore a brown houndstooth zip-up skirt and cashmere turtleneck with ankle boots. Her heels clacked hard across the wooden floor sending a Morse Code — Quadsters on Parade.

We weren't supposed to cut through the house; the sign outside read: *Party is in the backyard.* But Melissa wanted to assess the decor. "You can tell a lot about a guy from the interior, particularly artistic choices."

The bedroom doors were closed; there was a line for the bathroom. In the living room, the couches had been moved outside for the party, leaving only a pine accent table with a shade-less lamp in the corner of the dark-paneled room. There was a poster taped slightly crooked to one wall, showing rowers with the sun setting behind them. Another wall featured a black-and-white poster of an aerial view of a crew team from Cambridge, 1913.

"Bland," said Jill. "Not my type."

"What is your type?" asked Sheila.

"Brad Pitt," said Jill.

Melissa led us to the kegs on the back porch. "I'm not giving up hope. Maybe these rower dudes have some wall art in their bedrooms."

We filled our cups and dispersed into the crowd. I found Axel chatting with two guys and ran up and gave him a hug.

"Did you win?"

"Crushed it. Personal best by five seconds," he beamed and introduced me to his friends. "How'd your coffee gig go?"

"We made a killing until the coach's bench —"

Axel's friend Smitty blurted, "You weren't the coffee chick who got airlifted, were you?"

My face reddened. Axel tried to stifle his laugh by covering his mouth with his hand. "Busted!"

"Guilty," I said.

Smitty howled. "I heard the crane yo-yoed the coffee truck to the other side of the street!"

Melissa passed by with a tray of brownies. I took one and winked at Axel. "I used your special recipe."

"Ah, then I'll pass. I'm still in season."

"A man of discipline," said Melissa, working the crowd.

He was still laughing. "You left with a cop, I heard."

"He gave me a ride." I scanned the backyard crowd. "Where's Thalia?"

"I thought she was with you."

"No. We planned to meet here."

"She hasn't texted. She's usually the first one to congratulate me after a race."

I tried her again and it went to voicemail. "I need to talk to her. Someone trashed our rooms and stole our laptops when we were at the regatta."

"Seriously? That sucks."

I told Axel about Captain Biff's theory. "The Bauhaus thugs have been targeting me because they think I'm related to the McKim family. The McKims supposedly have secrets."

"Does he think you're in danger?"

"I'm being watched and followed. I don't know about danger but it sure feels creepy that someone went through our rooms. Captain Biff put eyes on the dorm."

Melissa circled back with the brownies. "You baked a weak batch, Paigester. I had two with zero impact. Hardly worth the calorie splurge."

"Don't eat any more. It takes a while," I warned. "Then it hits you hard."

"Speaking from experience?" She buzzed toward a new group of guys.

Axel called his mother to ask if Thalia was with them. His parents were driving back to New York and said they were disappointed Thalia hadn't stopped by the tent to visit. Then he called Xavier, hoping she was coming to the party with him. But he hadn't seen her either.

"Should I call Captain Biff? Or am I being paranoid?"

"This is a hundred percent out of character for her. Something's not right. I think you should call him."

I called Captain Biff who answered after one ring. "Now what?"

"My roommate is missing!"


Axel drove me and the Quadsters back to campus to organize a search party *sans* Melissa, who was stoned and useless. She passed out and we put her to bed. We went through the dorm asking if anyone had seen Thalia. I used a screenshot from our typewriter café photo to show the dorm residents.

The dorm search turned up squat. We tried to keep calm, but hysteria raced through the dorm like a case of crabs at an orgy. The residents freaked.

Louise, the residence director — we called her Wheezy — was furious with me. "You could have come to me first. There are better ways to handle things of this nature. I already have parents calling the college president!"

"My roommate is missing."

"And the police are handling it! Did you go to officer training school? You have no right to solicit information door-to-door."

"But —"

"Panic has set in. One father is screaming that he's withdrawing his daughter because of the kidnapping of one of our students. Kidnapping!"

I group-texted Axel and the Quadsters to meet back in my room. Jill arrived with a tissue box and red-rimmed eyes from crying. I made coffee for everyone.

"You need to pull it together," I said.

"I can't help it. Thalia could be dead," sobbed Jill.

"Are you the idiot that started the kidnapping rumor?"

Sheila nodded. "She told the girls in room 410 —"

"Those rude bitches weren't taking me seriously, so I ramped it up a notch," said Jill, dabbing the tissue around her eyes.

"You're supposed to be taking care of Melissa!"

Part of me wanted to strangle Jill, then part of me started to panic. It was past midnight and I hadn't seen Thalia since the afternoon when she was cleaning up litter around the memorial bench.

Axel stood to leave. "I can't sit around here drinking coffee. I'm going out to look for her."

"I'll go with you."

Captain Biff rang my cell at 2 a.m. "We have Thalia. She's fine. We're driving her back to the dorm."

"What happened?"

He handed his phone to Thalia. "I'm okay. I'll see you in a few."

Back at the dorm, Captain Biff worked swiftly with Wheezy to diffuse the rumors. He downplayed the incident, explaining that Thalia had lost her backpack and phone, etc.

We huddled around Thalia as she explained what really happened. When I went with Officer Delgado to deal with the coffee truck, a man in a green windbreaker who said he worked for the city, asked Thalia to help pick up the debris. He told her to bring her trash to his pickup truck.

"After we were done, he offered me a ride. I felt so grimy that I didn't want to visit my relatives at the tents. He was very nice and I wanted to get back to the dorm to cleanup before the party, so I accepted. The next thing I know, we went in the opposite direction and he took me to a rear entrance to the Museum of Fine Arts."

Sheila said, "Oh my God."

"I've never been so scared. But he kept being nice and told me not to worry, his boss had a few questions; they just needed some information. He brought me into a dark office where the boss kept his back turned the whole time. He wanted to know why I spent so much time studying the murals in the Boston Public Library."

I sighed. "Shit, you're being followed because of me —"

"Wait, does this mean the rest of us are being followed too?" asked Jill.

There was a knock on the door and Jill shrieked. The door swung open and it was Captain Biff who shot a look toward Jill. "Knock it off —"

"Sorry, Captain Biff. I'm a bundle of nerves," she said.

"Moving forward, you ladies need to be careful. Don't accept rides from anyone you don't know. I have an undercover crew on campus. Stay in groups," he said, leaving quickly.

Thalia continued. "The boss asked me why I came here from Greece. How I know Paige. Then he took my cell phone and set me free in the back alley. I started running and trying to figure out how to get back here. I had no money, no phone and no clue how to get back. It took me hours —"

"I dragged you into this mess."

"We're used to it," said Jill.


First thing the next morning, Hot Throat called. "I need you to deliver your printed column to me in person. Don't email. I can't risk your computer infiltrating *Lodestar's* network with a virus or spyware attack."

"I guess you heard my laptop was stolen. But don't you have firewall protection?"

She huffed, "I have loads of security, but don't underestimate hackers or whomever it was that raided your dorm."

I sat at my desk to generate new horoscope notes. Scorpio is the most transformative sign of the zodiac, a high time for personal evolution. It was difficult to produce a column because I was starting from scratch without my notes and wall charts, which were also stolen.

The new moon of the month was set to provide a chance to align our lives with new goals. I paused to reflect on what I should focus on. Axel and I were moving slowly. Really slowly. I wondered if I was giving too casual a vibe in my effort not to appear desperate. Or maybe I was reading too much into my actions; perhaps his focus needed to be on his crew goals, not love affairs. I made a note in Capricorn to loosen the reigns on the heart strings when the new moon appears.

The other thing speaking to my heart was all the negative energy from Bauhaus. I recalled that summer day when I'd left my apartment and stopped to report on the construction accident. What was I thinking? Why did I try to be a reporter? To impress Pilar for the *Lodestar*? I'd had it made. It was summer vacation, time to kickback and coast. Now I was involved in something I didn't understand and I'd put my friends in danger.

My visit to Hot Throat's office began with her usual question: "What's happening in Aries?"

"Your ruling planet Mars indicates it's time to get organized with medical appointments — dentist, dermatologist, etc. Toward the end of the month, you will negotiate contracts as more money is coming your way."

"I could use more money." Pilar jotted a note, reminding herself to make a dentist appointment. "I heard you've had run-ins with Bauhaus thugs. And you met Brenda Shepherd? Did you know she was a former *Lodestar* news reporter?"

"I don't know anything about her other than what Captain Biff told me — that she's with Bauhaus."

"We fired her. She was using her *Lodestar* connections to get in with the city's power players to advance her position with Bauhaus. It took me awhile to figure out what she was up to. She's slick."

"What did she do?"

"She'd schmooze with the city planning department, politicians, big business and bank executives for *off-the-record* details about building development deals. Then she'd feed the details to Bauhaus, so they could intervene with their own projects. I caught on when she stuck her nose into the undisclosed development plans of a 525,000-square-foot office building in Boston's Seaport Innovation District. She knew who was financing it, who'd signed pre-lease contracts, how many millions were given out in tax breaks and so on. I confiscated her *Lodestar* laptop and found private details that she was emailing to Bauhaus upper echelon. Bauhaus used her intel to sabotage the 17-story property from getting developed. Then they made moves to build one of their own compounds."

"Couldn't you trace the emails she sent to her Bauhaus contacts to figure out who they are?"

"We tried but my I.T. geeks couldn't hack their system. Their cyber-security is impenetrable."

"Captain Biff said she's low-level Bauhaus, but she doesn't seem so low-level to me."

"She's not to be taken lightly, but she is a minion. Bauhaus is in every major city with scores of Brendas doing their dirty work. You can see its influence everywhere you go. It's not difficult to spot their minions; it's the Bauhaus bosses who are well hidden."

"I noticed this symbol of a man's profile," I said, flipping over my horoscope copy to draw a face with lines and angles. "I've seen it on jackets and tattoos."

She nodded. "Bauhaus branding. What else have you noticed? Did anything in your dorm get damaged from the break-in?"

"They stole our laptops. Made a mess."

"I bet Brenda Shepherd ordered the hit. She's out to get revenge on anyone affiliated with the *Lodestar*." Hot Throat sifted through a desk drawer. "Don't use your *Lodestar* privilege pass anymore. Use this instead —"

She handed me a white credit card with a black barcode on one side. The other side read Governor's Courtesy Pass above the royal blue coat of arms featuring an Azure Native American holding a bow and arrow. The pass had the same benefits as my *Lodestar* pass, only this one covered the whole state, not just Boston.

"Maybe I should pay to get into places. Cash isn't traceable."

"Nonsense! Keep going to museums and libraries and whatever else you need to do to help the AOD. Don't let anyone intimidate you. If you discover anything, even some small detail, let me know. I've been around a long time; I can point you in the right direction." She handed me an envelope. "Here's tickets to a ghost tour of Boston. It's a blast. One of my favorite things to do for Halloween. Take some friends. But that doesn't mean let your guard down."


I sat in the doctor's waiting room, flipping through magazines for a half hour while I waited to get my arm checked. Dr. Alpha came in and made a sour face when he saw the water-damaged cast.

"The cast needs to come off and x-rays taken," he said.

The nurse escorted me down the corridor. When the cast was removed, my arm was purple and atrophied. Dr. Alpha reviewed the x-rays before he spun around on his stool.

"Can you flex your wrist? Up and down or side to side? Rotate it?"

It was sore and stiff. He squeezed the bone up and down my forearm. "You will have this bump for a while. But I think you are healed well enough to start physical therapy. Let's work on getting your range of motion back. And you need to build up the atrophied muscles."

"Can the athletic trainers at my college provide PT?" I asked, hoping to keep things simple.

"God no," he said. "This was a serious break. You need to go to Harborview Physical Therapy. The best in Boston. Twice a week and do the exercises they assign. That's mandatory."

He asked the nurse to get me an appointment that afternoon. She called, handed me the prescription and said, "They had a cancellation. They can take you now."

I checked in at the front desk and was taken into the PT room by a woman named Nadia, who had thick hands and forearms. She strapped a heat pack around my arm to relax the muscles. Then she measured the flexibility and made notes in the chart. The exercises were painful, but if it meant I would heal, then I was willing to tolerate it.

She bent my wrist and held it in place with a Velcro strap.

"That hurts a bit," I said

"If you're feeling sorry for yourself," she said, "just look at that man over in that corner."

"Geez, what happened to him?" I asked, although I wasn't really feeling sorry for myself. Nadia's wrist manipulation was nothing compared to the months-long misery I'd endured after sustaining a concussion in a high school soccer game.

"A construction accident."

The man grimaced and groaned while the therapist repositioned his arms and legs. A walker was placed in front of him while the therapist encouraged him to take a step. He slid one foot forward, paused for twenty seconds, then the other foot caught up. He white-knuckled the walker. One step and he was done, he asked to sit down.

Nadia sighed. "He's here for the long haul. It took four months to build him up to take that one step."

"Do you rehab a lot of construction accident patients?"

"We seem to get all the severe cases."

"Like what?"

"Guys falling from scaffolding, backfiring jackhammers, getting run over by trucks. Things of that nature," she said, peeling the Velcro strap from my wrist.

I wondered if these were truly accidents or the result of Bauhaus hits. I made a mental note to ask Captain Biff if there were any criminal investigations regarding these hits. I needed to make sense out of this mystery before anyone else got hurt.

Jill called for a meeting to discuss our plan for Halloween. We met in her and Melissa's room. It was spacious with a view of the front quad with an enlarged photograph of themselves leaning against the Peace Train van with the "Welcome to Wyoming" cowboy sign behind them from last year's road trip.

Melissa propped her dry-erase board against her chair and wrote "Halloween" in all caps in orange marker. "First, we need to decide on costumes. Second, venue. Third, we need a solid buddy system. We will each get assigned a person to be responsible for the night. We don't want another missing person."

"Good idea," said Sheila.

We drew names from a hat. I got Melissa, by far the toughest assignment.

Melissa cackled when she drew Sheila's name. "If there's a dancefloor, I'll know where to find Sheelz. Costume ideas? Anyone?"

Sheila suggested, "How about animal patterns? I've got plenty of cheetah prints."

"I'm thinking more of a hospital theme. Naughty nurses?" said Melissa.

"How about famous artists?" said Thalia.

Melissa shot it down. "A sexy one-eared Van Gogh would be tough to pull off. And Paige, we're not going as constellations, so don't even think about it."

Constellation costumes would be fun I thought, but suggested instead: "How about we go as a rock band? Dress up in black like KISS with big hair and painted faces —"

Everyone agreed. Melissa wrote KISS on the board under her costume theme category. "There's a campus party we could hit, unless anyone has a better idea."

"I have tickets for the Halloween ghost tour of Boston —"

Melissa's eyes spiraled. "Hello? How'd you score those? And when were you going to tell us? Jesus, there's a three-year waiting list for that tour on Halloween."

"My bad. I forgot about them."

Melissa smacked her forehead. "You should staple the tickets to your forehead, in case your room gets ransacked again."

On Halloween night, the Quadsters dressed in black leggings and tight, low-cut t-shirts. We found platform boots online that Thalia enhanced by hot-gluing silver ball-bearings down the legs. We made ball-bearing studded chokers, painted our faces white, and detailed black markings around our faces. Thalia painted a solid black star around my right eye. Melissa and Jill bought black wigs for us at a consignment shop that they teased and blasted with hairspray. The Gasoline Kisses' guitar perfected my costume.

Jill set up orange vodka Jell-O shots for us to pre-game. Melissa downed three and I started to dread being her buddy for the night.

"I've been reading about the Boston Strangler and nurse Jolly Jane who used morphine and atropine to kill her victims," I said.

"Leave it to Paige to bone up on serial killers," said Melissa. "She can't even remember she has the hottest Halloween event tickets, but she knows the names of every prostitute the Strangler murdered."

The ghost tour guide pulled up in our private trolley. He was dressed like Jack the Ripper in a black top hat and long black coattails. He had a wide neck and chiseled jawline. His brown hair was buzzed short so it looked spray-painted like a G.I. Joe doll.

"Is he seriously handsome or am I seeing an apparition?" whispered Melissa.

"Have you been doing this long?" I asked him.

"A few years. I love giving private tours. I feel like I'm hanging out with friends instead of working," he said, navigating the trolley as it rattled up the street. "I'm Hunter. I hope you're ready to hear some ghost stories!"

Melissa asked, "Are you a student?"

"MIT," he said. "My mother owns the ghost tour. I work whenever she needs me, which is quite often this time of year."

Melissa leaned forward in her seat, suddenly obsessed with the ghost hunter. I figured she'd added him to her list of future ex-husbands because one: ghost touring could be a lucrative business; two: MIT; and three: good looking. His only flaw was that he had a slight lisp.

Hunter wore a headset that projected his voice through the trolley speakers. "I have a question for you ladies. If there were a public hanging, would you watch it?"

Sheila said, "No way! That's gruesome. I couldn't watch a person suffer and die like that."

"It's too awful to even think about," Jill agreed.

"I might," said Melissa.

Hunter prodded, "What if that person broke into your house and murdered your husband and children while you were gagged, tied up, and forced to watch? Then the cops arrested the murderer and the judge sentenced him to hang. How about then?"

"Definitely," I said.

"Would you throw rocks if there was a stoning?" he asked.

"I'd hurl them like Cy Young straight at his head," I said. "Given the same murder parameters."

Melissa whispered to Jill, "Cy Young? Parameters? Why doesn't she talk like a normal person? We should stone her."

"She's already stoned. She pre-gamed with the brownies."

The trolley stopped near Washington Street in an area known as Boston Neck. Hunter pointed out a window. "There was a guardhouse in that area. Over there was Gallows Hill where so-called criminals were hung."

"Are you saying they weren't really criminals?" asked Sheila.

"In the mid-1600s the Quakers were governed by a theocracy that enforced literal biblical principles. The colony sent lots of dissenters to the gallows for heresy," he said.

"Paigester, this is right up your alley," said Melissa, flicking her thumb at me. "Meet the queen of biblical studies."

My face reddened. "I assume many of the victims were women accused of witchcraft?"

He nodded. "Exactly. This area is swarming with tormented and lost souls who struggle to rest in the next world."

"Have you seen any tormented souls?" Melissa asked. "Any pale-faced chicks with rope-burn necklaces in need of a trim and blowout?"

Hunter chuckled. "All the time! Apparitions haunt many historic streets and buildings around the city. There's hotels, theatres, and dead-end streets that have reports of paranormal activity."

He eased the trolley toward Boston Common, the site of numerous public hangings during Puritan and Colonial times. He explained that this was the first public park in America. The bodies were not buried after hangings. "Their souls are said to haunt the Common in search of justice," he told us.

"Do you camp out here, spying for ghosts?" asked Melissa. She whispered to Jill, "If you ask me, I think this is just a glorified Uber ride."

Hunter overheard her Uber comment and pulled over. "Normally, we keep the tours on the bus, but follow me ladies. Maybe we'll get lucky tonight."

Hunter took us into a rustic brick barroom called JM Curley's. The red-headed bartender lit up when Hunter led our group toward the bar. "Need a table?" she asked, nodding toward a closed velvet curtain.

"The works," he said.

She pulled back the curtain and showed us to a round corner table covered in a crisp white tablecloth. We sunk into the leather chairs. The room smelled like steak.

"Welcome, ladies. Love the costumes. Tonight, it's dealer's choice. Pick your spirit."

"Let's keep it simple," said Jill. "Gin all around."

I flashed back to my gin nightmare from freshman year at Stonehurst and hedged, "Can we go with vodka instead?"

"Shaken or stirred?"

"Surprise us," said Hunter, winking at her. "JM Curley was known as the Rascal King. He was the mayor of Boston and governor of Massachusetts — and big-time corrupt."

"Shocking news," said Melissa.

"Easy there," said Hunter. "Not everyone involved in Boston politics is a crook."

"There's a new angle — ghost hunter turned campaigner," she said.

The bartender served French gimlets in martini glasses with lime wheels. My drink, marked with a rosemary sprig, was primed with St. George vodka and apple-rosemary syrup. We clinked glasses as Hunter toasted, "Cheers! The problem with the world is that everyone is a few drinks behind."

"Great words from a future alcoholic congressman," Melissa said, gulping her cocktail.

I shot her a stern look.

"Relax, Paigester. It's a buddy system, not a chaperone service."

"I was quoting Humphrey Bogart," said Hunter.

A waitress placed the chef's sampler in the center of the table. "A little treat to go with the cocktails."

I tried to steer the conversation back to the ghost tour. "Is this bar haunted?"

"No," said Hunter. "I got the feeling you ladies weren't that into my ghost tour."

"Boston Commons is haunted, right?" asked Sheila.

"It's one giant anonymous grave. There's a plaque near the frog pond marking the spot where the Sons of Liberty assembled. It's also where the Great Elm once stood, where hangings took place. There's lots of ghost sightings there."

"Any specific ghosts? Or just random apparitions?" I asked.

"There were two sisters, Irish immigrants, who worked as maids in a local home. At night they prayed in Gaelic. The homeowners overheard them and assumed they were practicing dark arts," said Hunter. "When the kids started wildly misbehaving, the Irish maids got accused of putting curses on them. The sisters were hung together. Ever since, they've been seen sitting on a bench near the pond."

The waitress brought a third round of her dealer's choice that tasted like three parts booze, one part fruit splash. "Count Basie's Negroni for everyone except the vodka girl. For you, my special Three Lives."

I shuddered at the cough syrup taste. "What's in it?"

She rattled off the ingredients: Lunazul tequila, Campari, green chartreuse, maraschino and lime. "It's called Three Lives because it's supposed to intertwine and expose a person's private life, public life and secret life."

"That's exactly what we need!" Melissa bellowed. "I want to know about Paige's secret life!"

Thalia giggled. "She has an altar in her room. She lights candles and incense every night."

Sheila chimed in, "When she dances, it's devil worship."

"Yeah, the devil with double Ds," said Melissa.

I slid the drink toward the middle of the table. "May I have a beer instead?"

Melissa claimed the surrendered Three Lives and downed it in two gulps.

The waitress put out a charcuterie spread with a block of cheddar infused with truffle, which quickly disappeared. I headed to the ladies' room. The red-headed bartender entered the stall next to mine. When I washed my hands, I saw the bartender's phone by the sink where she left it while she used the toilet. A text message flashed across her screen: *Get ready to trick the lights near the pond. H.*

Back at the table, I noticed Melissa's wig had slid, making her look more like Identity Confusion than KISS. She waved her hand as if she were air-signing the bill. "Check, please."

"It's all set," said Hunter. "The tickets for the tour cover everything."

"How so?" I asked.

"Those are *Lodestar* passes. Every aspiring politician knows you have to play nice with the media. Who's the reporter?"

Melissa slurred, "The devil worshipper with the double —"

"What column do you write?"

"Paige writes horror-scopes," lisped Melissa. She wobbled past the crowded bar. She insisted on carrying the guitar prop which she clunked against the butts of customers ordering drinks.

"Hey, Joan Jett," said one guy with a wink.

"Not Joan Jett, dickwad — KISS!"

"Okay, keep moving," I said.

Outside, the cool night air smacked us in the face. We didn't get too far before Melissa stumbled, but Jill caught her elbow.

"These elevator boots are killing me!" said Melissa.

We guided her to a park bench so she could take off the boots. Hunter went back to the bar to get a bottle of water. We gathered around the bench near the pond. I noticed scaffolding near a building across from the pond. I moved closer to see what was going on because it seemed strange that there would be construction activity this late at night. There were gates protecting the construction site outside the Grand Lodge of Masons in Massachusetts. One of the details on the façade was the Freemason's signature compass and square surrounding the letter G. Inside the gates was a bright yellow vehicle labeled *Scorpion Concept Excavator*, with the long-armed scoop erratically rising and falling. I noticed that the Scorpion operator was a female wearing a hard hat. I did a double-take: She looked like the bartender...

Then there was a sudden flashing of white lights reflecting off the pond.

"What the hell?" gasped Jill. "Is anyone seeing what I'm seeing?"

The lights shaped into the aura of two women in Colonial-style dresses gliding straight toward us. Trick-or-Treaters dropped their plastic candy buckets and froze in terror.

"Get off their bench!" yelled Hunter, returning with a water bottle. "It's the sister ghosts!"

Melissa clutched the guitar, slashing it through the air at the sister ghosts. "Fuck off, Irish bitches!"

She chased the ghosts toward the pond, swinging the guitar as the sisters retreated, hovered, then lunged toward her. I grabbed Melissa's arm to pull her away from the apparition. She swung the guitar at me, but I ducked. Thwack! The guitar smacked hard against the side of Hunter's head. He staggered backward and tumbled into the pond.

The lights disappeared and I noticed the Scorpion excavator operator jump down from the truck, rushing toward the pond. It was the bartender; her red hair stuck out from under the yellow hard hat. "Hunter! Are you okay?"

A stream of blood gushed from Hunter's forehead, as he crawled from the pond. I reached for his hand to help him.

"The ghosts were a part of the tour! It's supposed to be fun! You bitches are psychos!" yelled Hunter.

"Grab the guitar," I yelled to Melissa. The Quadsters clambered away, clunking the platform boots against the sidewalk with Melissa swearing about being barefoot. We pushed ourselves into a crowded bar to call for a ride.

Thalia's art project left a winding trail from one end of the apartment to the other, starting in her bedroom with a mountain of sketch pads, stretching into the plum couch lounge with her oversized sheets of charcoal drawings taped to the walls, and meandering into the kitchen where three easels propped up half-finished canvases. Paint brushes stood bristle-side up in Mason jars. Tubes of jewel-toned acrylic paint spread across the newspaper-covered countertops.

Thalia's idea was to paint a John Singer Sargent-inspired triptych for her art class. Her interest in Sargent's murals had morphed into an obsession. Since the regatta, she'd shifted from a fun-loving adventure-seeker to intense artist-in-residence. She burrowed in her room with the door closed for hours at a time. Then she'd emerge, tape another drawing to the wall, and land in front of her easels. She would listen to the relaxation tones of Liquid Mind on repeat. I didn't dare interrupt her creative flow by flipping on my own music.

She drew charcoal images of men's hands, muscular arms, arched noses and soulful eyes. Some of the eyes looked straight out of the paper, others turned upward toward the ceiling.

One afternoon I made green tea with a dash of honey and lemon for us.

"I never should have committed to painting a triptych. It's overwhelming. Plus, I suck."

Each canvas was partially painted.

"Some fresh air can't hurt."

She swiped her brush against the canvas, then set it down. "Good idea. Want to come with me to the MFA? I can show you some Sargent murals."

"Are you sure you want to go there?"

"I'm sure. I won't be blocked from seeing Sargent because of some thugs," she said. "If the kidnappers were behind the ransacking of our rooms and they saw what was on my laptop, all my Dropbox files showed my interest in Sargent's murals. They should hire me to give tours at the museum. There's no reason for anyone to suspect me of anything. Besides you'll be my bodyguard."

"If that's what you want," I said, calling Logan with the *Lodestar* car service.

Inside the museum, she pointed toward a wing that looked like a white and gray shoebox. I noted that it was designed by Pei. I figured Bauhaus kept offices in there.

"That's where they took me," she said.

By the front entrance, she directed me toward Sargent murals depicting various scenes from Greek mythology. Phaeton asked his father, Helius, to allow him to drive the chariot of the sun. Helius advised his son to stay in the middle path, but Phaeton got thrown off course when he was frightened by a giant scorpion. He lost control and brought the sun too close to earth so it burned the cities. Zeus hit Phaeton with a thunderbolt to stop him from doing more damage.

"Perfect! It's October and the scorpion represents Scorpio. We're moving right along in our search for zodiac signs. I love that Sargent used the astrological signs of the night sky instead of just painting a field of stars," I said.

"I don't think Sargent was inspired by Halley's Comet in 1910 as some claim. He painted this mural in 1922 at a time when historians were looking for scientific basis involving ancient meteoroid impacts for understanding mythological stories," she said.

I admired Thalia's calmitude in returning to the museum. I looked over my shoulder to see if we were being followed. Anyone who came near us became a potential threat. I focused on Thalia's explanation of the next mural: Hercules fighting Hydra.

I mentioned, "Hercules has his lion skin in this mural just as we saw at the Monument of the Forefathers in Plymouth."

"You're right." She pointed out the mural of Atlas carrying the zodiac on his back and noted that he was between Taurus and Gemini.

We passed Apollo with his right arm raised, encircled by the muses. We looked up at a windowed dome where Sargent painted scenes in individual rounded frames. I honed in on one of the smaller paintings of Prometheus. This was the second Sargent painting of Prometheus, after the mural in the Boston Public Library. I wondered why Sargent would paint multiples of Prometheus chained to a rock with the eagle swooping down to devour his liver. What constellation did Prometheus represent? Was Prometheus part of the zodiac?

We shifted our focus to another part of the mural with Chiron and Achilles. "Chiron was a centaur who taught Achilles how to hunt —"

"You see Greek mythology and I see constellations. Sargent would have loved to take us out to dinner," I said.

She continued, "Centaurs were like the frat boys of the ancient world. But Chiron was sensitive, refined and educated. He had a deep love for his male students, especially Achilles. And speaking of Sargent taking us to dinner, there's a Greek diner up the block."

I was relieved to see Thalia relax, away from her project. We sat at a table by the window. Thalia impressed the waiter by ordering in Greek, making a new friend with her fellow countryman. He treated us to grilled octopus and salad as he flirted with Thalia. He winked at her when he served our chicken souvlaki. I realized she must be homesick.

"I'd love to visit Greece someday."

"How about next year when you're studying in Rome? Maybe we could be roommates again. I'll study art and, on the weekends, we explore."

"Sounds terrific, but there's just one issue. I haven't found the Winter Hexagon Salon yet. That's my ticket to Rome."

"A minor detail," she said, waving off my worry. "We'll figure it out. By the way, would you mind if I borrowed some of your ideas for my triptych?"

I doused the chicken with *tzatziki*. "Of course not. What ideas are you talking about?"

"I'm going to incorporate zodiac symbolism in my side panels to illustrate pagan beliefs. The center panel will capture a central figure gazing toward a constellation in the heavens, to show the progression toward Christianity."

I realized I was halfway through the zodiac and not even close to finding the key or figuring out where the Winter Hexagon Salon might be hidden. I wondered if Prometheus, Hercules and Atlas were clues. It couldn't be a coincidence that they kept showing up in paintings and sculptures. I made a mental note to pay attention to Greek gods as potential clues, along with the zodiac.

Axel and Xavier came to our place to watch Sunday football. We ordered pizza and sprawled out on the couches drinking Coors Lite. The Patriots were clobbering the Browns, so at halftime we went outside to toss a frisbee.

Xavier stopped to answer his phone. "Hi Mom, hold on, everyone's here, I'll let you ask them."

We huddled together to talk to Mrs. Adamos. "You're all invited to come to Long Island for Thanksgiving. There's plenty of room for everyone. You can see the parade in the morning — if you wake up for it this year."

The boys snickered. Xavier said, "Mom, you know Thanksgiving eve is a big night out."

Axel chimed in, "Everyone from high school meets at Gatsby's Pub. It's a bit of a tradition."

"Catching up with old friends is fine, but being hungover is a waste of time. You boys missed the parade and you looked an awful shade of green at dinner —"

"Okay Mom, we'll be good this year," said Axel. "Thalia will keep things under control."

"Don't worry, Aunt Amara, I'll make sure they're good. Going to the parade is on my list of American things to do."

"And what about Paige? Is she coming too?"

Axel muted the phone. "I was supposed to ask you earlier. It'll be a blast, I promise."

He switched the phone off mute and grinned at me. I wondered if Mrs. Adamos knew me as "Axel's girlfriend" or "Thalia's roommate" or both. I blurted, "I'd love to. Thank you for the invitation."

"Terrific," said Mrs. Adamos. "Daddy and I can't wait to have a full house for a few days. This empty-nest business is for the birds! Thalia, you'll let me know if you girls have any special requests, won't you?"

"Sure, I will. But I know you always think of everything."

I felt guilty for deciding to blow off my family Thanksgiving — for about five minutes, then got over it.

# Chapter Seven — Sagittarius

I was heading to the student center when Melissa's car pulled up with Jill riding shotgun. Melissa lowered the window and shouted, "What's shakin'?"

"Where're you going?"

"Grocery store. Need anything?"

"Beer, always."

Melissa ignored the car behind her. "What are you bringing to Axel's house for Thanksgiving? I doubt his mommy would appreciate your brownies."

It had not occurred to me that I should bring anything to his house. "What do you suggest?"

"Hop in. We'll help you assemble a custom gift basket for Mrs. Whatsherface —"

"Mrs. Adamos." I hopped into the backseat.

"Is there a Mr. Adamos?" asked Jill. "Or are they divorced?"

"Axel and Xavier refer to their dad as Titus. I'll use Mr. and Mrs. unless they tell me otherwise."

"The parental name game is a good indicator if the parents are cool or if they have poles up their asses," said Melissa. "If they say please call us by whatever their first names are, then that's a great sign. If you have to call them Mr. and Mrs., then they're probably total stiffs."

"What does a person put in a custom gift basket?"

Melissa parked over the lines. She dropped her Michael Kohrs mini-backpack in the toddler seat of the shopping cart and led us into Stop & Shop. "What types of snacks does Axel like?"

"Healthy ones. Baby carrots. He trains even in the off season."

"Boring." Melissa buzzed down the snack aisle. "What *ish* are they? Jewish? Irish? Polish?"

"Greekish."

Jill laughed. "Let's find the olives."

Twelve jars of Castelvetrano, Kalamata, Bella di Cerinola, artisanal seasoned blends, and Manzanilla stuffed olives landed in the cart. "This seems excessive, don't you think?"

"Trust me, Greeks are crazy for olives. It'll be the talk at the dinner table."

Jill said, "There's a dollar store next door. We can find a basket there. And ribbon and clear cellophane wrap."

I spent $63 on olives and $1.25 plus tax on a basket. We lined the basket with orange tissue paper, arranged the jars label up, and tied the wrapping with an orange ribbon.

Melissa elbowed me. "Stash some chips in your bag for midnight visitations."

"Midnight visitations?"

"Axel's childhood bedroom with his Little League trophies on the shelf — so hot."

"That's hot? Really?"

"What can I say, it's my kink. If you get the green light to call them by their first names, then it's a safe bet they'll let you shack up with little Axel or at least turn a blind eye. If they leave it at Mr. and Mrs., you better keep your Irish ass in line."

The traffic crawled through Connecticut and over the Throgs Neck Bridge. I sat in the back with Axel while Xavier drove and Thalia worked the playlist.

"I can't wait to dig into Mom's lasagna," said Xavier.

"Ditto." Axel tapped out a text to his mother, telling her we hit traffic. Instead of texting back, Mrs. Adamos called. He put her on speaker.

"You took the Throgs Neck, didn't you?"

"Yeah, it's all backed up," said Axel.

Mrs. Adamos blasted, "Did it not occur to anyone to listen to the traffic reports? I should just throw this lasagna in the trash. It'll be mush by the time —"

"Relax. We'll eat it even if it's mush," said Axel.

"How many times have I told you not to take the Frog's Bottleneck!"

I nodded off to sleep, waking only when I heard the Jeep wheels crunch along a stone driveway. I opened my eyes to the Adamos' waterfront estate on the North Shore of Long Island. The front door swung open and a golden retriever barreled across the lawn. Mr. and Mrs. Adamos sauntered behind, with Mr. Adamos holding Scotch on the rocks.

Mrs. Adamos hugged the boys and reached toward Thalia. "Give me a squeeze, Tay-Tay."

Thalia handed over a bottle of wine.

Mrs. Adamos shook my hand. "Paige, it's a pleasure to meet you."

I followed Thalia's lead and pulled out the gift basket. Mrs. Adamos peered through the cellophane wrap. "Jarred olives. Perfect for martinis."

The foyer was larger than my family's kitchen. A marble spiral staircase wound upstairs to the bedrooms. Mrs. Adamos side glanced my Lands' End canvas duffel bag. "Axel, honey, show the girls to the guesthouse."

A cottage was nestled in the corner of the expansive backyard. There were two bedrooms, a white-tiled bathroom and kitchenette with a stocked bar.

"I need a drink," I told Axel.

"Lasagna's waiting. My mom will freak if it gets soggy."

"We'll be right over," I said and poured vodka tonics for me and Thalia.

"Cheers," she said. "I hope you don't mind the dog house."

"Is this where you usually stay?"

"Normally I get an upstairs bedroom. I'm guessing she wants to assess you first."

"Was the gift basket a bust?"

"A sweet gesture, but —"

"But?"

"Olives should be from the Greek market, not jars. It's like you handed her boxed wine."

"She's an olive snob?"

"We all are."

In the kitchen, Mrs. Adamos told us to sit at the table. There were two fat bottles of chianti and stemless glasses that looked like they were for breakfast juice. She wore oven mitts that practically went up to her elbows and slid a steaming tray in the center of the table. She wacked slabs of lasagna with a spatula, then doled generous mounds to the men and ladylike slivers to the girls. I eyed the lasagna with suspicion as it was blond — *sans* red sauce.

"Honey, have you ever had Pastitsio before? It's Greek lasagna," said Mrs. Adamos. "Instead of marinara sauce, which gives everyone heartburn, this has creamy bechamel sauce with a hint of cinnamon."

"This is a first for me." I took a bite and burned my tongue. I chugged some wine to put out the fire. "Delicious. Just the right amount of cinnamon."

"It's a family recipe. The secret is combining freshly grated Kasseri and Kefalotiri."

"I thought I tasted a lamb and beef combo —"

"I was referring to the cheese."

On Thanksgiving morning, Mr. Adamos made pancakes. I wore a turtleneck under a thick fisherman's sweater. When I entered the kitchen, Mr. Adamos boomed, "That's some sweater. You look like a Viking!"

Mrs. Adamos looked up from the cranberry dish she was preparing and smiled. "Thalia, honey, you should wear my mink bomber jacket. It's adorable and warm enough for the parade. And Paige, you're welcome to borrow a ski jacket from the mudroom closet, although that sweater certainly looks toasty."

"Thanks. I think the sweater should be good enough."

Mr. Adamos pooled Vermont maple syrup on the dish and placed the pancakes on top, letting us in on his secret to the "world's best pancakes." I couldn't see what difference it could make, but I wasn't about to contradict him. When his "strapping young boys" finally showed up, Mr. Adamos fired up some eggs and bacon.

Mrs. Adamos fussed over what coats the boys should wear. Flurries were forecasted, she informed us. She whipped out a Neiman Marcus shopping bag with Gorski fur-trimmed parkas, one blue, the other gray, that were supposed to be Christmas gifts for the boys. She snipped off the $1,925 price tag on each jacket, making my eyes bulge. The brothers slipped into the parkas and zipped up the hoods so she could take a photo. They looked like they were ready for the Iditarod.

I cracked up and said, "You look like Nanook of the North."

Fair game after the Viking sweater comment, but Mrs. Adamos' retort hit me like an uppercut to the jaw. "My sons are not cold weather creatures. They're thoroughbred Greek."

We claimed a spot on 6$^{th}$ Avenue. The brothers and Thalia looked toasty in their coats while I froze in my "Viking" sweater.

"Take these. The mink pockets make my hands sweat," said Thalia, handing me her gloves.

After a few minutes, Axel noticed I was shivering and offered me his two-thousand-dollar parka.

"No thanks," I said, declining because I didn't want my Greek thoroughbred to freeze.

"Let's head to the apartment to warm up. We can watch it on the tv."

This was the greatest idea because one, my teeth chattered; two, I craved alone time with Axel; and three, the thought of him warming me up was the sexiest thing I'd ever thought about. Sure, we'd made out many times — came close to going all the way at the beach — but we took our time in this department because he was a gentleman, insisting we wait until the *perfect* time.

Xavier and Thalia stayed at the parade. We pressed through the crowded streets over to his parents' apartment in Kips Bay. The glass tower stuck up like a middle finger, another Bauhaus obscenity. I.M. Pei designed the building, he told me.

"I got off to a lousy start with your parents," I said.

Axel smiled. "Just be yourself. It takes them awhile to warm up to newbies. They like you."

"How do you know they like me?"

"You'd be getting it worse if they didn't."

The apartment's floor-to-ceiling windows gave a clear view of the crowded city. Axel opened a bottle of Redbreast Irish Whiskey and poured some in two Baccarat glasses.

"This will warm you up," he said, clinking his glass with mine. "Cheers to my Viking warrior!"

The whiskey and the fact that Axel put his arm around me warmed me all over. "You heard the Viking comment?"

"Tay-Tay texted me an alert from the kitchen. Titus means no harm, but the filter between his brain and mouth tends to disappear around the holidays. My mother's on edge from Thanksgiving through New Year's Day."

"Why do the holidays set them off?"

"The family business. Things heat up in the last quarter."

"What's the business?"

"Adamos Modern Air — heating, ventilation, air conditioning — it's an HVAC business."

He splashed more whiskey into our glasses and leaned in for a kiss. Before long we moved into the bedroom where he wrestled the Viking sweater over my head and peeled off my bra — a bit expertly, I must say. How many bras had he removed so adroitly? At that moment, I didn't care one whit. I started giggling thinking about the word "whit" while he nibbled my neck.

"What's so funny?"

"I didn't realize Greek thoroughbreds nibble."

"You're not going to let that one go, are you?"

"Never."

He wrapped his arms around me, so that I thought I'd melt under the sheets with him. Then, unlike the other times, I drew him closer so that he knew, without a doubt, that this was the *perfect* time.

We left the apartment and hailed a taxi. Axel told the driver to take us past 33 Thomas Street.

"It's a detour, but I want to show you the Long Lines building while we're in the city. My dad is obsessed with it."

The Long Lines building was a windowless concrete tower, another Bauhaus obscenity. "Wow. Now that's Brutalist to an extreme."

"Form follows function. It's considered the most secure building in the world. My dad is bidding on a big project there."

To me it seemed the perfect place for Bauhaus to hide the stolen key. "Do we have time for a look inside?"

"No one is allowed in there without security clearance." Axel told the driver to take us back to the parade.

I was happy to be in the warm taxi a little longer. We held hands, snuggling in the back seat. I wanted to stay in the apartment with Axel for the rest of the weekend, that's how great things went during our momentous *perfect* time, but there was turkey and relatives yet to come. The driver said he had to drop us near Grand Central Station because streets were blocked from the parade route. I had read an *Architectural Digest* magazine article about the *Beaux Arts* depot and its

Tiffany-blue celestial-mural ceiling. The article mentioned that the ceiling featured the signs of the zodiac, so I asked if we could take a quick look.

Axel paid the driver and we went inside. I had read that the orientation of the mural was from the point of view above the constellations, looking down on earth. I tried to mentally shift my earth-to-heavens perspective to view it as if I were in heaven. I examined the signs of the zodiac in the mural.

"This only shows the winter zodiac constellations," I said, noticing that Orion — club and lion skin slung over his shoulder — was included in the zodiac between Gemini and Taurus. This struck me as unusual: Orion isn't one of the zodiac constellations, so why was he painted in this mural? Did the Winter Hexagon include Orion as part of the zodiac? From the entrance of the terminal, I observed Orion's right arm and club raised straight into the path of the zodiac. The mural also included the dust cloud of the Milky Way. It intersected the path of the zodiac precisely at Orion between Gemini and Taurus. When I started my search in June with Gemini, I figured it would naturally end with the last sign, Taurus. It suddenly occurred to me that my search for zodiac signs might not end with Taurus as I had originally thought, but with Orion.

We found Thalia and Xavier drinking hot chocolate in the same spot at the parade.

"All warmed up?" asked Thalia, winking at me.

"On fire." I winked back.

We took photos as the Snoopy balloon floated by. Soon after Snoopy, a float that resembled a glass skyscraper rolled past. It had a giant red apple at the top to celebrate 100 years of modern architecture.

"Is that a Bauhaus float? There's no end to them!"

Xavier said, "I've had my parade fix. Want to head back?"

Thalia said, "Can we pass by Rockefeller Center? I'd love to skate for a bit."

Xavier called his dad to ask if his contacts at Seagrams could help us cut the line at the rink. Titus told us to see his guy at the front desk in the Seagram building where the Adamos' business had office space on the tenth floor. We headed up Park Avenue to the Seagram between 52$^{nd}$ and 53$^{rd}$.

"Another glass skyscraper," I muttered.

"Designed by Mies and Philip Johnson," said Axel, referring to Bauhaus architect Ludwig Mies van der Rohe.

"Johnson was the guy who designed the ugly addition on the Boston Public Library," I added.

An older gentleman greeted us and took us down to a basement exit. We followed him out to the rental counter where we were outfitted with skates.

"Could you tell me anything about the statue below the tree?" I pointed toward the massive gold statue of a man holding fire who was surrounded by the signs of the zodiac.

"That's Prometheus. He's been watching the skaters since 1934," he said, spraying my skates with Lysol. "Paul Manship was the sculptor. After the Statue of Liberty, it's the most celebrated sculpture in America."

I laced my skates and wondered why Manship sculpted this Art Deco Prometheus. Another reference to Prometheus, this time with a ring circling around him etched with all of the zodiac signs. I wondered if it had any connection with the Winter Hexagon Salon, but I couldn't connect the dots. In fact, I hadn't connected any dots. Maybe Manship was a member of the elite group? Who else was part of the salon? When were the meetings? How old was it? The biggest question: what were they *doing* in the salon?

It had been years since I went ice skating, so my ankles wobbled as I tried to balance on the blades. Axel gave me his arm to hold, which I clung to long after I felt stable. As we rounded the perimeter, I focused on Prometheus sprawled out on a rock, holding the fire that he stole to improve humanity. Thalia passed us skating backwards. She noticed I was staring at the statue.

"Prometheus again."

"Check out the ring around him — it has the sign for Sagittarius," I said.

"Now that you mention it. Yes. I see it."

She took over the rink with her spin moves and backward gliding.

"Where does a Greek girl learn to skate like that?" I called out.

She smiled. "I have a lot of hidden talents!"

Axel picked up his speed to chase after Thalia. I tried to go faster, a bad idea. I sprawled forward onto the ice. A man scraped his blades to stop in front of me, spraying ice flakes in my face, pressing a blade on top of my hand.

"Get off," I yelled.

He leaned toward my ear. "Who do you know inside Seagram?"

"Fuck off."

He pressed his skate harder. "What were you doing in there?"

Axel skated toward me. The man stepped off, pretending to help me up.

"Bauhaus is watching you," he whispered, before swiftly skating away.

"That fat bastard stepped on my hand on purpose. Another Bauhaus prick," I told Axel. "Let's go kick his ass —"

I tried to hustle off the ice, but I was too slow. The Bauhaus thug waddled past the rentals still wearing his skates. His head bobbed as he penetrated the tourist crowd, quickly moving out of sight.

"These Bauhaus jerks are starting to piss me off," said Axel.

While I unlaced my skates, Axel went back on the rink to get Thalia and Xavier. I searched the crowd for the slob who stepped on my hand, but noticed instead a different man in a black topcoat signaling like a third-base coach. A ground-level restaurant with a view of the rink was directly across from him. A man, sitting at a table drinking wine, returned a hand signal.

"All set with those skates, miss?" asked the rental attendant.

"Here you go, thanks," I said, handing over the skates.

"Exit this way, please."

"Can I wait here for my friends to finish?"

He shook his head. "Sorry. Move along, please."

The man drinking wine was staring in my direction. I held up my arms to signal an AOD greeting, like Captain Biff and the North Easton AOD had taught me. He signaled back a basic druid hello.

I hoped to spot the Bauhaus escapee with my camera. I took a few iPhone panoramic photos of Thalia and the brothers skating off the rink looking like bears on blades in their puffy coats. The phone indicator flashed a hold-steady line, so I tried taking another panoramic photo moving the lens slowly across the rink and ending at Prometheus. I snapped extra pictures of Prometheus holding fire in his raised right arm. It reminded me of Orion with his right arm and club raised into the path of the zodiac. Then it hit me: Is the fire Prometheus brought to mankind the sun? Did Prometheus put the sun into the zodiac?

A hand tapped my shoulder.

"Paige Moore?" It was the man in the topcoat.

"Who are you?" I said, slipping my phone into my back pocket.

He shook my sore hand. "Eli Stanton. The AOD contacted us to keep an eye on things. Are you on assignment?"

"No. I'm a tourist. Which AOD member contacted you?"

"Captain Biff. We go way back. He asked for a favor — a big one considering it's Thanksgiving."

"Ah, the good captain has taught me a lot. That's how I noticed you were communicating with the guy in the restaurant. Protocol is to let other druids know that I'm one, right?"

"Correct." Puffs of white swirled as his breath collided with the cold air. "Do you know what we were signaling?"

I blew warmth into my freezing hands. "Something about surveillance?"

"The man who stomped your hand caught my attention. I chased him, but he slipped away."

"Who was he?"

"I'm not sure. He put rubber coverings on his blades and disappeared. Did he say anything to you?"

"He said Bauhaus was watching me."

"Are you sure he said Bauhaus?"

"Absolutely. It's not the first time these pricks took a run at me. I'm close to something — I just don't know what yet."

"Captain Biff said that McKim told you to find the Winter Hexagon Salon. Do you think you're close to finding it?"

"Nope."

He faced the ice. "You should join us for the Feast Day of St. John the Evangelist on December 27th."

"Where?"

"At the Cathedral of St. John the Divine."

"I'd love to."

"It's a who's who among New York AOD. I'll see to it you get an invitation," he said, signaling a message to the man across the rink. Eli smacked his gloved hand against the railing. "Don't let Bauhaus distract you. They're just trying to rattle you. See you on the 27th."

Back at the guest house, I got dressed for dinner while Thalia showered. My light blue blouse and black pants were wrinkled from being stuffed in my duffle bag, so I searched for an iron. Thalia emerged from her room looking hot in a burgundy wool dress.

"Oh, damn."

"I should have warned you. But more importantly, you need to do something about that hickey on your neck. Hold on," she said, retreating to her room to rummage through the dresser drawers. "Let's try this —"

Thalia folded a nautical-patterned silk scarf around my neck as if she were doing *origami*. The blues complemented my blouse, hiding some of the wrinkles, as well as the love welt. She dabbed some concealer on my neck and rubbed it in with her pinky. It tickled so I jumped back. She pulled my arm and told me to hold still.

"Tuck in your shirt," she said, handing me a navy leather belt from the closet with a gold anchor buckle. "Better."

I checked my reflection in the mirror. "I went from an airline stewardess to a bank teller."

A navy cardigan folded in a drawer completed my outfit. I twirled around to show off my new look. That's when I realized I got dressed without closing the curtain. I saw a woman by the main house kitchen sink watching me. She looked the other way when I reached to close the curtains.

"But an elegant bank teller," she said.

"Oops. We're being watched," I said, closing the blind. "Won't your aunt mind that I ransacked her closet?"

"She'll have no clue."

Thalia squirted some Roja Parfums on my wrists and slid the dainty purple-topped bottle back on the bathroom vanity. We cut across the backyard. Smoke billowed from the chimney, the smell of burning firewood merging with the salty air. Inside, Mr. Adamos served Scotch by the fireplace with his sons, sitting with Axel's three uncles and four cousins. I followed Thalia into the kitchen where Amara was showing her two sisters and sister-in-law the final stages of turkey basting and gravy making.

The women gushed over Thalia. They hugged her, stroked her long hair, admired her slender physique and flawless complexion.

"It's the Greek olive oil that makes your skin so luminous," said one of the aunts.

"I'd like you to meet my roommate."

I wondered if there was a family buzz about Axel bringing home a lady friend or if I was just known as Thalia's roommate. They offered their hands for a shake then returned to peeling potatoes. Aunt Pasha, Amara's oldest sister, eyed me as if she had seen me before, but not in a good way. She was the one who'd been observing me from the kitchen window.

"Wine?" offered Aunt Pasha.

I hesitated, not wanting to appear the lush.

Thalia replied, "We would love some wine. Is it Greek?"

Aunt Pasha poured two goblets the size of fish bowls.

Amara smacked the peeler against the cutting board. "That's a 2018 Sassicaia, not Hawaiian Punch. Go easy on the pours, Wapasha."

"Relax, Amara. It's Thanksgiving, a time to indulge." Aunt Pasha winked at me. "Besides, they're college girls. They're used to alcohol, right girls?"

"Can we help?" offered Thalia.

I wanted to take my wine and sink into the leather club chairs by the fireplace with the men, but no: Amara assigned us water duty. "The chilled bottles are in the garage refrigerator. You can fill up the glasses on the dinner table. And add lemon wheels."

Was this a Greek thing, I wondered: guys in the living room, girls in the kitchen. Was Axel a closet patriarch?

We found a case of Greek Springs natural alkaline spring water on the bottom shelf. I whistled when I saw a silver Aston Martin convertible parked in the garage. I hopped in the driver's seat.

"Sweet," I said. "Very James Bond."

"That's Titus' summer ride. Don't let him see you in the driver's seat. He's super protective of that baby."

We lugged the cases of water into the dining room. Axel sauntered in from the den. "Mom put you to work, I see."

"Water girls," I said. "How's the manly talk?"

He helped pour the water into the long row of glasses on one side of the table. Mrs. Adamos' eyes bugged when she saw Axel in the dining room. She shooed him away. "The girls can handle this."

Thalia retreated to the kitchen to slice the fresh lemons while I finished filling the glasses. Axel's pimple-faced cousin Eddie, who looked to be about twelve, wandered into the dining room.

He squinted and stared at me, similar to Pasha, so I guessed he was her son. "When are we eating? I'm starving," he said.

"Soon, big guy."

"Is it true about you and Tay-Tay?" he asked.

"Is what true?"

"That you're lesbos?"

It was so unexpected, I cracked up.

"My mom saw you in the guest house." Eddie made a click-click sound with his tongue before running away giggling.

Amara set up the food buffet style and invited the men to fill up their plates. There were gold olive branch place card holders with each person's name written in calligraphy. I was seated between Thalia and Axel. To his right was Titus. I took a polite portion of turkey, but I wanted to eat the entire drumstick of dark meat like I normally would do if I weren't worried about looking like a vulture.

Mr. Adamos began a sloshed-sounding *God bless this food* that quickly rolled into an emotional paen to his beautiful family gathered around his table, especially his sons and dear wife. Everyone clinked glasses and said, *Ya mas.* Axel rubbed his foot against mine while Eddie and Aunt Pasha stole glimpses of me, presumably longing to touch Thalia.

The 2018 Sassicaia seemed to suddenly hit Aunt Pasha, who was doing more drinking than eating. She bragged about young Eddie's grades and how he would shatter Axel's rowing records at St. Blaise, where he was a freshman.

"Good for you," said Axel. "Coach P. is the best."

Aunt Pasha waved him off. "Eddie's going to the Olympic training center. Never mind your precious Coach P."

"I already beat your freshman personal best," bragged Eddie.

"Impressive," said Axel.

Mr. Adamos muttered, "The kid's obviously dyslexic. He probably reversed the numbers in his time. There's absolutely no way —"

"Dad, let it go."

Aunt Pasha reached for the wine bottle. "More wine, girls?"

After splashing some wine in our glasses, she plunked the bottle hard against the table in front of Mrs. Adamos. "So, Amara, I see you're re-gifting —"

"Re-gifting?"

Pasha leaned across the table, tugging on my scarf. "I gave you this Hermes scarf last Christmas!"

Mrs. Adamos glanced at my neck. "Honey, where did you find —"

My face deepened to a shade matching the Sassicaia. I had just taken a bite of turkey that was a bit dry. I was trying hard to swallow it, so I swigged the water.

"I hope it's okay, Aunt Amara," said Thalia, coming to my rescue, "but I found it in the closet in the guest house and offered to let Paige borrow it. The colors are gorgeous."

"Just watch the gravy stains," said Mrs. Adamos. "I was saving that for our winter getaway to Santorini."

"I hope you don't mind —" I blurted, swallowing the dry turkey. "I can take it off now —"

"There's a great idea," slurred Aunt Pasha. "Thalia can undo it for you."

Eddie laughed so hard his soda went up his nose and he snorted out Coke bubbles.

Mr. Adamos muttered, "Crew star, my ass. He can't even drink a soda without spazzing out."

I slipped off the scarf and folded it into a square. I followed Mrs. Adamos into the kitchen to hand it back to her. "I'm sorry —"

She put the dishes in the sink, snatched the scarf from my hand and stuffed it into my pants pocket.

"No, dear. I'm sorry about Wapasha. She turns into Pasha-the-Slosha when she drinks. I want you to have the scarf. It looks terrific on you. I had no intention of taking it on my trip."

"Are you sure?"

She ogled the hickey and pinched my cheek. "You're adorable, dear. I can see why Axel likes you."

As per the Adamos family tradition, the women enjoyed port wine by the fireplace while the men did the dishes. I felt relieved that they split the chores, but why separate men from women? Thalia and I sat next to each other on the sofa.

"You two are inseparable," observed Pasha-the-Slosha. "Are you an art major as well? Do you draw nudes of each other?"

"Every day. Thalia's my muse."

"Charming," said Pasha.

I found Axel in the kitchen. "Care for some fresh air before dessert?"

He spiraled his soggy dish towel and snapped it toward Eddie.

"Hey, watch out for my ball sack," squealed the little creep.

Titus smacked the back of Eddie's head. "Watch your language."

Outside, Axel took my hand and we strolled toward the water.

"Your aunt thinks me and Tay-Tay are lesbians."

He burst out laughing. "Aren't you?"

"She was spying on us in the guest house."

Axel pulled me into his arms, kissing me long and hard. "This will give her something to ponder. She'll have to change her scouting report."

I kissed him back, biting his neck and leaving a love welt for Aunt Pasha to ponder.

The night sky over Long Island Sound was clear, so I pointed out the winter circle composed of the bright stars: Rigel, Aldebaran, Capella, Pollux, Procyon, and Sirius.

"Sirius is the brightest star in the night sky. There's Orion and its bright stars Rigel and Betelgeuse," I said, glancing at him to make sure he was following my astronomy session. He was listening, but also glancing at my chest. I continued with Castor and Pollux, the bright stars of Gemini. "Okay, last one, there's the Pleiades star cluster above and to the right of Aldebaran. Aldebaran is known in mythology as the bloodshot eye of Taurus. It's the brightest star of Taurus."

"I thought you said it was the winter circle? These stars make more of an oval."

I started to show him the circle, but then I realized he was right. It was an oval. I played connect-the-dots, retraced the six points and wondered if it was the Star of David. If I removed Sirius, the other five stars made the shape of the five-pointed star of King Solomon. Then I considered the wild possibility that it was the compass and square of freemasonry, which like the Star of David is two intersecting triangles. I retraced it, thinking about which polygon has six sides. It was definitely six points intersecting two triangles.

"Holy shit, it's the Winter Hexagon!"

"I definitely see a hexagon, now that you traced it like that," he said.

"And in the center, those stars that make up Orion's club, form a G. That's always in the center of the freemason compass and square. It had to be the inspiration for the Winter Hexagon Salon. Remember what Chuck McKim told me before he died about finding the key? I bet the key has something to do with the compass, square and G."

"Sounds legit to me," he said, "but I need dessert."

Seeing the Winter Hexagon for the first time turned my thoughts to the hidden salon. The center of the winter hexagon is between Gemini and Taurus, the beginning and end of my search for zodiac signs. The more I thought about the Grand Central station mural that included Orion, the more I felt that the Orion constellation with his raised right arm and club would lead me to the Winter Hexagon Salon. But I couldn't dismiss Prometheus with his raised arm holding fire. I had a strong inclination that there was something with Orion and Prometheus that could help lead me to the salon.

The dessert table resembled the gates of heaven. The multitude of pie and cookie varieties would take a week to sample. I made my move on a piece of chocolate cream pie and added a sliver of apple pie.

Mr. Adamos polished off three desserts then pushed back his chair and crossed his thick legs. His plump fingers looked out of proportion with the dainty espresso cup and saucer.

"I increased my cryptocurrency portfolio. With the way our government prints money, I think the dollar will devalue in no time," he said.

Aunt Pasha butted in, "Theo bought Dogecoin and Ethereum."

"I'm talking Bitcoin, Pasha. Don't get involved with shitcoin," bellowed Titus. "The level of cyber-hacking and surveillance is over the top. It's not just nefarious foreign actors anymore. We're up against governments. We're up against our own government. Everyone and everything are being watched —"

"So how is Bitcoin a solution?" asked Theo.

"It allows me to be my own bank without having to trust a third party. It's the future of global enterprise. We all need to get our heads around this."

Mrs. Adamos collected some of the dessert dishes. "Titus, let's not talk business at the table."

Eddie pointed out the hickey on Axel's neck. "Are you dating *Jaws*? Is there a younger sister?"

"In your dreams, little man!" said Axel, adjusting his collar.

"Maybe I'm dating *Jaws*," said Thalia, winking at Eddie.

I reached for the strawberry-rhubarb pie, quickly returning to Titus' topic. "What's the purpose of all the surveillance?"

"You name it, they want to know about it!"

I thought about the druids communicating with hand signals in Rockefeller Center. I decided I should limit my cell phone usage to avoid Bauhaus tracking me.

"Can they hack a person's cell phone?"

"You could teach a chimp to hack a cell phone. Social media phishing is free and easy surveillance. Think about it. Pictures get posted. The social media controllers sell photos and information from personal accounts. Then the government came along and created a hash. It started as a means to troll photos and personal information to catch child pornographers," explained Mr. Adamos.

"Well, no one would argue against that," said Aunt Pasha.

"Exactly. But now there's no limits to what gets hashed. It's a free-for-all. It's rapidly turning authoritarian."

Axel said, "I'm convinced, Dad. I'm going to delete my Facebook account."

"I warned you boys not to set up any social media. Get rid of it," said Mr. Adamos.

"Eddie has nothing to do with social media," said Aunt Pasha, glancing at us. "He's too busy studying and rowing. The trash that's out there!"

"GoEdrowGo," mumbled Xavier, exposing Eddie's Instagram name.

Eddie slouched in his chair.

I took out my phone and powered it off. It was time to make things more difficult for Bauhaus.

# Chapter Eight — Capricorn

Back at campus, the post-turkey blues hit us hard. The looming reality of final exams and term papers with three weeks to go was a harsh reality check. I rummaged through the kitchen cabinets for a package of stale Oreos. I offered a cookie to Thalia, who was trying to finish her triptych.

"Can you picture Michelangelo dropping crumbs into his frescoes?" she asked, dabbing blue across her canvas.

"If I'm in Rome next year, I'll search the Sistine Chapel for traces of baguettes."

She glanced at her phone. "It's Melissa. There's a mandatory Quadster powwow in twenty minutes. As if we have time —"

"She's freaking over her econ final. If she fails, her dad will yank her out of Kew. Can you picture Melissa at community college?"

She rinsed her brush in the sink. "I can't imagine her not getting what she wants. Ever."

Their door was closed, which was unusual for them. We knocked and Jill whispered, "Who is it?"

I said, "Men in Speedos."

She whipped the door open to reveal Christmas Central: lights blinking around a four-foot faux pink spruce, pine-scented Yankee votives flickering on the table, Bing Crosby crooning.

"Impressive! Paige, we need to string up some lights."

While Sheila made hot chocolate, Melissa passed around a bottle of peppermint Schnapps and a can of whipped cream. Thalia and I skipped the Schnapps because we had a full night of studying ahead of us, but we splurged on the whipped cream and cocoa.

"By the way, *Jaws*, we heard about your epic Thanksgiving," said Melissa, winking at Thalia. "Way to shock Mr. and Mrs. Whatstheirfaces at the holiday table."

"You told?" I bugged my eyes at Thalia.

"*The Thanksgiving Hickey* would make a great film," said Jill. "The hickey could come to life and eat all the food like *The Blob*."

"We had to drag it out of your roommate," said Melissa. "But there's no secrets with the Quadsters!"

"Definitely, no secrets," said Sheila.

Thalia cackled. "It's too good not to share!"

Melissa propped her dry erase board with *Festivus Maximus* written in alternating red and green block letters in the center.

Jill said, "Festivus Maximus sounds totally Greek, right Thalia?"

"More like Latin. What is it?"

Sheila wrote our names on folded paper and dropped them in an elf hat. "Pick one for your secret Santa."

Melissa drew arrows explaining the rules. "You have to surprise your person before we head home for winter break. You can either buy something or do something special for your person."

"Great idea," I said.

Melissa swiped a napkin across her whipped-cream moustache. "It comes naturally to some of us."


Thalia put the finishing touches on her triptych. The side panels portrayed Greek mythology with Prometheus bringing fire to humanity on the left side and him chained to a rock on the right side. The center panel featured a magnificent banquet table with a funky rendition of DaVinci's Last Supper. There was an ornate gold chalice in the center of the table with golden rays reflecting from it. Thalia replaced Jesus and the Twelve Apostles with Orion and the twelve zodiac signs. She unified the three panels with a swirling teal-colored night sky with goldenrod stars. She used a straight edge to paint thin lines over Prometheus, setting him apart from the rest of the painting.

"Excellent detail," I gushed.

"I set up a *plein-air* easel by Trinity Church to capture the stone carving of the Last Supper. I was inspired by the carvings in the church, after you explained St. John to me that day. Remember?"

"Of course."

"The side panels show the mythological pagan beliefs and the center shows the movement toward Christianity."

"I love the color of the night sky," I said. "It's clearly the Last Supper. Are you worried about offending Bible thumpers?"

"My professor said art is supposed to make viewers uncomfortable. Provoke new thoughts on old ideas."

Once the paint dried, Thalia wrapped her canvases and headed out to meet her professor.

When she'd gone, I called Jill to tell her the coast was clear. Jill had pulled Thalia's name for her Secret Santa. She rifled through the piles of charcoal drawings, took a few of the larger pieces taped to the walls and scurried off to arrange her surprise.

Wheezy, the resident director, gave Jill permission to transform the first-floor foyer into an art gallery. Jill and Melissa fit the drawings into black mat-frames and tacked the work on the side walls. I wrote a blurb under her photo about our Greek artist-in-residence. Sheila helped to set up an ice cream social in the center of the foyer to attract the dorm residents to the gallery. There were about thirty students present to cheer when Thalia entered the foyer. Jill filmed her entrance to add to the college website.

Thalia cupped her hand over her mouth. "Oh my —"

Jill said, "Merry Festivus Maximus!"

"I can't believe you did this!"

Wheezy congratulated her on her art. "I think we should leave it on display through next semester. That is, if you're okay with it?"

"I'd be honored!" She excused herself to put away her backpack in our room.

Wheezy beamed about the dorm camaraderie, snapping photos to post on the dorm's social media sites. When Thalia returned, she handed Melissa a wrapped gift with a big red bow on it.

"I hope you like it," said Thalia.

Melissa shredded the wrapping paper. She howled when she saw what it was, then held it up for the rest of us. Thalia had painted a caricature of Melissa driving a golf cart with two wheels tilted off the ground, narrowly missing a tree, with her mouth agape in laughter.

"Do you like it?"

"I don't like it. I love it! More than my entire designer handbag collection."

Sheila handed an overstuffed giftbag to Jill — a terrycloth zebra bathrobe with a big pink J embroidered on the left lapel. There were a pair of fluffy zebra slippers to match.

Jill slipped it on. "Awesome!"

"It makes you look fresh out of Hollywood," said Sheila.

The following day, Melissa called the Quadsters to meet at the campus auditorium. I showed up, expecting some sort of secret Santa surprise, and I wasn't disappointed. She had arranged with her film professor for a private movie session in my honor. She passed around buckets of buttered popcorn, soda and M&Ms.

We howled when *Jaws* appeared on the screen. Each time the grinding, two-note motif sounded we chanted the *dun-dun, duuun-duuun, duuuun-duuuun* in unison.

When the movie ended, Melissa gifted me a hardcover copy of the Peter Benchley novel. I admired the cover art of the shark stalking the skinny-dipper. I said, "I'll treasure this."

"Someday you'll write your own *Jaws*, Paigester."

"And I'll turn it into a blockbuster," said Jill.

On the last night of the semester, I arranged for the *Lodestar* car service to drive the Quadsters to the L Street Beach in South Boston. As we huddled on the beach, I looked across the bay at the illuminated skyline, noting the JFK Library designed by IM Pei. It appeared to be another soulless Bauhaus design, but to be fair, I made a mental note that it needed further investigation. I had called that night's dress code: sweats and slippers. Sheila wore fluffy snow leopard Uggs. Jill rocked her new zebra slippers. Melissa donned green sweatpants with a red sweatshirt and fur-lined flipflops to show off her ruby toenails.

"I made one for everyone," said Jill, handing out silk-screened Festivus Maximus hoodies.

The beach was dark but for the moonlight. As a secret Santa gift, I bought Sheila a disco strobe light and portable party speaker to blast her favorite Korean boy band holiday remixes. Axel and Xavier brought four friends who were already drinking Corona from the pony keg. They passed a bottle of peppermint schnapps to keep us warm.

"Surprise!" I shouted to Sheila over the music, revealing the orb.

"You rock!" said Sheila, working her dance moves as the guys circled to dance with her.

Melissa's eyes popped. "Paigester, way to set the bar!"

We danced and drank, listening to the ramped-up Christmas playlist till midnight. Then I put on a Santa hat and plunked a pile of towels in the middle of the dance floor.

"Time for the Festivus Maximus Polar Plunge!"

"Wait, what?" said Melissa. "I didn't bring a swimsuit —"

"Skinny-dipping goes with our *Jaws* theme — *dun-dun, duuun-duuun, duuuun-duuuun.*"

We dropped our sweats on the beach and jumped butt-naked into the frigid Dorchester Bay.

"Way to bounce like *Bay Watch*, Paigester. Your milkshakes bring all the boys to the beach…or whatever that song is," said Melissa, dipping to her shoulders. "I'm not getting my hair wet. I just had a blowout."

We had a contest to see who could stay in the longest. Axel hugged me. One of his friends splashed Jill and she shrieked. Sheila was the first to get out of the water. She wanted to dance more to warm up.

Suddenly, Melissa flailed her arms. "What the fuck!"

She splashed toward the shore, screaming and pointing at the water. At first, I thought it was a black lab circling us to herd us out of the frigid water. Then I saw horns and heard bleating sounds coming from different directions.

"What the hell is that?" I shouted.

"Paige, get out!" screamed Melissa.

I got rammed in the back. Then something scraped the back of my legs. I raced toward the surf. Axel sped past me and reached to pull me from the water. I took another shot to the back of my legs and stumbled toward the sand.

"Are those fucking goats?" gasped Melissa.

I grabbed the flashlight to shine it into the water, seeing five sets of widespread eyes. The animals bleated and swam in a pack toward the shore. The wet goats looked like alien sea creatures. One had glow-in-the-dark crossed eyes. He appeared to be smiling in a perverted way. I was naked and shivering. Axel wrapped a towel around me.

"Was this part of your party plan?" asked Jill.

"No fucking way. Who could pull this off?" I looked around but nothing seemed out of the ordinary. "Where the hell did they come from?"

The goats lingered around the shallow water. I wondered if this was another demented Bauhaus stunt. But how could anyone know what I'd planned? The only one I had told was Axel. Otherwise, it was top secret. Did he tell his friends that joined us and they were trying to be funny?

I turned to him. "Did you let it slip to anyone about the midnight Polar Plunge?"

"No. I swear I kept your secret."

I believed him. His friends seemed just as shocked as the Quadsters. Then how had someone managed to sabotage my Polar Plunge? I decided to keep the mood festive and not get upset about the goats. The last thing I wanted was to appear uptight.

"Goats were not part of the Secret Santa Polar Plunge. But they're right up there with flying reindeer. I guess it's just Capricorn —"

"You and your zodiac signs," said Thalia, pulling on her sweats.

More like me and my battle with Bauhaus, I thought. Ever since Thanksgiving, I was conscientious about shutting off my cell phone to limit any potential for surveillance. I had also texted some of my plans to Axel to arrange for him to bring friends and schnaps. Maybe that was enough for Bauhaus to piece together what I was up to. I had also emailed my order and credit card payment for the keg with arrangements for where and when to deliver it. I wondered whether the laptop thief had access to my email account. This surveillance needed to stop.

I wanted to wait for whatever person was going to show up to pick up their goats, but Melissa was "bleeding and freezing" — her leg was barely scratched — and she demanded that we take her back to the dorm, so we packed up and took off.


Axel invited me to Manhattan after Christmas. When we arrived at his parents' apartment, the doorman handed Axel a cream-colored, wax-sealed envelope addressed to me. We took the elevator up to the apartment to drop our bags.

"Coffee?" he offered.

"You read my mind."

I opened the envelope. It was an embossed invitation to attend a ceremony celebrating the feast day of St. John the Evangelist at St. John's Cathedral.

"What's that all about?" asked Axel.

"An invitation to church."

"Are you religious?" Axel placed our coffees on the table, glancing at the invitation. "Or are you a Stop & Shop Catholic?"

"What's that?"

"A Catholic who only goes to church on holidays or when something is given away like palms on Palm Sunday or ashes on Ash Wednesday."

I smiled. "I'm a family Catholic. When I'm home, I go with my family every week. But when I'm on my own, never."

"What's special about St. John the Evangelist?"

"He wrote about the apocalypse in the book of Revelation. Revelation is loaded with references to the constellations and the movements of the stars and the planets. The book references the new and future temple, so most druids are St. John fanatics."

"What's it like being a druid? Or can you not share that?"

"I'm just a rookie. Captain Biff and Pilar are my mentors."

"Mentor for what? It's got to be more than secret handshakes."

"Druids are worldwide. Mostly I assist Captain Biff in the area of biblical relics."

"Biblical relics?"

"Believers think certain biblical relics have special powers," I explained. "They're considered gifts from God."

"Who sent you the invitation?"

I explained to Axel that Captain Biff had arranged to put "eyes on me" for protection at the Thanksgiving parade. I mentioned how I saw two druids communicating with sign language across the rink and how I met Eli Stanton. Since then, Captain Biff told Eli to follow me in the city, which is how the invitation got delivered to me.

"Come with me if you want to." I flipped the invitation. There was a handwritten note indicating I should meet Eli Stanton by the statue of Atlas near Rockefeller Center before the service.

"Excellent. We'll go to the Gramercy Tavern for lunch, see the Christmas windows on Fifth Ave., and then meet him near Atlas."

"You don't mind?"

He reached into his back pocket for the leather wallet that I gave him for Christmas. He pulled out two tickets. "But tomorrow: *Hamilton!*"

My eyes popped. "How did you get tickets? I heard it's impossible —"

He grinned. "Titus has connections."

On our way to Rockefeller Center, we ducked inside the New York Public Library to use the restrooms. The library was designed in *Beaux-Arts* style by John Carrere and Thomas Hastings, who both attended the *Ecole de Beaux Arts* and worked for McKim, Meade and White. There were no zodiac signs inside, but on the third floor there was a ceiling mural of Prometheus carrying fire in his outstretched right arm, just like at the ice rink. I knew it couldn't be a coincidence, but I felt as though I were not closer to finding the Winter Hexagon Salon.

We crossed the street and passed Salmon Tower — designed by the architectural firm York and Sawyer who once worked for McKim, Mead and White — where I noticed Capricorn and the rest of the zodiac signs by the front entrance. We were tight on time, so we moved along.

We waited by the entrance to Rockefeller Center, near where the Atlas sculpture depicted the Titan holding the celestial realm on his shoulders. Atlas taught astronomy to sailors to help them navigate the seas and to farmers to measure the seasons. Atlas was the god who turned the heavens on its axis, causing the stars to revolve. I noticed that one of the armillary rings had the symbols of the zodiac. Atlas was featured in one of the Sargent murals at the Museum of Fine Arts. I thought about Orion's posture — the way he stood below the zodiac with one bent knee — and wondered if Atlas was another myth based on the constellation Orion.

I considered Prometheus at the skating rink and Atlas near the entrance, which opened my thoughts to the possibility that the Winter Hexagon Salon intentionally left mythological signs around the city.

"Should we send smoke signals to let him know you're here?"

"Trust me, he already knows." I held up my phone to take a selfie with Atlas in the background. "Don't worry, I won't post on social media."

"I deleted all my accounts."

"I did the same."

Axel pointed toward Rockefeller Center. "I'll be working there next summer. Titus wants Xavier and me to learn the family business."

"That could be a cool job."

"He's all about 33 Thomas Street," Axel said, referring to the Brutalist windowless skyscraper in Tribeca — formerly called the AT&T Long Lines building — known as the most secure building in America, the hub for the National Security Agency. It was designed by architect John Carl Warnecke who took one year to complete a three-year master's degree in Harvard's architecture program, studying under Gropius.

"Why does Titus want to work on that project so badly?"

"Titus is mesmerized — 33 Thomas Street is protected from a nuclear blast. It has its own water and gas lines."

I felt three light taps on my shoulder. Eli Stanton wore a black topcoat, felt fedora, and he carried a blackthorn walking stick. He bowed his head and placed his hand over his heart in a formal druid greeting, so I did the same. Then he side-eyed Axel.

"Mr. Stanton, this is Axel Adamos, my boyfriend. I hope it's okay if he joins us?"

They shook hands. "I'm sorry. That won't do. It's a private affair. I have a car waiting, so if you'll excuse us —"

"I understand. Call me when you're done," said Axel.

We crawled through traffic to St. John the Divine Cathedral, where the driver dropped us off near the western façade.

"An impressive combination of gothic revival and Romanesque revival," I said.

Eli Stanton said, "Welcome to St. John the Unfinished."

While I admired the world's largest cathedral — designed by lead architect Ralph Adams Cram who also designed Boston University's Marsh Chapel — it occurred to me that Cram could have been a member of the Winter Hexagon Salon. I remembered seeing Solomon's temple and The Last Supper in the ornamental details at Marsh Chapel. Eli referred to the fact that there were towers above the western façade, the southern transept and a steeple above the crossing that were never completed due to funding issues.

I wondered about the unfinished aspects and the artistic detail above the entrance. My eye was drawn toward the stone carvings of four beasts, the same ones St. John wrote about in the *Book of Revelation*: "And the first beast was like a lion, and the second beast like a calf, and the third beast had a face as a man, and the fourth beast was like a flying eagle."

Eli tapped the brass tip of his walking stick against the edge of the entryway and mentioned that the cornerstone-laying ceremony was on St. John's Day, December 27th, 1892.

"The stone carvings are gorgeous. These beasts are from the *Book of Revelation.* Some say they represent the two equinoxes and two solstices in the age of Taurus: Leo, Taurus, Aquarius and Scorpio," I said, remaining skeptical because they were out of order — the man wasn't pouring water, and Scorpio should be a scorpion, not an eagle. With the Winter Hexagon constellation always on my mind, I was curious if the four beasts represented constellations surrounding Orion.

"Have you seen St. John standing atop the four horsemen of the apocalypse?"

He showed me the Portal of Paradise on the western façade where there are sculptures of the end of modern New York that were added between 1988 to 1997. The Brooklyn Bridge was breaking in two, with a bus plummeted from the bridge where waves met the toppling skyline. Included in the midst of the swaying skyline stood the World Trade Center.

"That's unsettling," I said, following Eli inside toward a black iron gate that he unlocked to show me rows of glass showcases, the cathedral crypt.

"One ecclesiastical item you'll find interesting is over here," said Eli, picking up a two-handled brass cup. "It dates back to the 1660s. It will be used in the service tonight."

He allowed me to hold it for a moment. "Does this symbolize the cup St. John held with the snake coming out of it?"

He placed the chalice back in the glass cabinet. "Captain Biff mentioned you're a whiz with the biblical references —"

"What's this?" I asked.

"That's a Mexican chalice from the mid-17th century," explained Eli. "I need to get ready for the service. Feel free to look around the cathedral. Find a seat with a good view of the altar."

I asked, "Do any of these relics have special powers?"

"They've been used in many religious services, but I'm not aware of any special powers. They certainly aren't the holy grail."

The church filled up for the service, so I found a pew in the back. The air was overridden with a musky aroma that I recognized from Tanya's herb-induced guided meditations. Tanya had explained that St. John's mugwort opened direct channels to lunar magic.

I sneezed. An old man next to me said, "Bless you."

"I think I'm allergic," I said, sneezing three more times.

The organ groaned its opening chords, signaling the choir to harmonize: *We are the light of the world; may our light shine before all ...*

The hushed priests, altar servers and robed celebrants proceeded up the center aisle. Priests gently swung brass censers emitting incense clouds. A priest boomed from the lectern, from the Gospel of St. John: *"In him was life; and the life was the light of men...and the light shineth in darkness; and the darkness comprehended it not."*

The priest delivered a sermon about St. John the Evangelist, how he committed to seeking the light. I perked up when the priest referenced a passage from *The Richardson Monitor of Free-Masonry*: "Master, to whom do modern masons dedicate their lodges? Senior Warden replied, to St. John the Baptist and St. John the Evangelist. Why so? Senior Warden explained, because they were the two most eminent Christian patrons of masonry. Since their time, in every well-regulated and governed lodge, there has been a certain point within the circle, which bounded on the east and west by two perpendicular lines, representing the anniversary of St. John the Baptist and St. John the Evangelist, who were perfect parallels, as well as in masonry as Christianity; on the vertex of which rests the Holy Scriptures, supporting Jacob's ladder, which is said to reach the watery clouds; and in passing around this circle, we naturally touch on these perpendicular parallel lines, as well as the Holy Scriptures, and while a mason keeps himself thus circumscribed, he cannot materially err."

In my mind the circle represented the constellations in the zodiac. A dozen hooded druids surrounded the priest, each holding a snake in their outstretched arms. The priest held up the chalice that Eli had showed me earlier. The sight of the snakes gave me the same nauseous feeling I got when there was a loose strand of hair in my food. I took custody of my thoughts, shifting from snakes and hair to pondering the two St. John's whom I began to think bookended the zodiac — with St. John the Evangelist representing Ophiuchus the serpent holder and St. John the Baptist representing Orion. I thought it was interesting that we were celebrating the Feast Day of St. John the Evangelist around the time when the sun was rising with Ophiuchus and the winter solstice. St. John the Baptist's feast day celebration happens six months later around the time the sun rises with Orion and the summer solstice.

The old man next to me struggled with the kneel-stand-kneel aspects of the ceremony, balancing himself on the pew to make the transitions. During the sign of peace, I shook his hand and started to say *peace be with you*, but he said, "Come with me after Mass. Stanton told me to bring you to the salon."

"Salon?"

"A private druid meeting. Stanton insists on your attendance."

An elderly woman behind us hissed, "Shhhh."

The hunchback next to me raised his cane at her. "You make more noise with your shushing!"

When the chorus sang the closing hymn, I left with the hunchback. His left foot slightly dragged, but he moved quicker than I expected toward his vintage car, which had a mean-looking, winged-out front grille.

"Nice ride," I said.

He opened the passenger door. "Dodge Dart. 1962. Hurry, honey. We can't be late."

I lingered on the curb. "First tell me: who are you and where are we going?"

"Timothy Edward Wexford of the New York City AOD, chapter 142. I serve under Eli Stanton. He told me to take you to the LaFarge Salon."

"As in John LaFarge, the stained-glass artist?"

"As in LaFarge's son, Christopher. He was one of the architects who designed this cathedral." He motioned his cane, encouraging me to get in.

I slid in. He shuffled around the car and got behind the oversized steering wheel, which he peered over. He pulled onto Amsterdam Avenue without looking. Horns blared at us the whole way, which he ignored.

Mr. Wexford pulled into a garage where the attendant waved him through to park the car himself. From there we took a subway to the end of the line, but we didn't get out. He signaled the subway operator who looped the subway car back to let us out at a private stop near an old abandoned station. I marveled at the vaulted ceilings with green and white tiled archways. Brass chandeliers lit the damp walkway along the tracks.

"This is beautiful," I said, keeping pace with his purposeful strides despite his lame left foot. LaFarge was the architect, he explained, along with George Lewis Heins, who designed the city's first subway in 1904. He banged his cane against an arched door.

A deep voice from inside said, "Password?"

"Deacon Darts," said Mr. Wexford. "Accompanied by Eli Stanton's guest."

Locks clicked and the door swung open. A short gentleman in a hooded monk's robe led us down a candle-lit hallway with a checkerboard marble floor. He announced our arrival as we entered the swankiest room I'd ever seen. A crystal chandelier shimmered above a twelve-stool bar with top-shelf liquor aligned on mahogany shelves ensconced by plush rust-colored velvet drapes. The chartreuse-hued walls featured a deco-style mural of men laying railroad tracks. Leather club chairs were arranged around a white marble-topped coffee table. A baby grand piano stood open in the back of the room with the pianist playing Duke Ellington.

There were eight men and two women, all middle-aged or older, sipping martinis and mingling around the bar. Eli

Stanton rested his elbow on the edge of the bar, stirring a three-olive stick in his drink.

"Did you enjoy the service?" he asked.

"Everything but the snakes." I accepted a vodka martini from Deacon Darts.

"And the incense made her sneeze," said Deacon Darts. "She's allergic to mugwort."

"Thank you for joining us. The purpose of our salon is for New York City AOD leaders to break away from the formal meetings so we can exchange ideas in small, private gatherings."

"It's a glamorous salon," I said.

The group gathered by the club chairs with their cocktails. The women had French-manicured nails and Ziegfeld-style cocktail rings. Their hair looked Blow Bar fresh and they wore silk skirts with navy blazers. They chatted until Eli announced the topic for discussion: biblical relics. Captain Biff had told me that Eli was trustworthy, so I felt relaxed in the salon.

"Eli, darling, haven't we exhausted this topic?" said Lillian, taking a long drag from her cigarette.

"The reason I bring it up tonight is because our guest is the North Easton druid who found the ark of the covenant —"

"That was you?" gasped Lillian. "Impressive work decoding Richardson's secrets. He was a clever fellow. How did you figure him out?"

I blushed. "Luck, mostly. I discovered his architecture was designed using the same dimensions as Solomon's temple. There was only one purpose for Solomon's temple: to protect the ark of the covenant. Once I had that calculated, then I applied my theory to his pyramid in Wyoming."

"You make it sound so easy," said Lillian. "What are you researching nowadays?"

The strength of the martini loosened my tongue. "A descendent of Charles McKim told me to find the key to a salon called the Winter Hexagon. He said Bauhaus stole the key. But finding the key is only half of it —"

She exhaled a puff of smoke. "Bauhaus bastards! What's the other half?"

"Locating the Winter Hexagon Salon," I said, searching their faces for any reactions. There weren't any which made me think they'd never heard of the salon. Deacon Darts was slack jawed.

Eli asked, "Do you have any theories?"

"Charles McKim attended Harvard and the *École des Beaux-Arts* in Paris. Richardson trained him as a draftsman when he built Trinity Church in Boston. I believe McKim hid symbols in his architecture, just like Richardson. I've recently discovered that the Winter Hexagon is composed of the stars of the winter circle that are part of the constellations Gemini, Taurus, Orion, Canis Major, Canis Minor and Auriga."

"Do you think McKim was building Solomon's temple?" asked Deacon Darts, handing me a second martini. I hadn't finished my first one.

"His symbols pertain to the zodiac. I think Solomon's temple has something to do with the Winter Hexagon. The Boston Public Library has a ton of zodiac signs. McKim built the library and John Singer Sargent painted murals in the library, which also depict zodiac signs. Those are the symbols that I'm trying to decode."

Eli said, "Let's take a step back. McKim was an architect long before Gropius arrived in America to start Bauhaus. What's the connection?"

"McKim, like Richardson, left symbols in his designs. Gropius arrived with his school of square-boxed architecture that was anti-bourgeoisie, geared toward the working man. I think he wanted to join the Winter Hexagon Salon, but he was shunned. Gropius stole the key to the salon and sent out his army of Harvard-minted architects to build bland Bauhaus boxes across the United States, without art or ornamentation."

"Why do you care so much about McKim's zodiac symbols?" asked Eli.

"Because it could lead me to the mystery salon," I explained. "Bauhaus wants total domination. If Bauhaus gains access to the hidden salon, then it could destroy the hidden secrets of early American druid architecture. Bauhaus would claim everything hidden in the salon for its own prosperity. It will demolish early American architecture."

Eli said, "Interesting theory. I don't disagree. Regarding the zodiac symbols, the ancients believed that after humans die their souls reside in the Milky Way waiting to be reincarnated."

"Exactly. The Gate of Man — the silver gate — is located at the intersection of the Milky Way and the zodiac. The entrance to heaven and Solomon's temple is through the center of the Winter Hexagon constellation. I think that's why the entrances to all the druid temples are marked by an image from the constellations of the Winter Hexagon."

"I'd like to hear more on that," said Deacon Darts.

"In Genesis it says, '*Let there be lights in the firmament of the heaven to divide the day from the night; and let them be for signs, and for seasons, and for days, and years.*' According to Isaiah it says: '*Thou art wearied in the multitude of thy counsels. Let now the astrologers, the stargazers, the monthly prognosticators, stand up, and save thee from these things that shall come upon thee.*'"

Eli said, "I think you're onto something."

"I've been researching murals and sculptures that were created by McKim's peers. Prometheus and Atlas keep appearing. There are two murals of Prometheus at the Boston Public Library, one at the Boston Museum of Fine Arts, a large ceiling mural at the New York Public Library and a gold statue of Prometheus at the Rockefeller Center ice rink. Perhaps Prometheus bringing fire to humanity is the constellation Orion holding the sun in his outstretched right arm. The sun passes through the club of Orion on its way through the zodiac. The

Rockefeller Center front entrance behind Prometheus has an Art Deco depiction of God holding the compass and square. I believe that the compass and square is a reference to the Winter Hexagon. In the middle of the Winter Hexagon at the intersection of the Milky Way dust cloud and the zodiac, the stars form the letter G. The most prolific symbol of freemasonry is the letter G enclosed by the compass and square. For all we know, the G could stand for grail."

I slid my martini glass onto the coffee table. The vodka was hitting me hard, loosening my tongue so my ideas spewed. Why had I just blurted out that detail about the G standing for grail? Most observers think it stands for God. This was the first time that had occurred to me. I wanted to leave, to go sit alone to mull this over. I was mad at myself for oversharing. It reminded me of the time I learned to play poker — *a card laid is a card played*. I just threw down an ace without even blinking.

Deacon Darts' eyes popped wide. "The grail?"

I tried to downplay it by discussing Atlas. "In Manhattan, both the Prometheus and Atlas statues are surrounded by a ring of zodiac symbols. I believe Atlas also portrays the constellation Orion, but instead of putting the sun into the zodiac path, he is carrying the zodiac on his shoulders."

Deacon Darts stared into my eyes so intently that I worried he was having a cardiac event. He asked, "Are you thinking the Winter Hexagon Salon is within Rockefeller Center?"

"Possibly, but the buildings and statues were designed well after the creation of the Winter Hexagon Salon. I'm going to continue searching for signs. I started with Gemini and I'm going to finish with the outstretched right arm of Orion."

Lillian puffed a few smoke rings, then stubbed out her lipstick-stained cigarette. "We got off track. What does any of this have to do with Bauhaus?"

"Bauhaus builds ziggurats — frightening corporate skyscrapers — to reach the heavens. Skyscrapers with no ornamentation are the proverbial middle finger toward old-school Solomon's temple designers. Gropius and Bauhaus only cared about maximizing square footage. The prophets reached for the stars. I'm not against the modern materials, but ornamental details should be included. For example, the metal gargoyles on the corners of the Chrysler Building are a visual game changer. It doesn't take much to improve aesthetics."

"I agree, dear," she said.

The meeting adjourned, so I left with Deacon Darts, exiting through the Surrogate's Courthouse where I recognized the main hall ceiling mural that had all twelve signs of the zodiac. The signs were appearing everywhere I turned, inching me closer to Orion, but I still needed to find the key. I was convinced Bauhaus was searching for the holy grail because it would give them access to its biblical powers. Bauhaus would have a field day learning what the early American architects discussed in their private think tank. What was it that they wanted to keep secret from Gropius? Who knows how much time and effort Bauhaus spent searching for secret rooms and worse, how many lives were taken in their desperate search? When I think back to the day Chuck McKim was shoved from the truck, I'd bet they were trying to scare the location of the Winter Hexagon Salon out of him. I doubt they wanted to kill him because he presumably knew the secret. Now with him dead, the Bauhaus plan was to search and destroy the Richardson and McKim buildings piece by piece until they found the salon. If I could locate the salon before summer, then we could save the historic buildings from demolition. But I was running out of time.

Axel surprised me with New Year's Eve plans: champagne dinner at Charlie Palmer, rooftop cocktails with deejays and dancing, and a terrific view of the Times Square ball-drop.

He booked a suite in the Knickerbocker Hotel, where his tuxedo hung in the closet. I wasn't prepared for a formal dinner party because I figured we'd do what I've always done — watch the ball drop on tv while lounging in sweats.

He opened the closet where an assortment of cocktail dresses awaited my selection: short-sleeved solid black, high-neck red, sequined full-length. The closet resembled Bloomingdale's designer racks. Shoeboxes were stacked on the closet floor along with a shopping bag stuffed with matching clutches.

"Selections from Amara's personal shopper," said Axel. "I hope you like the options."

I held up each dress, looking in the mirror to see which one worked on me. "They're all stunning. You choose."

"Most ladies wear black. But I vote for the gold sequins."

Axel made appointments for us in the hotel salon: a haircut and shave for him, a blowout and manicure for me. The hairdresser volumized my hair so that my head looked like it had been inflated with a bicycle tire pump. She worked a curling iron around the ends so they flounced off my shoulders with every movement. I chose *Not Red-y for Bed* for my polish. The manicurist advised a white-tipped classic French manicure so it would look like I had fingernails instead of the mowed-down stubs. When I met Axel back in our room, he was soaking in a lavender bubble bath. He whistled when I came in.

"Your hair looks like Carrie Underwood's."

I felt my face flush. "Thanks for spoiling me."

"I can't take all the credit; Amara gave me all the ideas."

"Should I get dressed now?"

He grinned. "Hop in. Plenty of room."

I tensed with hair-anoia: worse than a loose strand of head hair was a pubic hair floating in water.

"Can we save that idea for later? I don't want to muss my hair before the night gets started."

He threatened to splash. "Promise?"

"What time is dinner?"

He hopped out of the tub and toweled off the suds. Then he led me toward the bed where we kissed like we didn't care if we missed the ball drop. A knock on the door interrupted us.

"Damn, that's Xavier and Brett. They're a tad early."

Brett, stocky with a receding hairline, was a grad student at Columbia University where he was an assistant lacrosse coach. They had met years ago playing the summer tournament circuit. They'd reconnected at a bar in the city and hit it off. When they saw Axel with a towel around his waist, Xavier mumbled an apology for being early.

"Come in, raid the mini-bar. We're almost ready," said Axel.

I plucked my dress and shoes from the closet and ducked into the bathroom. There was a basket filled with toiletries and cosmetics. I stroked my lashes with mascara and ran a thin black pencil along my eyeline, like Melissa had taught me. There were three lip colors to choose from, so I went with pink blush. When I came out of the bathroom, Axel was fastening his onyx cufflinks. He flashed an opened jeweler's box with a pair of gold drop earrings.

"These were my idea," he said.

"They're gorgeous!" I smiled and slipped them on. "You're too much."

He offered his arm. "You look stunning. Let's roll."

Bouquets of gold and white balloons filled the corners of the candlelit dining room. A foodie's paradise banquet of every imaginable delicacy wrapped the perimeter of the room. Xavier ordered a bottle of Veuve Clicquot. I noticed there were two empty seats.

"Who's is joining us?" I asked, but the answer had just sashayed toward our table.

"Paige, you look ravishing. I knew you'd select the sequin." Mrs. Adamos scooched onto the chair next to me. "And your hair is to die for."

Xavier said, "Dad, do you remember Brett Campbell from my Lax Express days?"

Titus bellowed, "For Pete's sake! The stingy goalie from the Jersey Jets? Nothing got past you!"

Brett stood to exchange handshakes and back slaps. "Well, a few got past me in my day."

"Handsome *and* modest." Mrs. Adamos winked at Xavier.

After the pleasantries, we raided the banquet table. I loaded a plate that rivaled the men's servings. I elbowed Axel and whispered, "I didn't realize your parents were joining us."

"Who do you think is paying for all this?"

Mrs. Adamos side-glanced my dish. I noticed she had shrimp cocktail and fish salad. "Oh, to be young again!"

I doubted she'd ever wolfed down my calorie-dense portion in one sitting, young or not. I chomped into the prime rib, the best tasting beef I had ever swallowed. Mr. Adamos ordered a bottle of Argyros VinSanto, twenty-years barrel-aged in Santorini.

We shared the details of our adventures in the city before we returned to the banquet for a second pass; Brett whispered near my ear, "Easy on the carbs, darling. Amara might stroke watching you chow down."

"Heaven forbid!"

He giggled. "It's amusing to watch her ogling your fork-to-mouth marathon."

I wondered for a few seconds if I should be ladylike and just take a small plate of fruit. I shut down that idea because one: the food was topnotch; two: I was planning to burn calories on the dance floor; and three: my New Year's resolution to drop ten pounds was still a day away.

Back at the table, the waiter uncorked another bottle. I asked Titus about 33 Thomas Street.

"I'm on the short list to get the contract to renovate the HVAC systems," he said, eyeing Axel. "It's a big contract and would be a good look for the company."

"The Long Lines building was Warnecke's Project X," I said. "A twentieth century fortress with protons and neutrons protecting an army of machines on the inside."

"You seem to know it well," said Titus. "Why the interest?"

I shrugged. "It's rumored to be a covert monitoring hub to tap phones, internet data and more. Snowden didn't name the building, but his descriptions seem to be a match."

"You have a voracious —" Mrs. Adamos paused long enough for everyone to think the next word was appetite — "imagination."

After dinner we danced at the rooftop club. I worried that I misspoke with my Snowden reference. Then I recalled that the building had a three-level parking garage. This led me toward a new idea: underground access to the Long Lines building. I flashed back to when Deacon Darts had escorted me to the druid salon in a secret subway station. Could Bauhaus have its own underground lairs?

Axel pulled me close for a slow dance. I wanted to sink into the moment, but my mind raced. "I think I f'd up at dinner."

"Not at all. You're a big hit."

"The Snowden reference implied the wrong thing about your father's business. It's not what I meant —"

He spun me around. "You worry too much. Titus is impressed with your intelligence."

"And you? What do you think?"

"I'm spending New Year's Eve with a smoking-hot druid! Who's got it better than me?"

At 11:45 Titus gathered us onto the private balcony to watch the ball drop. A waiter brought us wool throws and champagne. The crowd below cheered through the final countdown. When midnight struck, we kissed. Mrs. Adamos asked the waiter to take a group shot. Then she snapped a shot of Axel and me with Times Square lit up behind us.

"What's your number? I'll text the photos to you," she said, adding me to her contact list. "Check your phone to make sure you got them."

I took my phone out of my purse and saw there were a slew of Happy New Year texts. I forwarded the new photos to the Quadsters. Melissa texted back: *The hair, the dress. You look so hot! Can't blame the woman for staring at your ass in the group shot!*

I zoomed in on the family photo and noticed there was a woman in the side doorway —staring at me. I had not seen her during the night. I looked around the room, but she wasn't there. I wanted to zoom in on the woman, but I didn't want to appear rude so I put the phone back in my purse.

"Did you get the pictures, sweetie?" slurred Mrs. Adamos, wobbling back on her high heels.

Titus balanced her from behind.

"Yes, they're terrific." I smiled. "I can't thank you and Mr. Adamos enough for a wonderful New Year's Eve. I'll never forget it."

"Honey, please. It's Amara and Titus —"

Titus kissed my cheek and shook hands with the guys. He whisked Amara away to their hotel room. "See you all for breakfast."

I went down the hall to use the ladies' room. I searched my purse for the blush lipstick to freshen up, then I answered the Quadsters' group text: *Axel's mother is smashed. She told me to call them by their first names. I'm officially in!*

Melissa texted: *We get all the credit for training you.*

I laughed thinking back to freshman year when Melissa and Jill dressed me like Wonder Woman to go on dates with Stoph. I'd come a long way with my fashion sense, although Melissa would probably disagree.

I was texting when I left the bathroom, so I didn't see the woman standing in the shadow by the door. She cornered me. "I see you've made some friends in New York City."

I startled and dropped my phone. The woman snatched it from the floor. She glanced at the screen. I stared in disbelief. It was Brenda Shepherd.

"Give it back!" I snapped, grabbing my phone.

"We know you went to the subway salon. Our eyes and ears are everywhere. You druids are pathetic. Bauhaus will find and destroy the secret salon. You are on the wrong side of this."

"Get out of my way, you crazy bitch!" I shouted.

She moved closer to my face. "We know what McKim told you. We know what you're up to."

I drilled the heel of my shoe into Brenda's shin. She howled from the pain and dropped my phone. I grabbed it and bolted down the hallway. Axel saw me running and rushed across the dance floor toward me.

"What's wrong?"

"Bauhaus is here. A lady cornered me outside the bathroom," I said, grabbing his arm. I had hoped she was still nursing her injury, maybe even rolling on the floor in pain. But by the time we reached the bathroom, she was gone.

I wanted to cry with anger and frustration. How did Brenda Shepherd know I'd be at the New Year's Eve reception? Bauhaus would do anything to find the Winter Hexagon Salon. They were spying on me, but I didn't want to ruin New Year's Eve by crying to Axel.

"I'm fine," I said. "Do you want to dance more or call it a night?"

"Honestly, you look so sexy tonight, I'm dying to cash in on your earlier promise —"

I took his hand and headed for the lavender soaking tub.

# Chapter Nine — Aquarius

Melissa texted us to meet her in front of the dorm. She had a surprise, she said. Ten minutes later she pulled up in a white BMW X1.

"Beep, beep, Bitch Cakes!"

My mouth dropped open. "Is this yours?"

The Beemer was Melissa's reward for pulling a C average last semester. I wondered what car her dad would have gotten her for an A. The BMW came with two rules for Melissa: keep up the grades and stay out of trouble.

Jill claimed the front. "I love the smell of new leather."

"What happened to your Toyota?" I asked, buckling up in the back. Sheila slid in the center and Thalia sandwiched her.

"The lease was up. My dad wanted me to have all-wheel drive for New England winters." She peeled out of the parking lot, heading toward the Big Y. "We need to stock the fridge. There's a blizzard coming."

"How many inches?" I asked.

"The snow or Axel?" She cackled, swerving around a parked car. "Sorry, Thalia, I shouldn't tease about your cousin's wiener."

"Flip on the news. I have to drop off my horoscopes tomorrow morning."

Jill glanced over her shoulder. "Can't you just email it?"

"Not since my laptop was stolen. Hot Throat thinks I'll corrupt the *Lodestar* system with a virus if I send an attachment."

Jill scanned the radio for traffic and weather. The weatherman called for a foot of snow.

"Crap. I'm screwed."

"Calm your tits, Paigester. I'll drive you. I'm dying to see how this baby handles in the snow." She parked crookedly, intentionally taking up two spots to eliminate the chance of someone dinging her doors.

"Thanks. I'll pick up the Lodestar box seat tickets to the Beanpot tournament while I'm there. I assume you all want to go?"

"Beanpot?" asked Thalia.

I explained that the Beanpot is an annual collegiate hockey tournament between Boston College, Boston University, Harvard and Northeastern held at the Garden.

"Men on blades, wouldn't miss it," said Melissa.

Thalia and I bought enough ramen noodles and apples to last for two weeks. She tossed in a box of Swiss Miss which reminded me to call Tanya Goforth to discuss winter coffee blends and the possibility of adding hot cocoa to the menu for the hockey tournament. We loaded our groceries in the BMW and headed back to campus where I hunkered in my room to finish writing the horoscopes.

I read about the processional wobbling of the earth's axis, slowly moving the vernal equinox westerly in a 26,000-year long circular path along the ecliptic. It moved roughly 30-degrees every 2,000 years. When astrology became an established practice under Claudius Ptolemy 2,000 years ago, the vernal equinox was embedded in Pisces, making it a Piscean Age. For the past two thousand years the sun has been in front of the constellation Pisces making it the Piscean Age. The sun at the equinox moved in front of Aquarius when we started the Age of Aquarius in March 2021. Individuals were free to choose a reality that aligned with their souls. It was time to focus on wellness and taking care of one another. It was also a time of pending chaos. Aquarius, the water-bearer, was the tenth largest constellation between Capricorn and Pisces. It was an air sign, reminding us to work with the wind.

I wondered if Saturn in conjunction with Uranus was the reason Bauhaus seemed to be on high alert. Perhaps that was how they always were, but I needed to find out what was on the other side of the Bauhaus chaos.

In the morning, a blinding white blanketed the campus. The Weeping Willow resembled the Abominable Snowman. The wind whipped ice pellets against the window. I curled under my covers, declaring it an official snow day. The world wouldn't come to an end if I missed a *Lodestar* deadline. My phone buzzed, but when I saw it was Hot Throat, I let it go to voicemail. I slept for another hour, then played the message: "Don't come in until after noon. The streets should be plowed by then."

After the great golf cart debacle, I worried about driving with Melissa into Boston. I told her I could call Logan with the *Lodestar* car service.

"Nonsense," she insisted. "I want to drive in the snow."

I hesitated, but decided to go. The city side streets were jammed with shovelers digging out their plowed-in cars. The sun poked through the snow clouds, blinding us as she barreled ahead. Melissa searched for parking across from the *Lodestar* headquarters.

"There's a spot. Can you jump out and move that fucking beach chair?" she asked.

There's an unwritten rule in Boston: when someone takes the time to dig their car out, then they claim that as their spot for the next 48 hours by marking it with a cone or some other object such as a beach chair.

"Haven't you heard of the Boston Space Savers rule? Let's just park in the *Lodestar* garage," I said.

"Move the chair. We'll be quick. Don't dilly-dally with your bitch editor. I want to hit Quincy Market for some chowder."

I tightened my scarf and lowered my pompom-topped knit hat against the whipping wind. I folded the chair and tossed it over the snowbank. Instead of parallel parking, Melissa eased in head first, parking on an angle so the rear bumper stuck out in the street.

My L.L. Bean duck boots squeaked down the corridor into the newsroom. Pilar waved me into her office.

"Whatcha got for Aries?"

"You need to harness the restless energy you're feeling by socializing with close friends. If you work tirelessly through this time of transition, you will start to feel blocked. The universe is telling you to take a break and enjoy life with friends and family. You need to laugh," I said, handing her my column.

"I'll schedule wine time with the girls." She jotted a note and stuffed it in her pocket. "I heard you met with a few Manhattan AOD. How'd that go?"

"They showed me their hidden subway station salon. It makes me wonder what else is under Manhattan."

"It's a major subway system. It shouldn't surprise you that there are little nooks and crannies here and there," she said. "What did they talk about?"

"Nothing concrete. But visiting New York got me thinking."

"About what?"

"My best guess is that Gropius got rejected by the Winter Hexagon Salon. Maybe he tried to infiltrate the salon but he was only able to steal the key. Bauhaus continues to search for the location of the salon."

"Why wouldn't they accept him?"

"Because he didn't design according to Solomon's temple specs. Gropius built trash."

"Gropius designed trash? That's harsh," she said, narrowing her eyes.

"In comparison to the founding fathers of American architecture who formed the Winter Hexagon Salon —"

"I've never heard of any Winter Hexagon Salon before you mentioned it. Is that what you dazzled the New York AOD with?"

"I don't know about dazzle, but I shared my theory that I think the holy grail is associated with the Winter Hexagon constellation. That's where the zodiac and the Milky Way intersect. It's the location of the silver gate where the ancients believed souls entered and exited the Milky Way in between incarnations."

"Listen, hon, the second you discover anything, you call me. Understood?" She stood with her thumbs hooked through the belt loops of her wide-wale corduroys. "Any more run-ins with strangers?"

I mentioned Brenda Shepherd showing up at the New Year's Eve gala. I showed her the picture on my phone. "She's a psychopath."

"That certainly looks like her," she said, studying the photo. "Gosh, you look terrific in that dress. Is that your boyfriend?"

"Yes."

She handed me an envelope with the hockey tournament tickets. "Box seats at the Garden. These extra four seats are in the nosebleed section if you want to give them away. Take your boyfriend."

I thanked her for the tickets and hustled away. I came upon an obscenity-filled argument, with Melissa yelling.

"Cut the shit with the snow! This is a brand new X1!"

Her car was surrounded by three guys armed with shovels who were heaping mounds of snow atop her SUV.

One guy raised his shovel. "It's our parking spot. We dug it out and marked it with that chair."

She flipped her middle finger. "I'm calling the cops!"

I jogged across the street. "This is my fault. I moved your chair. We'll leave now."

They stopped shoveling and started hurling snowballs at us. One of the guys drilled my shoulder with a snowball and mimicked my lame apology, "*I moved your chair.*"

They had an arsenal of ready-made snowballs that they peppered toward us and her car. Melissa retreated into her driver's seat. She leaned on the horn. They hurled snowballs against her driver's side window.

"Can we work this out?" I asked.

"Just because this rich bitch has New York plates doesn't entitle her to do whatever she wants in Boston."

"Do you guys like hockey?" I waved the four nosebleed tickets at them. "Here's four tickets to the Beanpot."

They lowered their ammunition. One guy in an oversized flannel shirt moved toward me while another guy cleaned the snow from the car with his gloved hand. The flannel guy took the tickets and locked eyes with mine. He inspected the tickets and said, "Are you coming?"

I smiled. "I'll be there, but in a different section."

"And what section will you be in?" He stuffed the envelope in his shirt pocket.

I flipped my thumb toward the *Lodestar* building. "The newspaper has box seats."

His eyes widened. "How'd you score those?"

"I write for the paper," I said.

"What's your byline? I read the *Lodestar* every day."

"Paige Moore. I write the horoscopes."

"Get out!" said the guy. "I'm Aquarius. You're scary accurate —"

"Thanks. I work hard at getting it right."

Melissa rolled down her window. "Let's go!"

"We'll see you there," he said, opening the door for me.

I hopped in the car and gave the guys a friendly wave.

"Let's get out of here," I said, noticing a snowplow barreling toward us. The driver pushed the snow up against Melissa's wheels. As he drove away, I noticed a bumper sticker with the Bauhaus emblem.

At the coffee shop, I poured two large Sister Winter blends, adding a heavy splash of cream to calm the powerful currents and spices.

"It tastes like grandma's fruitcake," said Melissa, scrunching her nose. She removed the lid from the takeout chowder and added gluten-free oyster crackers.

I agreed with her, sidelining Sister Winter from the hockey tournament. Tanya joined us at our table.

"Hockey is a rugged sport. We should go with robust flavors," I said.

Tanya agreed. "I've been experimenting with a new blend: a single origin bean from the Marcala region of Honduras that pairs well with a washed Ethiopian Hambela."

"Sounds like a heavy hitter. Let's call it The Goon," I said. "What else?"

"Let's take the El Salvador bourbon bean and blend it with a bourbon hybrid from the Kagomoini Cooperative in Kenya. Bourbon on bourbon beans from opposite sides of the world — too strong?"

"No, it's perfect. We'll call it The Hip Check," I said. "We need a decaf blend. We can call it the Penalty Box, for anyone who needs a timeout from caffeine."

Tanya ground the beans from Kenya, Honduras and Guatemala to serve in a French press. "What flavor notes do you taste?"

I thought it tasted similar to the Goforth holiday blend with a twist of chocolate. Melissa tasted molasses and sugar plum. She was spot on.

"The Hat Trick," I said, noting the three-bean combination.

"Great name," said Tanya. "By the way, the typewriter sold. I sent the antique store owner a check. Time for a new window display."

"I can brainstorm with Thalia if you'd like. Maybe a hockey theme? If these tournament blends are a hit, then it might attract customers."

"Go for it. Let me know how much money you need, but don't let it spin out of control."

"When haven't I let things spin out of control?"

Stella's Slacks-n-Such was going out of business in Faneuil Hall. Thalia and I needed a mannequin for the coffee shop window, so we asked the kid behind the counter:

"How much for the male mannequin?"

"Just the clothes are for sale."

"The sign says everything must go. Can you ask your boss?"

He phoned his boss and relayed the message. "He needs the male for his other store, but he'll sell the female for a hundred bucks, cash only."

"Will he take $75?"

He asked his boss. "$80 is as low as he'll go."

I slid the cash across the counter. I tilted the lady mannequin so Thalia caught her torso and I lifted the legs off the stand. She was wearing a denim skirt and denim jacket.

"Just the mannequin, not the clothes," he said.

"Seriously? For $80 we should get the whole shebang."

He called his boss. "No, the clothes are an extra twenty."

We wrestled the clothes off her body and carried the naked mannequin tits-up through Quincy Market.

Thalia asked, "How come you didn't want a female mannequin? Women play hockey, too."

"I said that to try to get a lower price. Once we dress her up in the hockey equipment, no one will know if it's male or female. We'll give her a gender-neutral name."

"How about Quinn? Short for mannequin?"

We borrowed goalie equipment from the local ice rink. Thalia painted ice rink lines on a white floor board. We bent Quinn into a goalie squat with the stick in position to block the puck and her outstretched glove hand raised shoulder high. Thalia designed Goforth Daily Grind hockey shirts for Quinn and for the staff to wear at the tournament.

"Quinn needs some action," said Thalia. She mixed epoxy resin with coffee-colored paint, added epoxy hardener, and spilled it across a piece of parchment paper. She glued a Daily Grind travel cup on the edge of the spill. Once the epoxy hardened, she positioned the cup in the goalie's glove.

"That looks like real spillage!"

We hung a sign: *Goforth's Daily Grind is a proud supporter of the Beanpot Tournament.*

Tanya drove us to the TD Garden with the vats of brewed coffee to set up for the first day of the tournament.

"Let's be quick. I don't want a ticket," she said, illegally parking to unload the Jeep.

We hauled everything inside and set up the coffee kiosk. I hustled back out to park in a legit spot. A parking ticket was tucked under her windshield. I plucked the ticket and tossed it on the passenger seat.

I drove around for fifteen minutes before finding a spot on Staniford Street near the Government Service Center — a Brutalist monstrosity that dominated the superblock — created when Boston's West End was demolished by urban renewal in the 1960s. I noted Paul Randolph's use of his signature ribbed, bush-hammered corduroy concrete. It gave the concrete texture, but it looked unattractive to me. Randolph studied with Gropius in the 1940s. I added it to my list of possible locations for the hidden key.

I jogged back to the Garden and tossed the keys to Tanya.

"No issues with parking?" she asked.

"All good," I lied, not wanting to ruin her morning. She was busy coordinating the two workers set to cover the morning shift, leaving me free to watch the tournament.

I looked down at the rink where some players were warming up. The *kish-kish* stroking of skates and pucks dinging the goalposts made me think about sports sounds: sneakers squeaking on a basketball court, helmets clacking in football, a soccer ball hitting the back of the net.

"What's your favorite sports sound?"

"I don't have one," said Thalia.

"Choose one."

"*Zoom zoom*. Monaco Grand Prix. What's yours?"

"Hockey stick smacking against the puck."

Tanya said, "Coffee slurping."

"That's not a sports sound."

"It is when it's slurped at a sporting event."


The *Lodestar* executive suite had a sports-themed bar and a sprawling buffet: sliders, hot dogs, subway sandwiches and a carving station with roast beef and turkey. Sliding glass doors opened to stadium seating where there were about twenty *Lodestar* staffers mingling with Melissa, Sheila and Jill. Melissa spotted me ordering drinks at the bar.

"I'll have a margarita, no salt." Melissa slipped a dollar in the bartender's tip jar. "Your reporter friends are nerds."

"They're not my friends. I've never seen them before."

"You're in denial. See that guy pounding brewskis in the front row? He seems to know all about you!" She flicked her thumb over her shoulder toward an older man in a Bruins baseball cap. "I overheard him say, 'How does a crappy-ass horoscope writer get the *Lodestar*-gold-star treatment?' His words not mine."

It was Fred, the reporter I met in Pilar's office after the construction accident. "I met him once. He's jealous because the city editor likes me better than him."

"He was perturbed you invited your friends to the luxury box. He brought his dorkwad son with him."

Fred meandered into the bar area trailed by his mini-me, who was wearing a Patriots ski hat.

"It's about time you got here. You've missed some great hockey," said Fred, acting like we were longtime friends. "This is my son Jeffrey. He's a freshman at Kew. Maybe you've seen each other around campus."

I shook his hand. "Nice to meet you, Jeff. What's your major?"

"It's Jeffrey. Not Jeff." He removed his wireframe eyeglasses, wiping them with the edge of his flannel shirt. "Math."

Fred said, "He's smart. Takes after his mother."

"Want a Sam Adams?" I offered.

"I'm not 21. And I'm guessing, as a sophomore, you're not either."

"Man, you really are quick with the math." I wondered how he knew I was a sophomore. I introduced him to the Quadsters and when Sheila called him Jeff, he corrected her, too.

"Dorkwad goes to Kew?" Melissa whispered. "The admissions committee should do personality tests. His old man is trying to fix him up with me."

"Play nice, please. I work with these people."

"I'll try. But not really."

Boston College took a one-goal lead against Harvard in the second period. An Eagle defender stick-checked a Harvard forward into the boards, drawing a trip to the penalty box. Fred sat next to me, biting into a slider that oozed catchup onto his leg.

"You've got Hot Throat wrapped around your little pinky," he said, chewing. "What's your secret?"

I shrugged.

"Come on, kid. How'd you win her over? She's tough on everyone except you."

I couldn't tell him that I'm a druid, so I lied. "Our mothers knew each other back-in-the-day."

He guffawed. "I'd love to know the dirt your mother has on Hot Throat. There's no way a newbie scores *Lodestar* perks like this. Especially for horoscopes."

I thought he'd stroke if he knew about the free summer apartment and beach house. "The paper has a huge horoscope following."

"As do the Sunday funnies." He dabbed the spilled catchup with a napkin. "You got off to a fast start with that construction accident. Did you ever follow up? It was weird that he called the newsroom looking to talk to you."

"I did, but he died while I was talking to him."

"There was definitely something fishy about that accident."

"Why do you say that?"

"Doesn't pass the sniff test. City developers and contractors. They're all in cahoots."

"With whom?"

"Don't get me started. The amount of bribery in Boston is appalling. It would blow your mind."

"Who's bribing who?"

"Developers, politicians, journalists, police. You name it. They're all dogs sniffing each other's butts."

"Journalists? Do you know anyone at the *Lodestar* taking bribes?"

"Are you kidding?" His unrestrained laugh turned heads from the seats below. He was distracted by a chippy play near the net as Harvard scored the tying goal. Players shoved each other; sticks dropped. I wondered how much beer he'd had because he shouted at the ref.

"Put your whistle away! Let 'em play for chrissake!"

"Who's taking bribes at the *Lodestar*?"

"Your girl Hot Throat for one."

"Seriously?"

"Let's just say she rubs elbows with the big boys. How do you think she affords her fancy house and that sweet cottage on the Cape? Editors don't make that much money."

"Maybe her husband —"

"Nah. That guy's a putz. She's the breadwinner."

"Who is she rubbing elbows with?"

The buzzer sounded the end of the period. Fred headed back to the bar for more beer. I followed. Stiffrey, as Melissa called him, slouched against the end of the bar with his hands jammed in his pockets. I stopped to chat with him.

"What's it like having a reporter as a father?" I asked, attempting to give him a chance, something my friends couldn't be bothered with.

"As long as he pays the bills, who cares?"

"My dad's an architect. He influenced me a lot — the way I look at buildings and analyze their form and function. I'd think it'd be cool having a dad who's a journalist. You probably have the inside scoop on everything."

"The inside scoop?"

"Whatever stories he's covering."

"I don't snoop through his desk, if that's what you're implying."

I bugged my eyes toward the Quadsters, sending an S.O.S. They ordered another round of drinks, ignoring my plea.

"Have you ever met his editor?"

"There's a bunch. Which one?"

"The city editor, Pilar Kuhlkoat."

He smirked. "We live in the same town. Why?"

"Just asking." I nodded toward the stadium seats. "Let's watch the last period."

Melissa buzzed past us. "Save me a seat. I need to pee. Be back in a jiffy, Jeffrey."

His face instantly reddened. He grabbed a sandwich and followed me, grumbling, "She's got no respect for personal space."

"Who?"

"Hot Throat. She waddles her fat ass past our house with her yappy mutts crapping on our lawn until my dad heads out for her private sidewalk meetings."

"And what does she want?"

"How would I know?"

Fred pounded another beer. He sat behind us with his co-workers. I overheard him say, "Jeffrey's making the moves on little miss horoscope. They go to Kew together. Kid takes after his old man!"

Was Fred just blowing off steam when he said Hot Throat took bribes? She must confide in him during their sidewalk meetings, so he must know what she's up to. Or maybe she's telling him what angle he needs to take for his interviews and articles. I needed to research what Fred's reporting and keep a closer eye on them.

Melissa returned from the bathroom accompanied by four clean-cut college guys wearing hockey t-shirts and unbuttoned flannel shirts. "Look who I found loitering outside our box!"

I didn't recognize them at first, until one guy shook my hand. "From the snowball fight?"

"It's not really a fight if one side doesn't return fire," I said. "I never did get your name."

The guys introduced themselves and I invited them to join us for beer and sandwiches. Melissa whispered, "B.U. grad students. The one in blue plaid is in law school — meet my future ex-husband."

I noticed Fred glaring in our direction. I overheard him complain to Jeffrey, "Who does she think she is? It's *Lodestar* only."

"Dad, technically I'm not staff," said Jeffrey.

"Don't you get it, son? The extra guys are killing your chances. It's a sausage party up there —"

When Boston College scored the go-ahead goal with a minute left, our luxury box and the Quadsters roared. Someone in the row behind me jumped to cheer a play and spilled his beer down my back. Fred dabbed napkins on my back but I insisted it was fine, mainly to get him to stop touching me. The cameraman zoomed in on the Quadsters. They hammed it up: Sheila and Thalia boogied to the blaring music, Jill flung her hair like a wild child, Melissa — who had quaffed a bucket of margaritas with her future ex-husband — whipped her shirt up to flash her red pushup bra. The arena went wild, and suddenly no one cared about the game, it was all about Melissa's boobs bouncing across the Jumbotron.

Jeffrey gasped. "She didn't just —"

"Yep. Tits-up."


Thalia and I left the hockey tournament to bring the cash box back to the Daily Grind.

"Did everything go okay?" asked Tanya.

"We didn't count the money, but the staff said we had steady customers," I said.

"I saw the Jumbotron episode," she said, pointing to the tv behind the service counter. "Your friend is a wild child."

"Melissa strikes again," I said, chuckling. "You'd think she'd learned her lesson after her streaking debacle at the Harvard-Yale game."

"Did security say anything to her?"

"Nope. That would suck if she got hit with community service again."

Thalia said, "The second she flashed her boobs, I scrambled to the bathroom. I didn't want any part of that show."

Tanya said. "You'll never guess who popped in for coffee today."

"Who?"

"Officer Delgado."

"Really? What for?"

"Hello? Parking ticket on the front seat! I kept his contact information after your regatta episode. I called him to ask if he could squash the ticket."

"And?"

"Not only is he going to kill the ticket," she said, grinning. "But he asked me on a date. He drank two cups of coffee and asked me about my blends. He's a connoisseur."

I laughed. "A cop! After all the grief they gave you in North Easton?"

"Grief about what?" asked Thalia.

I told Thalia about the local police officers' suspicions about Tanya's mushrooms. "They kept a close watch on things and popped in for a few *drug raids*."

"A hottie with handcuffs," Thalia blurted, "When's the big date?"

"Friday night."

"We'll close for you so you can get ready."

"Thanks, but trust me, I'll be ready."


Thalia wanted to stop by Trinity Church for inspiration for her next painting. I became engrossed with a stone carving of St. John the Baptist holding a vessel over Jesus' head as he baptized him.

"What are you seeing?"

"The next sign, Aquarius," I said. "But I don't think St. John the Baptist is Aquarius. He is way too important to be associated with a dim sign that has no bright stars."

"Is the Age of Aquarius really a thing or is it just a hippie song?"

"It's for real. Mercury retrogrades in the air signs," I said. "An astrological age shifts every 2,150 years when the earth's rotation moves into a new zodiac sign around the spring equinox."

"How does it translate into your horoscopes?"

"In the Age of Aquarius, there's power when you align with your soul's purpose. It's a time for all the signs to care for each other."

Thalia dug through her bag for a pad and charcoal pencil. "I'm focusing on St. John holding the cup with the snake. Could make a cool painting."

I watched Thalia's quick strokes. She drew versions of the cup upright, tilted, upside down and sideways. I found it interesting that she repositioned the cups to be something other than vertical.

I wondered about the cups in biblical times: St. John's cup, the cup Jesus used at the Last Supper, the chalices in protected glass cases at St. John's Cathedral and the multitude that must be stashed away inside the Vatican. I once read that the cup Jesus used at the Last Supper was taken by Joseph of Arimathea, the man in charge of Jesus' burial, to collect Christ's blood at the cross. Considering all the cups from biblical times, I wondered what detail differentiated the holy grail from the others. How could one prove it was the actual grail?

Then it occurred to me: what if Bauhaus was searching for the holy grail? Maybe that's why they planned to start demolition on the early American architecture, so it forced anyone hiding secrets to make a move. It could expose what they're looking for — including the location of Winter Hexagon Salon. I need to start moving with a greater sense of urgency before they destroyed the historic buildings.

We left the church and headed through Boston Common. A patinaed statue called *Learning* caught my eye: it was a boy sitting on a sphere reading a book. The sphere was encircled with a band that had all of the zodiac signs. Underneath the sphere was a wave pattern that I interpreted as water.

"Check this out," I said, pointing to the zodiac symbol centered under the boy. "That's Aquarius."

"That didn't take you too long to find," she said.

We strolled through Parkman Plaza and stopped to look at the Boston Massacre Monument — a woman with her right arm raised holding a broken chain.

"This reminds me of the Plymouth Forefathers statue," I said, posing with my right arm raised. "Maybe your next art project should focus on fist pumps."


Axel texted, inviting us to meet him at Chauhaus — a cafeteria in Gund Hall, the Harvard Graduate School of Design.

"I thought it'd be ironic to eat here, considering your issues with Bauhaus," he said. "Anything on the menu can get turned into a panini."

I ordered a burger which was dumb because I'd eaten my share of sliders at the game. Gund Hall itself looked like a giant panini with its boring flat-pressed concrete walls.

"I heard B.C. won in the last minute," he said.

"It was exciting," said Thalia. "We got on the Jumbotron dancing and cheering, but then Melissa flashed."

Axel cracked up. "Again!"

"Can you imagine if I pulled that crap in front of her co-workers at her summer job? I'd never hear the end of it," I said.

When we finished eating, we looked around Gund Hall's design research labs, the fabrication lab and Frances Loeb Library.

"Do you have access to the special collections department?" I asked.

"Of course, why?"

"I'd like to see what they have on the Long Lines Building. I'm obsessed with it."

"What's that?" asked Thalia.

"It's a strange skyscraper with no windows on 33 Thomas Street in Manhattan. When it was being built, it was referred to as Project X because it was designed to withstand an atomic blast. It's a fortress protecting the most important telecommunications hub in the country."

Inside the special collections department, Axel sweet-talked the woman working the desk, and she brought us to the section where we could access the design plans. We spread the copies of the building specs on the table to review the 29 floors with three basement levels.

"There aren't any lights on the outside, so at night it turns into a 550-foot shadow," I said. "And the vents emit a harmonic resonance like an opera singer shattering a glass."

"Ominous," said Axel.

I explained that most Bauhaus architecture was designed for human functionality in the form of offices and schools, but the Long Lines Building was designed for machines, not humans.

"I bet they're mining Bitcoin in there," said Axel. "I'd love to see how much electricity the building gobbles up."

"You can't just go in that building. How does your dad plan to renovate the HVAC systems?" I asked.

"No idea. I imagine they'll give him access and security clearance."

I flipped through photographs of the building's lobby ceiling, designed in mosaic and colored plaster. There were four Art Deco figures personifying Europe, Asia, Africa and Australia. The continents were linked by long gold lines to an eagle, a condor, and two females facing in opposite directions. Inside the main entrance, a brown tiled map of the world took up the entire wall, called *Telephone Wires and Radio Unite to Make Neighbors of Nations*.

"Check it out. This room is marked with that Bauhaus logo that I keep seeing everywhere."

Thalia and Axel looked closer.

"If Bauhaus has the key, I bet it's in this room," I said. "Tucked away where no humans have access to it."

Axel nodded. "It is the most secure civilian building in New York, if not the whole country."

"That's exactly why I need to get in there."

"Impossible," said Thalia, glancing up to meet my eye. "For the average person, I mean."

# Chapter Ten — Pisces

We opened the windows to welcome in the first hint of fresh spring air. Melissa breezed into our apartment to deliver her whiteboard with erasable green markers and give us a special assignment.

"Paige, you're it," she said, appointing me host of the next Quadster meeting on the St. Patrick's Day parade.

"What are we serving?" asked Thalia.

"How about Irish coffee? I have a bottle of Tullamore Dew Irish Whiskey. We can grind Goforth's Breakfast Blend."

Thalia flopped on the couch. "What's so big about St. Patrick's Day?"

"It's mainly a midwinter excuse to breakout your Shenaniganator," I said, experimenting in the kitchen with Irish coffee. I found heatproof glass mugs jammed in the back of a cabinet, poured a generous shot of whiskey in each glass, filled three-quarters with hot coffee, and added two white sugar cubes. The Quadsters arrived while I was whipping heavy cream with a milk-frother.

"Whip it, Paigester! Whip it good!" Melissa tossed a loaf of soda bread on the counter. "There's nothing sexier than a woman whipping cream."

"If you say so."

I poured the cream over a spoon to maintain a layered look. She took a picture and posted it on Instagram.

"Hashtag *crème de la crème*?" I suggested.

"I can't spell Gaelic. How about hashtag got cream?"

The Quadsters sunk into the couches, sipping their coffees. I took the green marker and wrote: CHARITY.

Melissa groaned, "This is supposed to be about St. Patrick's Day, not a Catholic Daughter's meeting."

"Hear me out," I said. "I arranged with the Daily Grind to sell coffee at the parade. It's just for a few hours. We can donate our tips to YAM, the city's youth arts movement. It helps underprivileged teens pursue their art and design dreams."

"Great idea," said Sheila. "Sign me up."

Melissa and Jill exchanged eyerolls. "Way to drag your Catholic guilt complex into this," said Melissa. "How many hours are we talking?"

I explained that we would set up in the morning. "At the start of the parade, we'll pack it up and watch the shenanigans."

"Are we talking McGoforth Irish coffee or just plain old coffee?" asked Melissa.

"The usual themed blends. Customers love it. I doubt we could get a liquor license to serve Irish coffee."

"There's always a workaround. Think about it. We'd make a killing selling Irish coffee-to-go. This stuff is killer. If you're serious about donating to a charity, then let's not futz around," said Melissa, sliding her empty glass on the guitar coffin. "Teach us how to do it."

I demonstrated my Irish coffee-making technique.

Jill studied the whiskey bottle. "My cousin owns a liquor distribution center in Queens," she said. "I'll call him to see if he can hook us up with sample bottles."

Melissa grabbed the marker, drew an offshoot from CHARITY and wrote: LEPROCHAUN LASSIES.

"What's that?" asked Thalia.

"Cheer Girls." Melissa tapped the cap back onto the marker. "Jill and I will get cute matching green outfits with deep pockets. We can stash sample bottles in our pockets and offer a shot to anyone who wants to ramp up their McGoforths."

"But if we get caught —"

"Try lightening up once in a while, Paigester," said Melissa, licking her milk moustache. "We're not selling them. We'll suggest a McShot for a McTip. Bring battery-operated frothers, this cream is to die for."

Melissa pointed at Sheila. "Can you Irish stepdance? If not, learn. We'll haul in beaucoup tips for a dancing-coffee lass."

"Of course, I can kick."

"What's the plan after we're done selling coffee?" asked Thalia.

"Guinness and watch the parade," I said.


I'd settled on three blends for parade day: Lucky Leprechaun light roast, Irish Clover dark roast and Peppermint Patty with chocolatey-minty nuances. We dressed Quinn like a leprechaun in the shop window, adding a curly red wig under a top hat. Thalia painted a rainbow with a pot of coffee instead of a pot of gold at the end. A sign informed the patrons that Goforth's coffee truck would be parked on the corner of West Broadway and Perkins Square at the parade.

Tanya loved the idea of donating to a charity while promoting the Daily Grind at the same time. I didn't mention anything about the Irish McShot coffee-to-go because I knew she would squash the idea. Jill's cousin donated five hundred mini-bottles of whiskey to our fundraiser. I got a permit to park the coffee truck on the corner of West Broadway and Perkins Square. I bought extra batteries to keep the frothers operating at full force. Thalia helped me set up early before the crowds filled the streets along the parade route.

We started serving our regular coffee, but before long I spied the Leprechaun Lassies gunning for the coffee truck. Sheila, dressed in step-dancer's garb with green cheetah-print knee socks, lugged a boombox down West Broadway, an instrument case in her other hand. She put the music on and flipped open her fiddle case for onlookers to toss in coins. She clacked her heels against the tap board we'd set up in front of the truck.

"I didn't know you play the fiddle," I said.

"I don't. It's just for show." She cranked up her reels and danced for the coffee line.

The guys cheered and hooted and clapped in beat.

Melissa and Jill, dressed as Irish milkmaids, were carrying big wooden buckets filled with enough miniature whiskey bottles to sink the Titanic. They grinned at the patrons, offering shots of whiskey in exchange for charitable contributions. The first few customers balked, but then a group of balding men decided to indulge. They dropped ten-dollar bills into the tip jar.

"I could watch you milkmaids all day," raved one of the men. "To hell with the parade."

Droves of coffee drinkers stopped at the truck to watch Sheila dance. Most ordered our Bootlegger's Blend, as the milkmaids started calling it.

We had to empty the tip jar every thirty minutes. Sheila's violin case overflowed with ten- and twenty-dollar bills. She only knew a few jigs, so she switched to her own freestyle that looked like hybrid Riverdance-meets-Harry-Styles. She ditched the stiff upper body for head swirling and arm swaying that thrilled the crowd.

Suddenly, Jill and Melissa scrambled to throw tartan-plaid blankets over their whisky buckets.

"Five-o on wheels," announced Jill, nodding toward two uniformed cops navigating their bikes toward us.

"Just play it cool," I said.

"Should I keep dancing?" Sheila lowered the music volume.

"Hell yes, and you two join her. Make it like that's what you're here for," I said.

The cops dismounted and approached the truck. I recognized the one cop as Tanya's new love interest.

"Officer Delgado, what can I get you? Clover dark roast, cream, no sugar?"

"And one for my partner too," he said, skipping the line. "Tanya mentioned you'd be here."

"On the house," I said, handing over the cups. Delgado's partner grimaced like he was trying to hold back laughter or maybe he just needed a bathroom break.

"Thanks. It's a shame we're on duty, though," said Delgado.

"Why's that?"

"Because I'd love to sample the Bootlegger's Blend."

My shocked expression reflected in his sunglass lenses. Delgado smirked and nodded toward the Leprechaun Lassies. When they were out of sight, Melissa and Jill picked up their buckets.

"Do you need to change your McBritches, Paigester?" Melissa cackled.

"Do you think he'll rat us out to Tanya?"

Thalia nodded. "We're screwed."


The Leprechaun Lassies headed off to enjoy the parade while Thalia and I returned the truck and money to the Daily Grind. We'd sold all the coffee and ran out of whiskey bottles before the parade; the tips totaled $3,118.

"We could buy roundtrip tickets to Greece for spring break," said Thalia.

"If only. But hopefully this will do some good for YAM."

"That's a lot of art supplies."

I was relieved that Tanya was out so we could drop and dash. We hustled back to the parade, finding Melissa already bored with the marching bands.

"Anyone down for a Southie pub crawl?"

"The guys are meeting us here in a few," I said.

"All righty. Jill and I will go secure some real estate in a pub. Can't we use your Crapstar newspaper connections? I'm surprised you're not on the *Lodestar* parade float waving like a homecoming queen."

"We'll have to slum it. I'm lucky I didn't get fired after you went tits-up in the Garden luxury box."

Melissa cackled. "If we don't live large now, then when will we? Before you know it, you'll be married to the Axeman with little Axelrods buzzing around your backyard."

I laughed at her idea of living large. "Text us which pub. Order a round of Guinness on me."

Axel arrived wearing a gray cashmere sweater, jeans and Chelsea boots. Xavier and Brett trailed him wearing fisherman knit sweaters.

"No green for you today?" I asked.

"Green boxers with white shamrocks. Want to see?"

"Yes, but later."

We watched the parade until Melissa texted: *Craic House. Guinness and Smithwick on tap. Chop-chop.*

We pushed through the crowded streets, finding the Craic House. It had an upper-level balcony where rugby players in striped game jerseys chanted the chorus to "Black Velvet Band." They swayed with their raised beer pints, singing: *Her eyes, they shone like diamonds...you'd think her the queen of the land...*

Some of the guys formed a scrum. I wasn't surprised to see them hoist the Leprechaun Lassies over their heads, Melissa and Jill howling with laughter. The others continued: *As I went walking down Broadway…not meaning to stay very long…I met with a frolicsome damsel…as she came a-traipsing along.*

Parade viewers cheered for the ruckus and Melissa and Jill waved at the crowd as they got tossed around.

"You watch. She'll seize the opportunity to go tits-up," I said.

"Let's not wait for it. I'm dying for a beer," said Axel.

We crammed around the high-top they'd reserved for us. Melissa came away from the balcony scene with two phone numbers.

"Bad idea," said Brett. "Rugby players are animals. The love'em-and-leave'em type."

"Maybe I like animals." Melissa winked at him.

She loosened her hair tie, tussling her locks with her fingers. "Maybe I'm the love'em-and-leave'em type. Maybe they should be worried about me."

"*Touch*é." Brett grinned at her.

"How about a round of Irish Car Bombs?" suggested the waitress who wheeled up her bar cart stocked with our pints. We upgraded to boilermakers and she dropped shots of Irish cream and whiskey into the stout.

Melissa toasted: "Cheers to the Leprechaun Lassies."

The rugby players chanted their names. Melissa nudged Jill out of the booth. "We're summoned to the balcony for more rugby rebelry."

"I think you mean revelry," said Brett.

"Whatever. Live large, lassies."


I awoke the next morning shivering in Axel's room because he preferred to sleep with the window open. He also hogged the blankets, so I rummaged through his closet for a hoodie. I felt bloated and hungover, the residual effects of the Irish car bombs and a late-night pepperoni pizza.

I fell back asleep until noon when I awoke to the sound of Axel getting dressed into shorts and a crew sweatshirt.

"Top of the morning," he said. "It looks like we missed breakfast at the Hair of the Dog."

"There's no way in hell I could meet Melissa and Jill for Bloody Mary's with their rugby buddies."

Axel pulled on tube socks and running sneakers. "Best way to burn off a hangover is to sweat it out. Care to join me for a run?"

I wore sneakers to the parade because I was on my feet all day, so I borrowed a pair of Axel's sweatpants. The cold air stung my cheeks and ears as we trotted across the campus toward the Weld boathouse. My stomach cramped after the first two miles.

"You go ahead. I need a break," I said.

I gimped toward the entrance to the boathouse. A *beaux-arts* style stone carving above the main doors captured my attention: a boat emerging through a cascading wave with two dolphin fish carved beneath it. I recognized the fish to mean that I'd entered into Pisces.

To ease my guilt about serving the Bootlegger's Blend, I invited Tanya to kayak on the Charles River. We rented kayaks near Kendall Square and started paddling side-by-side so we could chat. I doubted whether Delgado had shared the detail about our boozy coffee because Tanya didn't mention it.

The view of the sun-soaked skyline was majestic, despite the looming presence of Bauhaus. When we passed the MIT Green building — another I.M. Pei travesty — I thought about Galahad. According to the legend, when the grail was lost, the countryside turned to a wasteland. Bauhaus was Boston's wasteland.

"Don't the central towers look like salt-and-pepper shakers?" I suggested, as we paddled toward Longfellow Bridge, squinting against the sun.

I noticed a stone carving similar to the one at the boathouse, sculpted on the main piers of the bridge. The prows of a Viking ship protruded from the bridge. Two large-mouthed dolphin fish were carved on the sides of the ship. I glided along, studying the sculpture.

"Check out the Viking ship — it's the same one that's carved at Harvard's boathouse. Legend has it that Leif Eriksson voyaged up the Charles River in 1000 AD. I looked it up, but there's zero evidence Leif Eriksson ever set foot in Cambridge."

"Remind me to do a special blend on Leif Erikson Day," she said, pulling ahead of me as the wind whipped against our faces.

"October 9$^{th}$, plenty of time to concoct something robust."

I figured the carvings could be Solomon's ship that Galahad traveled on to get to the island of Sarras where he claimed the holy grail. I wondered if I would need to take a ship somewhere to find the holy grail. The shape of the boat looked like a creative representation of the Winter Hexagon constellation. The bridge was designed by Edmond Wheelwright, another student of the *École des Beaux-Arts*. I tried to think of a building on a mystical island like Sarras that I'd need to take a boat trip to get to…

"What are you staring at?" She called back.

"I'm thinking that this has nothing to do with Leif Eriksson and everything to do with Solomon's ship that sailed Galahad to Sarras."

"If you say so."

"Oh crap!" I shouted, pointing at a tour boat — a supersized Hummer pimped out to troll the river — heading toward us. The passengers hung over the sides staring at us.

One man in an overstuffed Gore-tex coat pounded his gloved fists against the boat. His angry scowl roared: "Let's flip the bitches! Flip the bitches!"

The other passengers hooted approval. The boat picked up speed, creating a wake that bounced us backward. We struggled to balance the kayaks with the paddles. The boat circled us again, faster and closer. The nose of my kayak plunged under water. I leaned back so hard I almost fell out. The water smacked against the kayak and flooded into my seat. The boat passed so close, my face got sprayed with a shock of cold water. The wakes, large and rapid, bounced us backward and I crashed into Tanya. The passengers cheered when Tanya's kayak landed on top of mine. Another wake flipped us both into the frigid Charles. My limbs went numb but I was buoyed by the lifejacket. The boat idled long enough and I wondered if they were going to help us.

"Tell us what you know!" shouted the man in the Gore-tex,.

"You're a fat bastard!"

"We'll be back!"

"Grab your paddle, quick," yelled Tanya. "We need to get back to land before we get hypothermia."

Our soaked clothing weighed us down, making it difficult to flex our bodies back into the kayak. I sprawled against the deck and shimmied my sneakers toward the opening. I shivered so much I could barely work the paddle.

"Who was that?" she asked, pulling swift strokes.

"Bauhaus bastards. The same jerks that put the hit on the coffee truck."

"I'll call David as soon as we get warmed up."

I assumed David was Officer Delgado but my teeth were chattering too hard to ask. When we reached the dock, the guy at the boat rental eyed us.

"You both fell in?" He dragged our boats toward the rack, then squeezed the excess water from our life jackets. "The hut is heated if you want to warm up in there."

"We'll crank the heat in my van," said Tanya, heading toward her hippie van, the Peace Train. She peeled off the drenched layers and changed into sweats. She scrounged through the camping equipment. "Here's some thermal pajamas. Get changed."

I dressed in the back and listened to Tanya on the speaker phone with Delgado. I expected him to kick into action: rev up his cop cruiser and barrel-ass to the kayak rental. Instead, I heard him say, "Wanna warm up at my place or yours?"

"Come over. I'll crank the hot tub."

"Can't wait," he said.

"I have to drop off Paige. See you in a few."

She glanced at me when I slid into the front seat. "So: Bootlegger's Blend?"

"Ah." I warmed my hands against the heat vent.

"Did you really think he wouldn't tell me?"

"It was for charity." I slumped in my seat. The Bauhaus hit left me exhausted and nauseous. Was I ever going to find the Winter Hexagon Salon? I was running out of zodiac signs with only two remaining. Was any of this going to stop the Bauhaus architectural wasteland and their planned demolition? Would I ever get to study in Rome?

She sighed pleasantly. "Bootlegger's Blend! The shit you think up!"

Back at the dorm, I piled on the blankets for a post-kayaking power-nap. The chills ran through me like a raging river, along with my anger toward Bauhaus. The kayak attack pushed me closer to giving in to Brenda Shepherd and the Bauhaus thugs. I was starting to realize I was outnumbered. I needed to end their harassment. If Bauhaus figured out where the Winter Hexagon Salon was before me and the AOD, then more power to them. Their intimidation tactics had worn me down. I drifted into a deep slumber.

It was late afternoon when Thalia called into my room. "Sushi?"

"Funny you should mention that," I said, rolling out of bed. "I've had fish on my mind all day. It's the sign for Pisces."

"Fat Baby?"

"Excuse me?"

"A Southie sushi place," she said.

"I thought you meant me. I feel like a blob after yesterday."

"You look great, as always," she said, flashing a smile. "I'm craving Hamachi crudo and some *sake*."

Thalia, in truth, was the one who consistently looked amazing. I wondered how she looked so put-together without ever fussing over her hair or working out like Melissa and Jill did. She turned heads when she sashayed across campus. Aside from looking great, Thalia was the kindest friend I'd ever had.

"I don't want to be a killjoy, but I think I'll skip the *sake*. We have a big drinking night ahead of us. Howl at the Moon has frozen drinks to die for, but they're strong as hell," I said.

"Then I'll skip the *sake*, too."

We ordered rolls at the bar inside the modern wood-paneled Asian fusion restaurant. I shared with Thalia the details about the kayak attack. "Damn Bauhaus. We could have frozen to death."

"You must have been petrified."

"Scared and angry. The guy was yelling at me to tell them what I know. If they can figure it out, who cares? I can't take it anymore."

"What do you have to lose?"

"The opportunity to study art and architecture in Rome. And the potential to make another great discovery for the AOD. You see the perks I get from being a druid. Imagine if I discover something epic with the Winter Hexagon Salon —"

"I've got your back, if that's any comfort."

"It is."

I told the waitress to put it on the *Lodestar* tab and called an Uber to take us to Howl at the Moon, a bar with live music and bucket drinks. A bouncer checked the driver's license that I borrowed from a brown-haired senior who looked nothing like me. It passed, but Thalia's real identification from Greece sparked his suspicion. He grilled her on the details, then called over his manager. She had to speak Greek to convince them it was real.

At the bar we ordered drinks that came in beach pails with the Howl at the Moon wolf image printed on the side. I ordered "Sex on the Moon" and Thalia got a "Broken Heart Zombie." We found Sheila on the dance floor, and Melissa and Jill were gabbing with their new rugby friends, Murph and Carlton.

"Are those your first names or last?" I shouted over the bar noise.

"Are you running a security check on us?" asked Carlton.

"Don't mind her, she's permanently uptight," said Jill.

"I'm not uptight!" I fired back.

Jill laughed. "See what I mean."

I sipped my drink through the straw, wondering if I was in fact, uptight. The live music was set to start and my mouth fell open when I heard the announcement: "Let's give a howl for Gasoline Kisses!"

Jill launched a high-pitch screech that sounded like a distressed seagull. The rugby friends thought it was hilarious, which encouraged her to continue the tortured gull sound.

Nova, perched high behind his drums, thumped the opening Reggae love-bump *riddim*. Kurt snatched the mic from the stand. "It's great to be back in Bean Town!"

I clutched Melissa's elbow to pull her closer. "If these dicks announce they need a place to stay —"

"Say no more," she said, making the zip-my-lips motion.

Thalia huddled with us. "Should we bounce? What if they see us and want their music case back?"

"They can have it. I just don't want them crashing on my floor."

"But we used up their stash."

I shrugged. "Payback for storing their case for six months."

Axel, Xavier and Brett joined us. I handed Axel an extra straw to share my bucket drink. Xavier and Brett swigged Angry Orchards.

The rugby dudes roared to the Bob Marley tribute, shouting out the lyrics to "No Woman, No Cry." I wanted to tell them the song was about women having a strong backbone, toughing it out through difficult times, not about the misconception that if there is no woman in your life, then there's no reason to cry. But if I dropped that little info-nugget, I would appear uptight and unwilling to live large.

I wondered why they called me uptight. Was it because I wasn't an exhibitionist? Was it because I took on more responsibilities with my academics and the *Lodestar* than they did, not to mention my druid investigations? But I partied just as much as they did. They didn't date one guy at a time; they were wild with guys. I felt happy with my relationship with Axel and I doubted I could be comfortable fooling around, like they did. I was satisfied with my study-work-social life balance, even if it made me "uptight" by their definition.

Kurt's lady friend Lydia danced through the crowd shaking her tambourine. Sheila started in with her signature hip swivel and in no time, Lydia pulled Sheila up to the stage. Lydia passed a smaller tambourine to Sheila and they danced like gypsy sisters, until Sheila broke free with her electrocution-style hair-whipping. Gasoline Kisses shifted from reggae to electro-Tropicalia beats that inspired Sheila's feet to defy gravity.

"Give it up for Lil Miss Crazy Feet!" Kurt bellowed. "Howl at the Moon should name a bucket drink after her."

Gasoline Kisses took a break. The Quadsters started in on naming the new bucket drink: Sheila Sauce, Micro-Moves Booze bucket, Sheilectro-Tropicalia Punch.

"How about Kinky Feet?" said Murph.

His words blurred in the barroom din. I asked, "Why Stinky Feet?"

He shouted near my ear. "Kinky. Not Stinky."

I wanted to ask why Kinky Feet, but I didn't want to hear about his foot fetish. A bouncer approached us and said, "Kurt's invited you backstage. Follow me."

"Brett and I will hang here to keep our spot," said Xavier. I realized he was avoiding a potential awkward moment with love'em and leav'em Carl.

Kurt hugged us as if we'd known each other since childhood. "Oh man, I missed you guys."

Axel bro-hugged him. "How's life on the road?"

"Ups and downs," he said. "Our van died, we all got the flu and had to cancel a few gigs. We got in here tonight because of a last-minute cancellation."

"Sweet," said Sheila.

"Where'd you learn those dance moves?" asked Lydia.

"Streaming Soul Train re-runs on You Tube."

"You got *riddim*, girl," said Kurt. He kicked open the ice-filled cooler. "Grab one."

We each took a Lagunitas, clinking our bottles. "We like your idea that they should name a bucket drink after Sheila," I said.

He took my straw and gulped from my bucket. "Slurpee brain freeze."

"You can finish it," I said, skeeved by his germs. "Did you get our messages about your guitar coffin?"

"What messages?"

"You forgot your guitar coffin at my apartment. We left messages on Carl's phone."

Carl perked up. "Dude, that was you? I thought it was some fan-stalker."

I laughed at the thought that this small-fry musician assumed he had a crazed fan base.

"Can we swing buy your apartment and pick it up after the show?" asked Kurt.

"I moved back to campus. I have it in my dorm room."

"Can we stop by the dorm late tonight?"

"Paigester, tell him why his case is a tad lighter," blurted Jill. I shot her a look. She continued, "She made hash brownies with your stash."

Kurt looked as if I kicked his puppy. "You did?"

A tidal wave of guilt flooded my head. "I did."

His eyes narrowed. "And I thought we were cool."

"Stop by later. I'll repay you."

He nodded. "Alright, but that was some quality shit you Betty Crockered."

He sucked down the rest of my boozy Slurpee and dropped the bucket on the floor. "Let's crush this last set," he said, charging toward the stage door entrance.

"Kurt's pissed," said Melissa.

"Did you not inhale your fair share of the brownies? Why is this all on me?"

"You're the one who went Julia Child on his stash."

I started to panic, but then talked myself down. I whispered to Thalia, "Do you think Tanya's counted the tip money from the parade yet?"

"No. She put the box in a cabinet in her office."

"Let's go back to the Daily Grind and take out $500 from the tips to repay Gasoline Kisses. She'll never know."

"That feels like we're stealing from the charity."

"I'll donate money from future paychecks."

I told the others to head back to the dorm while Thalia and I went to Goforth's. When we passed the shop window Thalia said, "I guess we'll have to do an Easter theme with Quinn."

"Maybe a generic spring theme. Something to go with the vernal equinox," I said, unlocking the door. There was a night light glowing behind the counter. I hushed Thalia. "Someone's here."

"The cleaning crew?"

We tiptoed toward the service counter. We heard heavy breathing turn to gasps, as if someone were choking. I peered over the counter to see Tanya on the floor writhing in ecstasy under Delgado's grunting thrusts. I gasped. Her eyes popped open and she screamed when she saw us staring at her.

"What are you doing?"

"Not ordering caramel macchiatos," I said, bursting with laughter.

"Or double espressos!" added Thalia, cackling.

Delgado rolled off Tanya and crawled for the back room, scrambling to zip his fly.

Tanya grabbed her clothes to cover up. "Get out of here! You idiots!"

Thalia quickly covered for us. "Sorry! I forgot my phone. Here it is, we'll leave. Carry on."

We turned and hustled from the café, locking the door behind us. Our cackles echoed across Quincy Market. I had to refrain from calling back, "Welcome to the Bang-Bang Barista! May I take your order?"

I put on the music as the Quadsters gathered around the guitar coffin to brainstorm Operation Payback.

"How much do you think that stash was worth?" I asked.

"A lot," said Thalia.

Wheezy, making last rounds through the dorm for the night, tapped her key on our door. "Please turn down the music."

She stood in the hallway peering in at us. The music wasn't that loud, so I figured she was making sure we weren't breaking any rules. Then it hit me.

"Come in," I said. "Can I run an idea past you?"

Wheezy hesitated. "Make it quick. I need to finish my rounds."

"What's planned for the Battle of the Dorms for Spring Fling?"

"The R.A.s suggested a greased flag pole competition in the courtyard. The team that makes it to the top wins a prize."

"Sounds dangerous. Someone could break a leg. Are you open for further suggestions?"

She shrugged. "Like what?"

"We could take up a collection to host a band in the courtyard for the last night of Spring Fling."

"That's too difficult to coordinate on short notice. Bands are usually booked months in advance."

"But for the right price, I could get a kickass band to play for a few hours. C'mon Wheez, whaddya say?"

"What band are you referring to?"

"Gasoline Kisses. They played at Howl at the Moon tonight and they rocked out the Sinclair last fall."

"Are you joking? They rock. We could never get Gasoline Kisses."

"Trust me. For the right price, I can make it happen. How much money's left in the dorm dues?"

"Around a thousand bucks."

"What if I offer $500 to book them tonight, and we'll sort out the rest with a collection or fundraiser?"

"We'll need permits and security, though."

Jill hopped up. "I'm the queen event coordinator. I worked in the alumni relations office last summer. I practically coordinated the whole Bushfoot Country Club alumni golf outing. I know who's who around Kew."

"Okay, let's do it. I'm counting on you ladies to help pull it off."

"We will. Can I get the $500 now? The band is stopping by to pick up their gear. I'll book them with a down payment."

"Make them sign a contract. I'm trusting you to do the right thing."

"We always do," I said, winking at the Quadsters. I followed Wheezy to her room to get the cash.

Gasoline Kisses pulled their van into the dorm parking lot at 3 a.m. stoned and hungry. I offered a bag of chips to Kurt and Lydia.

"I want to pay you back for the hash. How much do I owe you?"

Kurt's eyes were bloodshot. "Dunno. How much was there?"

"It was about the size of a grapefruit."

"Geez. Lyds, whattya think?"

Lydia squinted as if the lights were too bright while she thought about it. "A hundred bucks and we'll call it even."

I was relieved. I paid Kurt. "Now here's an offer. We want to hire Gasoline Kisses to play at our campus Spring Fling next month. Can you fit us in?"

Kurt popped open the case and took out the guitar. He fiddled with the tuning knobs. "We can work something out."

"How much?"

"We'll do a two-hour gig for three grand, plus food and lodging."

I handed him the remaining $400 as a deposit. Thalia wrote a receipt and asked him to sign it for proof of the partial payment for Wheezy's accounting records.

"Who's the artist?" asked Lydia, staring at the charcoal sketches taped to the wall.

"It's something I've been playing around with," said Thalia.

"Can you draw something trippy?" Lydia's eyes were red slits that she struggled to keep open.

"Trippy?"

"We're recording a CD. We need cover art. Something with colors that pop so it feels trippy, but not full-blown psychedelic."

"I can try," said Thalia.

Lydia crashed on the couch next to Kurt who was strumming his guitar. "Can you crank it out now? We sorta need it, like, yesterday."

"Let it fly, girl," said Kurt, humming a tune to go with the chords.

Lydia curled up closer to Kurt. "What are you playing? I like that."

"A new song about a fly girl. I should write this down before I forget it."

Thalia handed him paper and a pen. She went to her easel and painted a girl's face with juicy red lips and oversized sunglasses with kaleidoscope lenses. She added mustard, teal and black for spaghetti-string hair. She drew her right arm holding a torch pumped toward the sky. She finished the painting in a half hour, then quick-dried the acrylic with a hairdryer.

She held it up for them. "It's a trippy fly girl."

"Awesome sauce," said Kurt. "If you let us use that, we'll knock a thousand bucks off the concert tab. Deal?"

"Deal."

Thalia and I headed into work Sunday morning at the North Easton Daily Grind. "Do you think Tanya's punishing us with the early shift?" I asked.

"Totally." Thalia kicked a rock toward the curb. "I don't blame her for being pissed. We busted up her hump sesh."

"Shit. There she is," I said.

Tanya propped the sign promoting the day's blends on the lawn. She glanced at us and turned to head back inside.

"Good morning!" I called out with feigned enthusiasm.

"Sit," she commanded. "What were you two doing at the shop after hours?"

I scrambled for an excuse. "We were at a bar in Quincy Market and thought we'd pop in for coffee and change up the front window."

"We didn't really see anything. Well, not that much," added Thalia. "We're super sorry."

"Super sorry? Next time give me the heads up what you're doing. It's been a long time since I did it in the coffee shop. I've been waiting years to find the right cop. You ruined it! You stepped all over my fantasy."

"That wasn't a first?" I asked, struggling to keep a straight face.

"Hell no! Do you know how sexy it is to do it with a cop in a coffee shop?"

"Ah. No. But I'll take your word for it," I said.

"Are handcuffs optional?" asked Thalia, realizing she took it too far. "Never mind, let's brew some coffee."

# Chapter Eleven — Aries

"It's just a loaner," said Axel, getting out of a bold orange Ram 1500 TRX. "The Jeep is getting an oil change and brake job."

"Badass!" I said, checking out the menacing black grille. The RAM reminded me that I had officially entered Aries.

We drove to his parents' Manhattan apartment for the first few days of spring break. Amara insisted on taking me and Thalia to lunch and shopping while Axel went to the office with Titus. We met her at Le Bernardin. The *maître-de* looked us over as if we were junkyard strays squatting in the Westminster show ring. When we mentioned the Adamos name for the reservation, he whisked us to our corner table where Amara was halfway through a glass of chardonnay.

"Thank you, Henri. Aren't they beauties?" She batted her eyes at him. "Send the *sommelier*, please."

The *maître-de* placated her with an ingratiating smile. "Certainly."

"I hope you like seafood," said Amara. "I took the liberty of ordering the chef's tasting with a wine pairing."

"Sounds great," I said, eyeing the empty chair.

The *sommelier* delivered a textbook-thick binder. Amara flipped pages before deciding. "*Cent dix-huit, s'il vous plaît.*"

"*Bon choix*," he said, scurrying to the wine vault.

"As if there's a bad choice." Amara chuckled to herself before her sister Pasha breezed toward our table carrying gift bags stuffed with pastel tissue paper.

Pasha distributed the gifts, knocking over a water glass. "A little something for you ladies. Open them."

The gifts were matching Hermes silk scarves. Thalia adjusted hers around her neck with little fussing. She knew I had no idea how to fashionably wear the scarf, so she tied it for me. Pasha side-glanced Thalia's nimble fingers smoothing the silk folds across my shoulders, adding more proof to her suspicions that we were more than gal pals.

"Where's my handsome nephew?"

"He's with Titus," said Amara.

The *sommelier* returned with the bottle, flashed the label and plucked the cork with a welcome pop. Relief was on the way, I thought to myself. He poured a sample in his silver-plated tastevin.

"This is a lean and restrained wine with puckery tannins. It has a velvety mouth-feel," he said, pouring a taste for Amara's approval. He angled the bottle so she could review the label.

"This Pomerol is more cloying than a Barry Manilow ballad," she said, flaring her nostrils like a bull. "I expected more of a gritty Bordeaux terroir."

"Would you prefer something else?"

She shook her head. "It needs to breathe. Proceed with the pour."

He remained stone-faced as he distributed the wine in even servings, making sure Amara received the last drop. "Enjoy, ladies."

"A velvety mouth-feel? What a cork dork," said Pasha, practically snorting her first sip.

"Pasha, lower your voice. I think he heard that."

"Is Titus still bidding for the HVAC renovation contract in that weird building? This has been dragging on for months."

"He won the project. The work starts soon."

A demitasse cup of seafoam was placed alongside Hamachi tartare with a bonito flake and soy ginger sauce, the best Japanese yellowtail money could buy, in America at least.

The server said, "Enjoy an amuse-bouche, compliments from the chef."

"It doesn't take much to amuse my mouth." Pasha cackled. "Where's the cork dork with another bottle?"

Amara whispered, "We have a pairing with each course."

I took some warm brioche from the bread server. Pasha's eyes popped when I slathered it with butter. "When you get to be our age, bread is a big no-no. It goes straight from the lips to the hips."

"Is the building you're referring to the Long Lines building?" I asked, chomping into the roll.

"Yes, that's the one," said Amara. "He's taking Axel with him to get introduced to the building's mechanical systems. We've been contracted to upgrade the entire heating —"

Pasha butted in. "Eddie's been selected to compete at the Stotesbury Cup."

"That's terrific," gushed Amara. "We had such fun when Axel was in high school and his boat won at Stotesbury. But beware, the college recruiters will be out in full force."

"Eddie's already on the Ivy League radar. It's simply a question of Yale or Harvard." Pasha excused herself to go powder her nose.

Amara leaned in. "I heard he's the equipment manager."

Thalia smiled. "I love Aunt Pasha!"

"She's a pain in the you know what, but I love her, too," said Amara, dabbing the corners of her mouth and leaving plum lipstick on her white cloth napkin.

We worked our way through the seafood and wine with each course. The passion fruit mousse with lemon sorbet arrived for desert and spring solstice melted in my mouth.

"For your finale, enjoy our signature *mignardises*," said the server, setting down plates filled with caramel chocolate truffles, rose macarons, vanilla bean custards and miniature *éclairs*.

Pasha said, "I'm stuffed."

Amara pushed her plate away. "Me too."

I wanted to ask for their deserts, but erred on the side of politeness. It wasn't until we stood to leave when I realized my head spun from the wine. Thalia and I headed for the bathroom while Amara settled the bill.

"I'm such a food slut," I said.

"Aunt Amara knows her restaurants," said Thalia.

"And Titus knows his HVAC — no one gets into the Long Lines building!"

Pasha left us alone with Amara who led the way to Tory Burch to shop for spring layers. Inside, she motioned for the salesperson to assist us.

"Let's start a dressing room. The young ladies need coming-and-going looks," she said.

I wasn't sure what that look was, so I followed Thalia's lead as she flipped through the racks. I thought Tory Sportswear looked like Yoga Barbie desperate to seduce Ken with a downward dog. The salesperson pointed out an embroidered tunic with matching striped cinched ankle pants.

"The Miller Cloud sandals look cute with this outfit. They're a best seller," she said.

Amara insisted we try on the outfits. She chaperoned us inside the dressing room. I thought the bright tunic made me look like a celebrant at a Diwali festival. The signature double-Ts on the sandals resembled Toyota hubcaps. Thalia tried on a tunic dress that looked like a grandmother's housecoat.

"Adorable!" said Amara, springing from the velour chair to adjust the tassel drape on my tunic. "We'll take it."

I glanced at the price tags: $228 hubcap sandals, $598 tunic and $398 ankle pants. That was more than I spent on my entire college wardrobe courtesy of Target. And we weren't done.

"Lily Pulitzer next. Her color schemes will pop on your cute figures."

The only thing popping inside Lily Pulitzer were my eyeballs. The color schemes looked like melted rainbow sherbet. It wasn't long before I was in the dressing room trying on the Adalina high-collar shift romper in blue and pink, a cute number if I were to attend a baby gender-reveal party. Thalia rocked a sleeveless navy-blue shift dress with white embroidered detailing down the front.

"The Tory Burch sandals will look stylish with these dresses — unless you'd prefer something a tad dressier?"

Thalia said we were set with sandals. We headed out to meet the men for cocktails at Garfunkel's, a 1920s speakeasy. We found Axel and Titus were in the library sipping Scotch on the rocks. I ordered an aged-rum drink called 1933.

"I'll have the same," said Thalia.

"Chardonnay for me. Something buttery, please," said Amara. "We had the most pleasant afternoon, didn't we girls?"

"Le Bernardin is my new favorite," I said, laughing to myself because any restaurant with a menu not on the wall was a step above my typical fare.

Titus guffawed. "Axe, you better start working for me right away. Your lady friend has expensive taste."

"She's worth every penny," said Amara, narrowing her eyes at her husband.

"How did things work out at 33 Thomas Street?" I asked.

Titus slipped a keycard from his pocket and grinned. "We met with the owners today. We can start working right away."

"I'd love to see it," I said.

His eyes lit up. "We are on a tight schedule and could use more help. Axel and I start surveying the building on Monday. Would you two like to assist? I'll pay, of course. We have to document all the existing equipment to see if we can salvage anything."

"Sure, I'd love to help. What does it look like inside?"

Axel shrugged. "The foyer is funky with the art on the ceiling, but upstairs are bland server rooms. Totally Kafkaesque."

"There's nothing out of the ordinary? No super secure room? Suspicious custodial closet?"

Titus ordered another round. "Why would there be a secure room within the most secure building ever built?"

"Maybe there's an object of significant historical value that needs to be protected?"

Titus rolled his eyes. "Such as?"

I restrained from blurting "the holy grail" and said, "Maybe an Andy Warhol —"

Titus laughed. "I'll keep a lookout for soup-can paintings."


Back at the apartment, I pressed Axel for more details about the Long Lines building. "I have a hunch that Bauhaus might have hidden some important artifacts there."

He sighed. "We've reviewed the plans in the Harvard archives. I've been inside the building. There's nothing in there except telephone securities, so far as I can tell."

Thalia said, "Remember when we looked at the architectural drawings the other day and noticed the Bauhaus marking in one of the rooms? The building is Bauhaus design, one room is marked with its symbol. There must be something interesting in there."

"What room?"

"The top floor," I said. "Can you get us in there?"

He shrugged. "We have to survey the entire building, so there's a good chance we'll get inside. Thankfully we have the existing drawings. We can only hope they're close to what was actually installed. If not, then everything has to be redrawn by hand and then go back to the office to draw it on the computer."

"What will Thalia and I be doing?"

"Documenting the charts with all the measurements."

"We're on it!"


First thing Monday morning, we donned our Adamos Modern Air t-shirts and baseball caps and met the crew in the foyer to check through security — body scans and metal detectors. After clearing security, we were equipped with clipboards, architectural drawings and ballpoint pens. The electricians and plumbing engineers were on hand to process the survey as well. We followed the building superintendent to the mechanical rooms. Axel led his team, which included Thalia and me, where we had to record the nameplate tags of all the air handlers, fans, pumps and all other major equipment. I measured each pipe and duct to see if the sizes matched the drawings.

Axel checked my clipboard. "Good. The existing drawings are accurate so far."

We climbed up and down ladders, working the measuring tape like ninjas. After a quick lunch break, we finally reached the top floor.

While the other doors were all keyed entries, we arrived at one room that was secured by a pass code. The superintendent made a call and said, "It'll be a few minutes. We need a suit to open this one."

A man in a navy pinstripe suit clacked his dress shoes down the corridor. He double-checked our security clearance, punched in a four-digit code, and dismissed the superintendent. "I'll monitor the workers in this room," he said.

Inside the room, a twelve-foot wall resembled a detective's office: surveillance photographs of pedestrians, blueprints of buildings, and lists of names with birthdates. A chalkboard was marked with Xs and Os like a coach's game-day plan.

"Start in this corner," said Axel, setting up the ladder.

I climbed the ladder while keeping an eye on the main wall. I tried to memorize what was posted, but it was difficult with The Suit staring at me. I almost fell off the ladder when I noticed a photograph of me and Thalia at the front entrance to the Boston Public Library.

I kept my back turned to The Suit who watched us so closely that I thought he could see the sweat beading on the back of my neck. I recorded the measurements of the pipes and moved the ladder closer to a side wall where there was a built-in black safe next to an Ikea-style block desk. Thalia called out her measurements to Axel. He borrowed my ladder to double check her measurements. I took out my cellphone and managed to take a few quick shots of the wall while I steadied the ladder for Axel.

"Are you close to finishing up in here?" asked The Suit. He answered his cell phone and stepped into the hallway to continue his conversation.

When Axel came down, I moved the ladder closer to the desk, glanced at the door to make sure he wasn't watching, and opened the top desk drawer. There was an assortment of pens, pencils and paperclips, along with pads of paper and manila folders. Then I noticed the safe had a number code. The Suit's voice carried from the hallway, so I swiftly attempted 5/18/1883 for Gropius' birthday. That was too many numbers; shortening it to 5/18/83 didn't work either. I tried 1969 for the year construction began on the Long Lines building, then 1974 for when it was completed. No luck. I retreated toward my ladder when I heard The Suit finish his call.

He returned to the room. "Nearly done?"

"We shouldn't be much longer," said Axel.

The Suit leaned against the wall, studying Axel who was advising Thalia how to mark the drawings with the measurements. He grumbled when his phone rang again and took the call in the hallway. I moved back to the safe, punched in 1919 — the year Bauhaus was founded — and gasped when the safe clicked open. I peered inside: a stack of black binders, blueprints, and a gold compass and square. I snatched the compass and square, stuffed it in my pants pocket and shut the safe door. I was all business again at the top of the ladder measuring pipes, until Axel checked our final measurements.

He whispered. "Titus will murder me if you snoop."

The Suit returned, clearing his throat.

"All set," said Axel, folding the ladder.

I followed him out, praying the Suit didn't notice the compass and square in my pocket.

Later that evening, we ate New York style pizza in the apartment. Axel was relieved that there was no need to draw new plans, making the project less tedious. I showed Thalia the photos I snapped.

Axel squinted at my phone screen. "Wait, you took photos?"

"Don't worry. Everything's cool."

"Snapping photos was a huge risk. You could've blown my dad's contract!" His phone rang and he answered it in the kitchen when he saw it was his father.

I showed Thalia the compass and square. "Look what I found in the Bauhaus room."

Her eyes bulged. "You stole it?"

"More like borrowed."

"You shouldn't have —"

"And they shouldn't have stolen our laptops," I said. "Do you recognize this symbol?"

There was an engraved masonic compass and square centered with a capital G. Thalia shrugged. "No. What is it?"

"It's the same symbol as the one in front of The Grand Lodge of Masons of Massachusetts. I've seen the symbol on many headstones in historic cemeteries around New England. I think this could be the key McKim told me to find."

"Gingbo," she said, handing it back to me. "I can't believe you found it."

"The compass and square are architects' tools. They have symbolic meaning in Freemasonry. There is no official understanding of the letter G. Some say it's for God while others claim it's for Geometry or Grand Architect. But I believe the compass and square with the G represents the Winter Hexagon," I explained, turning it to study. I noticed it had worn lettering engraved: WH RMH.

"Do you think the WH stands for Winter Hexagon?" asked Thalia.

"That's exactly what I'm thinking," I said, slipping it back into my pocket when I heard Axel ending his call. "I'm just not sure what the RMH stands for. And you're right, let's keep this between us."

We headed back to Boston for the marathon. Thalia and I dressed Quinn in a Boston Marathon t-shirt, running tights and Asics. We made sure to get it pre-approved by Tanya. We placed a water bottle in one hand and a travel cup of Goforth's coffee in the other.

"We need to talk. Meet me in the booth when you're done with this," said Tanya, eyeballing Quinn's marathon outfit.

"Do you think she's still pissed about St. Patrick's Day?" asked Thalia.

"Nah, she's over it."

We waited in the booth for Tanya to present her marathon blends. She slid four French presses on the table with homemade protein bars for us to sample.

"I've been brainstorming recipes with the owner of Quincy Pastry. What do you think?"

I chomped into a bar and amused myself with thoughts of a potential Quadster fundraiser: hash protein bars. The bars were chewy with a heavy nut-butter taste, but they crumbled easily. I brushed the crumbs onto my napkin and sipped the Barefoot blend.

"Delicious. I'm guessing they're gluten free by the way they crumble?"

"I was hoping the almond butter would hold them together. We need to tweak the recipe," said Tanya, tying her hair back with a scrunchie. "The coffee blends are similar to what we served at the parade. Without the booze, of course."

I felt my face redden. "No booze, got it."

"Officer Delgado will be on bike patrol, so make sure."

"We'll hook him up with free coffee." I crossed my heart like a Girl Scout and regretted that I used the phrase *hook up*.

Thalia asked, "How are things going with the hottie officer?"

I swallowed hard to stifle a laugh, recalling Delgado's naked butt behind the coffee bar.

"He helped get the permit to set up at the Athlete's Village, not far from the start line. Most marathoners know the benefits of drinking coffee before an event. It boosts speed and endurance. I added Cordyceps — the energy and endurance mushroom — to a Kenyan bold roast for a supercharged blend."

"Smooth and nutty," I said, drinking half a cup.

"We'll need to staff up. It's going to be a mob scene. I need you two to drive the truck there by 6 a.m. Then I'll shuttle the staffers and backup supplies. No partying the night before."

"Got it. No partying."


We joined Jill and Melissa in Sheila's room for pizza night. Her walls were plastered with Korean boy band posters, a *Parasite* movie poster and Korean soap opera stars.

"How did you get so into Korean culture?" asked Jill, who was half-Korean.

"K-dramas on YouTube," said Sheila. "We should do Korean barbecue sometime."

"I'm game," said Thalia, sighing when she saw the dry erase board propped up against the lower bunkbed. A unicorn was drawn in the center representing the Boston marathon.

"What's your problem? My unicorn isn't up to your artistic standards?" snapped Melissa.

"The drawing is fine, but has anyone noticed that every time we make a plan on the dry erase board, it turns into a mini-disaster?"

Melissa rolled her eyes. "What mini-disasters are you talking about?"

"Cops inspecting our bootleg coffee shop?" said Thalia.

"Trust me, the only thing the cops were checking out were the milkmaids."

Melissa gave Sheila the go-ahead nod. Sheila drew offshoots from the marathon unicorn and wrote *Kew Sports Drink Tunnel*.

"Wellesley College students cheer the runners in a scream tunnel. I think we should represent Kew by offering sports drinks to the runners. Jill's cousin is contacting his vendors for supplies."

Melissa said, "I'll ask Wheezy to announce the need for volunteers. We can get them to do the dirty work serving the sticky sports drinks while we flirt."

Sheila drew an arrow to Kew College hoodies. "Let's keep it simple: jeans, hoodies and sneakers."

Melissa kicked her feet in the air to flash hideous highlighter-yellow sneakers. "I already bought my pair of top-notch running skips. Hokas are a party on the feet. I want to look like Rosie Ruiz on race day."

"Who's Rosie Ruiz?" asked Sheila.

"She won the Boston marathon in 1980 but they found out she took a subway for part of the race. My kind of girl."

I said, "Thalia and I already committed to selling coffee for Goforth's. We can help you coordinate things, but on the day of the race, you're on your own."

Melissa flashed a dismissive wave. "No worries. I've got this."


Thalia and I parked the coffee truck in the center of Athletes' Village on the town common, where other vendors were selling t-shirts and running gear. Within an hour there was a mob surrounding our truck. I called Tanya wondering why she hadn't dropped off the support staff yet. The call went to voicemail.

I handed coffee to a customer and glanced across the crowd at a Kew College minibus, rolling into the commons. Students in Kew hoodies hefted coolers filled with sports drinks toward our truck. Four football players carried portable folding tables.

Melissa stormed ahead, ordering pedestrians to get out of the way like Moses parting the Red Sea.

She shouted, "Set the tables next to the coffee truck. Chop-chop."

"What are you doing?"

"We tried to set up next to the scream tunnel but the Wellesley bitches told us to get lost. Some bullshit about us needing a permit," she whined. "I said fuck it, we'll one-up them in the Athletes' Village."

Within minutes the Kew *tunnel* was in full operation with the volunteers handing out sample bottles of light green sports drink labeled Kewade.

I stared at Melissa in disbelief. "Kewade?"

"Chill out, Paigester. It's one hundred percent Gatorade with a redesigned label. It's all about marketing." She marched around in her yellow sneakers and running tights.

"Can I grab a free coffee?" One of the Kew volunteers popped his head inside the back of our truck. I spun around to see it was Jeffrey. I wanted to tell him to drink the Kewade, but I was inundated with orders so I ignored him. He came into the truck and poured coffee for himself.

"It's a tight squeeze," said Thalia. "Could you step out?"

"I used to work at Starbucks in high school," he said. "Looks like you could use some help."

Jeffrey sported Maui Jim sunglasses, a Red Sox baseball cap and blue Polo shirt. He wore shorts and I noticed he had muscular legs. He seemed less dorky and we needed the help, so I accepted his offer.

Melissa came to the back of the truck. "How come I wasn't invited to the gang bang?"

"We're slammed. Any chance we can use one of the tables you brought? Jeffrey offered to help sell coffee for us," I said.

She huffed, "You both need event-planning lessons. Let me see what I can do."

Thalia elbowed me. "Isn't she the one piggy-backing off our permit?"

"Exactly."

It took Melissa less than two minutes to clear space for us. Two police officers rode their bikes toward the truck. I blushed when I saw it was Delgado, remembering his tight buns.

"Have you tried Tanya's Cordyceps blend yet?" I asked.

"Of course, I'm her human guinea pig," he said.

Thalia whispered, "More like her rabbit."

I kicked her behind the counter. "Here you go, one for your partner as well."

He asked, "Where's Tanya? She said she'd be here by now."

"I haven't heard from her all morning."

"I'll text her," he said, staring at the Kewade table. "Are they supposed to be here?"

"Um…"

"As long as there's no alcohol."

"We would never," I said, but I wasn't sure what Melissa was up to with her Kewade.


When we ran out of coffee, Thalia and I sprawled out on the lawn. Jeffrey handed me the cigar box overflowing with dollar bills.

"Thanks for the help," I said.

"Don't mention it. Maybe you could get me a job at the Goforth's near campus. I could use some cash. My dad's a tightwad."

"I'll put in a good word for you."

Melissa rounded up the army of volunteers and called for the school bus to pick them up. "Are you coming, Jeffrey?"

He looked at me. "You need help packing up?"

Thalia answered before I could think it through. "Definitely. You can drive to Quincy Market with us to help unload."

Back at the coffee shop, we couldn't find Tanya. The crew she was supposed to bring over was hanging out in the back room.

"You guys couldn't come over on your own?"

"We had no clue where you were," said one staffer.

I held up my phone. "You could've called!"

"I guess."

Jeffrey brought in the rest of the gear. "That's okay, you can introduce me to the boss another time."

"If she's alive," I said, worrying Bauhaus kidnapped her.


The *Patriot Lodestar* had a press table not far from the finish line. Jeffrey and Thalia came with me to check in with Hot Throat. Fred was hunkered behind his laptop, checking the times of the top finishers so far. He grinned when he saw his son with us.

"Jeffrey and the ladies," said Fred.

"Dad, please."

Fred laughed. "I call it like I see it, son."

Hot Throat encouraged us to eat. "Italian Stallion or chicken cutlet. They're both delicious, so take one of each if you're hungry."

"Starving," said Jeffrey.

I moved closer to Hot Throat. "Did you hear about any car accidents this morning?"

"There are always car accidents. Why?"

I put some of the sandwich and a handful of chips on a plate. "Tanya Goforth was a no-show. I haven't heard from her. I'm worried."

"Fred, pull up the police blotter."

A few minutes later he reported, "Nothing but a few fender benders."

I munched the Italian Stallion. "If you don't mind, I'm going to catch the next train back to North Easton to check on Tanya at her house. Maybe she has the flu."

"I'm done here. I'll drive you."

Thalia went off to watch Xavier's lacrosse game in Cambridge. I told her I would meet her and Axel there by halftime. Fred chewed his pen cap and glared at us when we left Jeffrey in the press tent.

"Thanks again for your help. See you around campus," I said.

Hot Throat's breathing sounded strained, as if she were running the marathon, so I slowed my getaway pace. Her white Sketchers looked fresh out of the box. We had several blocks to go before we reached the *Lodestar* parking garage.

She bent against the wall of Trinity Church. Straight above her was a stone carving of Moses with horns protruding from his head, similar to the Michelangelo sculpture of Moses at the Vatican. I recalled that when Moses came down from Mount Sinai carrying the Ten Commandments tablets, he was horned. He became enraged when he saw the Israelites worshipping a golden calf. Some interpret his fury to signify Moses ending the age of Taurus and leading the way into the age of Aries. He reached his hand over the Red Sea similar to Orion's outstretched hand in the Milky Way. Could Moses be connected with Orion?

On one of the towers was the symbol of a sheep holding a cross which matched the one I saw at Marsh Chapel. I knew I was in Aries — one zodiac sign away from finding the Winter Hexagon Salon.

"Did you ever wonder about the sheep carrying the cross?"

She followed my gaze. "I never noticed. But now that you mention it —"

"It's one of the symbols of the Knights Templar. The Freemasons claim to be descendants of the Templars and Richardson was a Freemason. I noticed the Templar cross sits above the entrance pediment."

"Go figure," she said, swigging from her water bottle.

We were on the move again. "Do you have any birthday plans?"

"My husband's taking me to Manhattan. I love the tulips and cherry trees in bloom in Central Park."

She caught a pebble in her shoe, so she sat on a bench across from Richardson's Brattle Square Church.

"Take your time," I said, crossing the street to admire the stone carvings.

A beautiful frieze wrapped around the four sides of the bell tower, depicting the sacraments of baptism, communion, marriage and death. Ralph Waldo Emerson, Henry Wadsworth Longfellow and Nathaniel Hawthorne were included in the communion frieze scene. Charles Sumner was in the baptism panel and Abraham Lincoln and Giuseppe Garabaldi were in the marriage panel.

She asked, "Any more signs of Aries?"

"Not Aries, but —" I showed her the church's bell tower frieze that was designed by Frederic Auguste Bartholdi. "He sculpted the Statue of Liberty as well."

Hot Throat said, "I've never visited the Statue of Liberty. Maybe I'll take the ferry to Liberty Island while I'm there."

Then it hit me. Richard Morris Hunt — the founding father of American architecture — designed the Statue of Liberty's pedestal. His initials were RMH, the same letters engraved on the compass and square. A chill ran through my body. I studied the frieze details for a few more minutes. What was I sensing?

Hot Throat's heavy breathing was a distraction, so I checked my phone again — still no word from Tanya.

A few minutes later, Hot Throat directed her Prius through stop-and-go traffic. I closed my eyes so I could think. McKim told me to get the key that would open the salon. I started in Gemini and was entering into the last sign, Taurus. Orion's right arm reached into the zodiac path in between Gemini and Taurus. I recalled my sightings of various godlike images with outstretched right arms: Prometheus at both the Boston and New York public libraries, Prometheus at Rockefeller Center, Phaeton at the Boston Museum of Fine Arts, the lady statue at the Monument of the Forefathers and the Woman Boston Massacre Memorial statue in Boston Common. It couldn't be random. I wondered if my gut reaction had something to do with the Statue of Liberty's outstretched arm holding the torch. Did her figure represent the brightest constellation Orion? The same Orion constellation that is located within the Winter Hexagon constellation?

I recalled the Emma Lazarus poem: "Give me your tired, your poor, your huddled masses…" It ends with the line: "I lift my lamp beside the golden door!"

Could the Statue of Liberty be the entrance to the Winter Hexagon Salon? In Abbey's mural of Galahad's quest for the holy grail, Galahad takes a boat to a mystical island called Sarras. Was it possible that the Winter Hexagon Salon was hidden under Orion on Bedloe Island — also known as the Statue of Liberty on Liberty Island?

343

I Googled "Liberty" while Hot Throat pumped her brakes. "Did you know that the Liberty pedestal was designed by Richard Morris Hunt? He was the first American to attend the *École Beaux-Arts* in Paris. Richardson followed Hunt, and McKim learned from Richardson."

"Where are you going with this?"

I read her some facts — that a stone box was incorporated in the pedestal where a copy of the Declaration of Independence was kept and other items during a Freemason ceremony hosted by William Brodie the Grand Master of the Grand Lodge of New York.

"And?"

"There must be something in the pedestal," I said, bracing my hands against the dashboard when Hot Throat accelerated.

"Write up a report with all your findings and get it to me by EOD tomorrow."

"EOD?"

"End of Day."

Hot Throat pulled into Tanya's driveway. I dashed up the front steps, but the door was locked. I rang the bell and peeked into the windows, then jogged around to the back of her house. I worried that Bauhaus was harassing Tanya now. Then I noticed that the Peace Train VW van was gone.

Hot Throat tooted her horn. "Anything?"

"Nothing. I'm going to call Captain Biff. Maybe he knows something."

"I don't think you need to trouble the captain. He's a busy man."

"Too busy to pursue a missing person?"

"She's not a child or a senior citizen. Leave the good captain alone."

I hedged. "I think I should share my latest thoughts about the Statue of Liberty pedestal."

"New York is out of his jurisdiction. I have a guy who can cross state lines. We'll set up a meeting in my office tomorrow. In the meantime, get cracking on my report. You're this much closer to winning a year in Italy," she said, holding her fingers an inch apart.

# Chapter Twelve — Taurus

"What now?" said Captain Biff, coughing and clearing his throat.

"Tanya Goforth never showed up at the marathon. She was supposed to meet us there. Nobody's heard from her in two days. It's out of character for her."

"My educated guess — she's out foraging mushrooms," he said.

"You're not going to send out a search team?"

He huffed. "You said you went to her house and it looked undisturbed?"

"Yes."

"You said her van was gone?"

"Yes."

"She took a trip. She'll be back."

I wasn't convinced. "I'm worried that Bauhaus may have targeted her because she's affiliated with me. Maybe they're holding her hostage, messing with her the way they did with Thalia."

"Trust me, a mushroom-coffee hippie like her is not on the Bauhaus radar. Speaking of Bauhaus, any updates?"

I hesitated. "Pilar Kuhlkoat told me not to bother you with my latest theories."

"Give me the rundown."

"She said that New York is out of your jurisdiction. She wants to meet in her office today. She said she has a guy who can cross state lines."

"She has a guy, my foot! Kuhlkoat's disgruntled because I introduced you to Eli Stanton. She's always wanted to expand into New York druid affairs. She goes galivanting like a tourist and thinks she knows the Big Apple."

"I didn't realize she felt that way about New York druids."

"What did you come up with?"

I explained how I used the zodiac and the Orion constellation to deduce that the Winter Hexagon Salon could be inside the Statue of Liberty's pedestal. There was a long pause.

"Did you tell any of that to Kuhlkoat?"

"Fragments. I was going to go all in during today's meeting," I said.

"Who's her guy? Is he a druid?"

"She didn't give his name."

He sighed. "Go meet with Kuhlkoat and her guy, but don't share all of your ideas just yet. Call me after the meeting and let me know who he is. Got it?"

"Got it."

Hot Throat called at noon. "Meet in my office in an hour," she said.

"So soon? I'm not sure I can get there that quickly."

"An all-expenses paid year in Rome is on the line and you're whining?"

Pilar was waiting in her office with her door open.

When I passed Fred's desk, he grumbled, "Did your coffee boss ever show up?"

I leaned against his cubicle wall. "Jeffrey told you about her?"

"Good thing he was there. He saved the day. If she needs a boyrista who can also do her bookkeeping, tell her to hire Jeffrey. He's a math whiz."

"I'll mention it to her."

"She'll need to give him a better wage than anyone working there, including you."

"Why more than me?" I said, exaggerating three blinks.

"Jeffrey brings a lot to the table. High skill set, genius IQ."

"Goforth's Daily Grind would be lucky to have him," I said, remaining diplomatic even though I wanted to break him the news that his son was even a larger tool than his dad.

Hot Throat motioned for me to move along. I closed the door behind me. I sat across from her and reiterated some of my basic theories. She looked stern, jotting notes the whole time.

"Okay, I'm not sure there's enough to go with here, but I'll tell you what," she said, sliding her reading glasses on top of her head. "I'll arrange for a little field trip for you and me to visit Manhattan. I need visuals to wrap my head around your ideas."

I scanned the newsroom. "Is your guy running late?"

She tapped her knuckles on the desk. "I don't want to get him involved until I think we're onto something. This idea of following the zodiac to the Statue of Liberty is a tad woo-woo."

My face reddened. I wish I hadn't shared my insights with her, but she'd baited the hook with a trip to Italy. "I'll go to New York anytime you want."

"I'll set something up," she said, eyeing the blinking desk phone. "One more thing before you go."

"Yes?"

She leaned across her desk. "McKim told you to find the key to the salon. Did you?"

"Not yet."

"If you do, leave it with me. I have more resources for keeping it safe."

"That's not something I would lose," I said, standing to leave.

Hot Throat nodded. "Sure. Your laptop was stolen. You've had about five run-ins with Bauhaus. And you think the key's safe? I think it would be best if we kept it in the *Lodestar* bank vault."

I wondered if she knew about the recent kayak attack because I hadn't mentioned it. "You're right. The *Lodestar* vault it is. You'll be the first call I make. But as you said, my ideas are a tad woo-woo."

"Well, you did find the ark of the covenant," she said, as if arguing with herself.

"Yeah, I did."

I stopped by Quincy Market and almost fell over when I saw Tanya cleaning the espresso machine. She casually acknowledged me with a nod.

"Are you okay?" I asked, feeling like a panic-stricken mother torn between scolding the child and crying with joy.

"Why wouldn't I be okay?"

Her nonchalance was off-putting. I said, "You disappeared for three days! I was worried! I called the cops! Didn't you get my voicemails?"

"A friend invited me to Burning Woman. You must go next year."

"Burning Woman?"

"A festival with cool vibes. It swarms with artists, musicians, writers. I'm surprised you never heard of it. It's like Burning Man but without the douchebags."

I wanted to scold her for not telling me ahead of time, but I could hear the Quadsters' voices reminding me I'm uptight.

"Sounds awesome."

"You'd love it. I can't wait for you to meet Feather Faraday. She runs the festival. We meditated together. Now we're dynamic sisters."

"Dynamic sisters?"

"Spiritually looped," she said, smiling in a relaxed way I hadn't seen since she'd opened the shop in Quincy Market. "I'm going to live in the Burning Woman community. My mushroom coffee blends will be a hit."

Feather Faraday? Burning Woman? Spiritually looped? Tanya's eyes were clear, so she wasn't on quaaludes. In fact, she looked more at peace than the times I saw her meditating.

"What about your house? The coffee shops?"

"I contacted a realtor to put the house on the market. I have interested buyers for the coffee shops. I'll put in a good word for you. But you're heading to Rome next year."

"Thanks, but Rome isn't a guaranteed thing," I said, watching her reassemble the espresso machine. "Where's Burning Woman?"

"Fire Island. You take a ferry to get there. No cars. No noise. Pristine beach for miles."

"Sounds epic."

"Come visit once I'm settled. Feather would get a charge out of you. But I'm warning you, it's like 'Hotel California.'"

"How so?"

She laughed. "You can check out any time you like, but you can never leave."


At the North Easton police precinct, I waited by the front dispatch for Captain Biff.

"The captain will be with you soon. Help yourself to coffee while you wait," said the receptionist. I stared at the Keurig machine, feeling uninspired. Once you Goforth, you never go back.

"Moore!" Captain Biff called from his office. "Get in here."

The receptionist bolted upright at her desk. "The captain will see you now."

I stepped inside his office — beige, filled with old wooden filing cabinets, an oak desk covered with stacks of case reports and an aerial photograph of North Easton. He noticed I was eyeing a Royal typewriter on top of a cabinet.

"It looks just like the one we had at Goforth's Daily Grind," I said.

"It is. I bought it." He rocked back in his chair with his hands interlocked behind his head. "Did Goforth return from her mushroom-foraging?"

"She's back. And you were right. Total hippie excursion. Now she's selling her house and the coffee shops," I said, noticing a framed family picture on the corner of his desk. He had an army of kids which surprised me because he never mentioned them.

"Really? Just when I was getting used to my daily Lion's Mane." He reviewed a memo his secretary handed him, folded it and slid it inside his blazer pocket.

"What happened with Kuhlkoat?"

"She's pushing for me to find the key and give it to her for safekeeping in the *Lodestar* vault. She thinks it will get stolen from me in another Bauhaus hit."

"Interesting." He looked over the rim of his glasses. "Who's her guy?"

"He was a no-show. She wants to go to Manhattan with me. Then if she's convinced about my theories, she'll bring him in."

"Contact Eli Stanton. It's time to further explore your ideas in New York. Eli knows Manhattan better than anyone."

"Should I take Kuhlkoat with me? What if I find the Winter Hexagon Salon without her? I feel like I owe her."

"She used her *Lodestar* resources to groom you in the Boston AOD. She just wanted to keep you motivated. The penthouse apartment, the beach house, the expensed services — that was all on the *Lodestar* dime," he said, shuffling around his desk for a folded newspaper. "Did you ever miss a deadline?"

"Nope."

"You were hired to write horoscopes for the paper. You fulfilled that responsibility and you remained committed to the AOD. You don't owe her anything."

"Still —"

"Fine. Take her with you. I guess it can't hurt. Plus, she can drive you."

"If you say so," I hedged, clearing my throat. "I think I found the key."

His eyebrows raised. "Do you have it with you?"

I slipped the compass and square into his hand. He squinted at it, furrowing his brow into deep wrinkles. He rummaged through a drawer until he found a magnifying glass. He chewed on a toothpick while he examined it. "What makes you think this is a key?"

"See the engraved letters?" I pointed to the inner edge. "I think it stands for Winter Hexagon Salon and Richard Morris Hunt. The compass and square with the G make the symbol for Freemasons."

He inspected the tool for at least a minute. "What does G stand for?"

"Some say God or Grand Architect. I think Grail. As in, the holy grail. It could also just represent a star image in the center of the winter hexagon. The points on the compass and square are formed by six bright stars that surround an arc of stars shaping the G. That's the location of Orion's club at the intersection of the milky way and the zodiac."

"I'll contact Eli Stanton. You should take this tool and your ideas to him. Don't breathe a word of this to anyone until you meet with him, not your boyfriend, not Kuhlkoat, not Goforth. No one! Got it?"

"Got it."

Liberty Enlightening the World is the official name of the Statue of Liberty, made in 1886 out of copper, gold, steel and cast iron. She was modeled after Libertas, the Roman goddess of freedom, with twenty-five windows in her crown and seven spikes for the continents. Broken chains and shackles near her feet symbolize freedom from oppression.

Thalia and I cut across campus to the student center, making sure no one was following us. I checked my mailbox and was happy to find a magazine. We headed out to the parking lot where Hot Throat waited for us in her Prius. I rode shotgun while Thalia hopped in the backseat.

"I packed some sandwiches and snacks in the back," she said, sounding like a mom. "Help yourselves."

"Thanks." I lowered the volume on the radio. "Are we going to listen to the news and weather reports all the way?"

"You got a problem with that?"

"Just asking."

She flipped on the baseball game. "How's this? First home game of the season."

"I don't understand baseball. You'll have to teach it to me," said Thalia, flipping pages in my magazine while we sped toward New York. Hot Throat grumbled about an infield error that almost cost the Red Sox a run and horse-lipped when they escaped the inning unscathed.

"What's the plan once we get to New York?" She eyed Thalia in the rearview mirror. "Hon, pass some chips up here."

"Stanton will meet us in Battery Park. We'll take his boat to Liberty Island once it closes to the public."

"And if we find the salon?" asked Thalia.

"I'm thinking Eli will contact high-level druids to take over," I said.

"Ladies, let's just get there first —"

"Could I ever get appointed to the AOD like Paige?"

"Hon, if we find the salon, you'll be a shoe-in."

"So let's go find it."


We parked in a garage, headed toward Battery Park, and I pointed out the charging bull bronze statue on Wall Street.

"Taurus, the final sign of the zodiac. If I'm right, we should now be on the brink of finding the secret salon. I also think that Orion between Gemini and Taurus holds the holy grail. In Ancient Egypt, Orion was Osiris, the gatekeeper to heaven. Lady Liberty is the gatekeeper of the new world."

"I hope you're right," said Thalia.

I could smell the hot dogs and pretzels long before we approached the corner vendor.

"Can I get a hot dog?" Thalia asked, sounding childish.

Hot Throat checked the time. "Make it three. We're a little early."

The vendor plucked the hot dogs with his tongs. "Ketchup? Mustard?"

"Plain. And a salted pretzel." She paid the vendor. "Keep the change, pal."

"Big spender."

The crosswalk signal flashed for us to cross into Battery Park. We jumped two steps back when an old black Dodge peeled around the corner.

"Moron! You could kill someone driving like that," screamed Thalia.

"True, but that's a sweet ride," I said.

"No airbags," said Hot Throat, squashing my appreciation for the slick angles and whitewall tires. "Probably no seatbelts either. Under federal law, all cars had to be fitted with seatbelts starting in 1968. But it took another fifteen years before most passengers started to use them."

"We've come a long way since then," I said, splitting the pretzel into thirds. The kosher salt crystals and warm dough tasted so heavenly I thought it should be an item included in the Le Bernardin tasting menu. The last ferry dropped off the tourists in the park. I checked the time again. Thalia pulled a container of Tic-Tacs from her pocket and started chomping. The mints rattling in the plastic container and her nervous crunching was irritating.

"What's with the mints?"

"Mint relaxes me. Where is this guy?"

A lean man in a black trench coat moved with purposeful strides across the park. He carried a closed hardwood-handled umbrella that doubled as a walking stick. I flashed a druid greeting.

"That's him," I said. Hot Throat quickly applied lipstick and adjusted her hair.

Eli Stanton hooked the umbrella on his wrist to signal back to us. He strode past us without speaking, so we followed fifteen feet behind him toward the dock. He reached a boat and waited for us to catch up.

"I'm Pilar Kuhlkoat. So nice to finally meet you," she said, shaking his hand. "And this is Paige's assistant Thalia."

"Ladies, the pleasure is mine," he said, boarding the Phaeton, the private druid speedboat set to escort us to the island. The boat was an open-topped wooden Chris-Craft runabout with red leather seats. An American flag flapped from the stern, reminding me of photos I'd seen of Jackie and JFK cruising around Hyannis Port.

"Is it vintage?" I asked when we climbed into the back seat.

"Custom 1939 Barrel Back," said Eli. "Restored her myself."

"Impressive."

The engine rumbled. Thalia sat next to me in the back seat while Hot Throat sat up front. I focused on Liberty's patinaed colossal form and felt my heart pounding as we cruised toward the island. Lady Liberty was illuminated by floodlights. I imagined what it must have been like to watch her get welded together when she was erected atop the pedestal.

"She's a beauty," said Eli.

I wanted to ask if he was referring to Lady Liberty or Thalia, but I remained focused on the mission. Thunder clouds rolled toward Lady Liberty who gazed off into the lonely starlit hours. A light drizzle started, prompting Eli to snap open his umbrella to hold over our heads. He struggled against the wind to keep the umbrella from turning inside out, so he closed it and focused on steering the boat.

"Thanks anyway," I said, pulling on my sweatshirt hood.

Eli sped toward the island. Water sprayed from the bow into our faces. We bounced across the choppy water until he eased the Phaeton alongside the dock, bringing us as close to the shore as he could. He tied a rope to a wood post and hooked an easy deploy fire escape ladder to the dock. Eli climbed the ladder onto the dock. "Hand me the flashlights."

Eli helped us from the boat, first Hot Throat, then Thalia and me. We followed him down the dock and sloshed across the soggy lawn toward Liberty's stone pedestal. The island was closed to visitors at night, so we had the place to ourselves.

"Are there security cameras? A night-watchman?" I asked, my heart pounding with excitement.

He jingled a set of keys. "I know people. I got after-hours clearance to inspect the pedestal."

He unlocked the lobby door to the Statue of Liberty Museum where Liberty's original leaky torch was kept on display. It was replaced in 1986 by a copper flame covered in 24-karat gold. We searched through the main lobby, looking for an unusual door or entryway. Nothing seemed out of the ordinary. We left the museum to search Hunt's pedestal.

Eli exhaled. "Thoughts?"

"Let's try the mechanical rooms. There's no way the salon entrance would be exposed to the public," I said.

Eli sorted through the keys to open the main mechanical room. I ran my hands along the stone, poked my pinky inside small holes, and kicked away cobwebs in the corners. Residue — a mix of water, rust and oil — dripped from the old pipes. It smelled like mold. The residue runoff sloped away from the furnace toward a round floor drain the size of a city manhole cover. I dragged my sneaker across the cover to clear away some of the sludge.

I crouched for a closer look at the raised detailing in the drain cover. There was a starburst line pattern extending from a center compass and square symbol. Along the perimeter were evenly spaced line segments with images inside.

"This is the line symbol for Aries," I said, revealing a curling V. I scraped away more sludge to find an etched circle with horns, the line symbol for a bull. "Taurus is here."

We continued the sludge clearing until all twelve signs were revealed.

"What does it mean?" asked Hot Throat.

"I've been following the signs all along!" I tried to control my emotions. "And they're all right here."

Thalia shouted, "This could be it!"

The Sagittarius arrow pointed toward a side wall that was blocked by a supply cabinet. We unloaded the boxes, filled mostly with cleaning products. I noticed another box had wooden baseball bats and baseballs.

"That's odd," I said, pulling a bat from the box. "Who would stash sports equipment here?"

Eli shrugged. "Maybe the workers play on their lunch break."

Hot Throat rummaged through the other boxes, then dusted her hands on her slacks when she found nothing.

We lightened the load of the cabinet enough to drag it away from the wall to reveal a black vault door. I tugged on the silver handle but it didn't open. Next to the handle was an old brass bank safe vault lock with decorated gears marked Yale Lock Mfg Co. I shined the flashlight on the lock and noticed a dime-sized circle with a slit in its center.

"I'm going to try the compass pointer in that slit," I said.

"What compass pointer?" snapped Hot Throat, leaning over my shoulder.

I took the compass from my pocket and showed her and Eli.

"And where did we find that item?"

"I came across it in my research."

"And I'm hearing about it now? This should have been brought to my attention —"

"Nevertheless," interrupted Eli. "Please proceed."

I inserted the pointed end into the slit. The gears clicked, retracting the locking pins.

"It works!" I said, putting the compass and square back in my pocket for safekeeping. The door opened to a cement staircase. "This has to lead to the Winter Hexagon Salon!"

"Let's check it out," Eli suggested, heading down the steps ahead of us.

"Are you sure we should we go down there? It could be overrun with rats," said Thalia.

"We came this far, we can't stop now," I said.

Hot Throat pushed past me to follow closely behind Eli. We descended the winding staircase with the flashlights pointing ahead of us, reminding me that the entrance to Solomon's temple had a winding staircase. Thalia clung to my arm.

Brick archways opened to a winding hallway. Wrought iron sconces held remnants of wax candle drippings. The corridor led to a rounded foyer. There was a magnificent ceiling mural of a Viking ship that resembled the ships I noticed at the boathouse in Cambridge. In the center of the mural, above the ship, was Orion surrounded by the four *living creatures.* At the far end of the mural was a man that resembled Prometheus, holding fire in his outstretched right hand.

There was a bull, lion, eagle and man painted above a silver door with the same vault lock as the door upstairs. I slipped the compass point into the slit, slowly twisting clockwise until the gears clicked. I pushed the door open, then stepped inside a chamber with marble floors. A crystal candelabra hung from the ceiling. On one wall there was an oil painting portrait of a man with a handlebar moustache and a narrow patch of beard. A placard underneath said Richard Morris Hunt. The opposite wall had a gold-framed painting of a rotund man wearing a hooded monk's robe. I recognized it was H.H. Richardson. Next to Richardson was a head-and-shoulder portrait of a bald man with a moustache, Charles McKim.

We passed through the rounded archway into a library loaded with stacks of leatherbound books. In each corner of the room were glass cases containing scaled models of Solomon's temple, Trinity Church, Chartres Cathedral, and the Boston Public Library. Antique draftsman cabinets had drawers filled with architectural plans signed by Richardson, McKim, Hunt and other architects. I found Richardson's sketchbook with drawings of Memorial Hall in North Easton. He'd sketched multiple pages of the tower frieze with all the zodiac signs. There were blueprints of detailed druid architectural design. McKim's sketches of the Boston Public Library had specific details on where each inlaid zodiac sign needed to go in the floor design.

"Check out the ceiling. It shows different symbols of the Winter Hexagon," I said.

Thalia scanned the ceiling with her flashlight. "Mezzo fresco. Gorgeous."

I went into the next room while Thalia studied the ceiling and Eli and Hot Throat looked through the drawers. I was awestruck by an altar staged in the center of the room set upon a jewel-toned oriental rug. A gold tabernacle covered in dust sat on the altar surrounded by candles with wax drips stuck in time, their wicks long since extinguished. I sneezed three times. I thought I caught a whiff of St. John's mugwort, but I couldn't figure out where it was coming from. It was probably mold. Presumably, no one had been in the room for a hundred years. Cobwebs had formed in the corners of the ceiling. The dusty floors were black-and-white checkerboard marble. The walls were coated with thick swirls of gray stucco. There was a loose brick in a wall, so I removed it. I pulled out more bricks to discover a reserve of gold. I slid back the bricks to cover the gold.

There were six high-backed, velvet chairs semi-circled in front of the altar with the names of the salon members: Richard Morris Hunt, Henry Hobson Richardson, Charles McKim, John Singer Sargent, Augustus Saint-Gaudens and Daniel Chester French. They'd signed a document that stated their mission statement: *the entrance to heaven is through the winter hexagon in the night sky...preserve ancient wisdom through art and architecture...teach future generations the principals of the founding fathers...*

The ceiling above the altar had a painted human eye like the one in Memorial Hall in North Easton. My throat tightened as I approached the altar. I opened the tabernacle that housed a book and wooden chalice. I took them out and stroked my fingers around the rim of the cup. Could this be the holy grail? I thumbed through the book, noticing illustrations of Solomon's temple. My hands trembled, so I slid the book and cup back into the tabernacle.

"You need to see this," I called. "I think it's the holy grail."

"You can't be serious," said Hot Throat, rushing into the room.

We gathered on the altar where we pointed our flashlights on the tabernacle. I took out the chalice and book. I said, "In the *Holy Bible* it says Jesus took a cup, gave thanks and told his apostles to drink from it, it's the blood of the covenant, which is poured out for many for the forgiveness of sins."

Eli raised the chalice to study it.

I gently turned the pages, stopping to show them the illustrations. "This must be the *Book of Kings*; it shows the dimensions to Solomon's temple. Druid architects like Hunt, Richardson, and McKim all designed according to Solomon's temple. I think this book was the original AOD *Bible*."

Eli said, "This room is definitely where the American druid architects had their secret society meetings. It's absolutely the Winter Hexagon Salon, only it's more spectacular than I'd imagined."

"It all makes sense. Bauhaus stole the golden compass and square, but they couldn't figure out where this room was. McKim was the last architect to have the key before it got stolen. The McKim family held the secret to this room. The only way to get in here was to unlock it with the compass and square. The door is otherwise impenetrable, designed by Richard Morris Hunt."

"Hunt was the founding father of American architecture," agreed Eli. "And now the druids have access to the greatest minds in early American architecture."

"And the grail," said Thalia.

Hot Throat went slack jawed. She didn't speak. It was as if she were in a trance.

"Are you okay?" I asked her.

She nodded.

Eli said, "Let's lock up and head to the subway salon to share our findings."

I took photos with my cell phone of the grail, book and tabernacle. I filmed a short video of the rooms as evidence to show Captain Biff. We put the book and cup in the tabernacle. I locked the door and stashed the key in my pocket. Eli shined his light above the foyer door where a quote from the *Book of Kings* was painted: *According to the grace of God which is given unto me, as a wise master builder I have laid the foundation, and another buildeth thereon. But let every man take heed how he buildeth thereupon.*

On our way out of the mechanical room, I asked Hot Throat, "So does this mean I get to study in Rome next year?"

"That was the deal," she said, maintaining her flat expression.

"Can I become part of the AOD now, like Paige?"

"That can be arranged. You can go with her to Rome seeing that you work well together."

Eli hushed us. "What's that? Do you hear something?"

"Someone's out there," said Thalia.

Eli grabbed a baseball bat from the box. We peered out to see what was happening.

Two figures dressed in dark clothing were running toward us like Walmart shoppers on Black Friday. I startled when I felt something cold press into the back of my neck. "Everyone stay right where you are," growled Hot Throat.

Eli shined the flashlight toward Hot Throat. "Put down the gun!"

"You move and I'll shoot her."

"What the hell?" I shouted.

"Silence!" She shoved the barrel harder into my neck. My heart pounded like jungle drums.

The two intruders approached us with pistols pointed toward us. "Did you find the salon?" called out a man's voice.

"Deacon Darts?" shouted Eli, squinting into the dark space between us. "What are —"

Hot Throat shouted, "Shut up! All of you just shut the fuck up! Brenda, move in on the right."

The third person ran wide to flank us. It was Brenda Shepherd hustling to take her post, assuming an attack stance. She pointed a pistol at us and said, "The salon and everything in it belongs to Bauhaus!"

"Bauhaus?" said Eli. "Deacon Darts, have you lost your mind?"

Deacon Darts stepped closer to Eli. "Bauhaus has the power. The AOD is obsolete!"

Hot Throat held the gun in the air and cocked the trigger. "Shut up! Get on your knees!"

Hot Throat stepped in front of us steadying her aim. Thalia quickly knelt. I slowly dropped to my knees and stared at her in disbelief.

"Don't get all doe-eyed. It's nothing personal. Bauhaus bankrolls the *Lodestar*. You of all people know the perks!"

Eli bent toward the ground, but in one swift motion he reached for his gun strapped under his pant leg. He drop-rolled to his stomach and fired a shot at Hot Throat that missed, but sent her stumbling backward onto her butt. Her gun slipped from her hand, landing three feet away from her. I grabbed it from the barrel end, flipped it around for a proper grip and pointed it at her.

Brenda hollered, "Stop or I'll shoot!"

Brenda misfired a shot. Thalia sprung to her feet, making a mad dash toward Brenda. She drilled Brenda with a body shot. Brenda slipped backwards and dropped the gun. Thalia scrambled to grab it.

"Stay right there," I commanded, pointing the gun at Hot Throat.

"You stupid bitch. If you had half a brain you'd join Bauhaus —"

"Shut up!" I hollered.

Eli dove to tackle Deacon Darts. The men wrestled before Eli managed to put a choke hold on him. Deacon Darts flailed his arms as Eli tightened the squeeze around his neck. Deacon Darts gagged and his body went limp.

"You murdered a druid!" Hot Throat screeched.

"He's not dead, you idiot." Eli let go and Deacon Darts slumped to the floor. "Keep them right where they are!"

Eli stepped over the body and ran outside toward the boat. Deacon Darts twitched as he regained consciousness. Eli returned with rope and duct tape. He tossed the rope toward me to tie up Hot Throat. When I put the gun in my waistband, Hot Throat swung her fist at my head. I grabbed her wrist, pulled it behind her back and tied a knot around her right wrist, wrapped the excess rope around the left and made a knot.

"You can kiss Rome goodbye," she yelled. "That deal is dead!"

Eli drove his knee into Brenda's back while he tied up her hands and ankles. Thalia duct-taped Brenda's mouth, then did the same to Hot Throat. She taped Hot Throat's ankles together, then tied up Deacon Darts.

"I radioed for backup," he said. "Just hold them right where they are."

"But won't the NYPD do an investigation? They'll probe into what we were doing."

"I called druid cops. Nobody will find out," he said.

Moments later a distant chuff-chuff-chuff sounded when a helicopter circled past Lady Liberty's head, descending toward the lawn. Three men hopped down and rushed toward us. As they closed in on us, I recognized Captain Biff so I opened the door.

"Are you injured?" he asked us.

"No!" I called back.

A second helicopter landed with more AOD police. Captain Biff ordered them to take Hot Throat, Deacon Darts and Brenda Shepherd to their precinct.

"Give me those guns. What did you find?"

"The Winter Hexagon Salon," I said. "The holy grail and the druid's *Book of Kings*. The place is loaded with American architecture artifacts."

"How big is the grail?"

"Larger than a wine glass."

"Gold or brass?"

"Wood."

"What condition?"

"Mint. A miracle when you think of its age," I said.

"Where's the salon?"

"The main entrance is in the mechanical room. The salon is underground."

Deacon Darts resisted the police escorting him to the chopper. "You've got the wrong guy! I'm a druid!"

"Pipe down! Get him out of here," commanded Captain Biff to the two officers.

"Just hold on a minute. This is all a misunderstanding," said Hot Throat. "We were helping Paige —"

"You were working against her from the start!"

"I admit I may have over-reacted..."

"Over-reacted? Was shoving McKim from the back of the truck an over-reaction? What about the attacks on Paige? Kidnapping her roommate?"

"McKim slipped on his own. Brenda Shepherd saw Paige talking to McKim. All Paige had to do was share —"

"Enough. Don't try to twist this to look like it's Paige's fault. You've been surveilling her from the start, haven't you?"

Then it hit me. That's how Bauhaus followed me. Logan, the *Lodestar* chauffeur! He informed Hot Throat about my every move. I wanted to club Hot Throat with a baseball bat. She was linked to Brenda Shepherd and all the Bauhaus attacks: getting shoved in the harbor...the ransacking of my dorm room...the coffee truck debacle. She'd used me as a pawn in her twisted Bauhaus chess match. We locked eyes but neither of us spoke. A cop escorted her to the helicopter.

When the helicopter lifted off, Eli and Thalia joined us inside the mechanical room. I showed Captain Biff the drain cover with the zodiac signs, then took him down to the Winter Hexagon Salon.

"These drawers and books are loaded with insight into early American architecture. But I want you to see the altar," I said, leading him across the checkerboard floor into the back room.

He peered into the tabernacle. "Don't touch anything. We should leave everything undisturbed for a proper AOD investigation."

Eli said, "Do you think —"

Captain Biff nodded. "It must be. It's the holy grail."

An hour later, twelve high-ranking druids arrived on Liberty Island by helicopter.

"Look at this place," said Eli, showing them the library. "It's a miracle we found it."

I side-glanced Captain Biff. "*We?*"

"Don't worry," he whispered. "The Winter Hexagon Salon is your discovery. Your accomplishment will be recognized in ways you can't even begin to imagine."

Inside the Winter Hexagon Salon twelve hooded druids gathered in a semi-circle around the altar that they draped with lambskin. St. John's mugwort incense overpowered the room with renewed energy. I sneezed.

There was a low-level buzz, a sound hovering between prayer and chanting. They lifted the cup and passed it around to each other, holding it in reverence. One druid passed a different cup of red wine, symbolizing lamb blood, and offered a druid blessing. The rest of the druids recited a prayer while the wine was passed around for each druid to drink, including me, Captain Biff, Eli and Thalia.

They passed the *Book of Kings*, taking turns reading passages. When the ceremony ended, they looked through the drawers and books.

One of the druids spoke to Captain Biff about Pilar, Deacon Darts and Brenda Shepherd. "There will be criminal charges. They will be stripped of their druid rites and barred from all domestic and druid chapters. They will pay the price for betrayal."

"Pilar was slick," said Captain Biff, shaking his head.

"We never suspected Deacon Darts," said the druid. "And as for you, Paige, you will be rewarded for your accomplishment. No one ever thought to search for the Winter Hexagon Salon under Lady Liberty. Remarkable. Utterly, remarkable."

I smiled and wondered what he and Captain Biff meant — how my find would be recognized in ways I couldn't imagine.

# *Epilogue*

The Quadsters pounded on my bedroom door.

Melissa barged in first. "You alone or is Axe humping you under the covers?"

I pulled the pillow over my head. "Go away."

"Hell no! It's Spring Fling," said Jill.

"Put on your dancing shoes," said Sheila.

"Flip flops will do. Chop-chop," said Melissa. "There are hot bagels in the kitchen. Pull yourself together."

After I showered, Melissa tossed a t-shirt to me that read *Gasoline Kisses Roadies* across the back. The front of the shirt sported Thalia's fly girl design.

"Bras are optional. Things could roll into a wet t-shirt contest during intermission," said Melissa.

"The things you think of," I mumbled.

I peeked outside my bedroom window where the frat bros were rolling in kegs of Corona Extra. A stage was set for the band with JBL tower speakers aimed straight at the dorm.

"Are you ready yet? We have to greet Gasoline Kisses," said Thalia.

"I wonder why no one ever thought of having a concert behind the dorms…"

"It's one of your best ideas to date," said Thalia.

The green space was already mobbed with Kew College students tossing Frisbees, footballs and Hacky Sacks. Someone tossed inflated beach balls out the windows to the students below.

We came across campus security in the lobby, arguing with Wheezy about capacity rules.

"But it's an outdoor event," she protested. "It's within regulation."

The head of security raised his voice. "We don't have enough manpower if this thing turns into Woodstock."

I stepped in. "How much backup do you need?"

He shot an annoyed look at me. "At least a dozen boots on the ground. And we need four more for rooftop surveillance."

"Give me a minute. Let me see what I can do."

He rolled his eyes. "Yeah, right."

I stepped outside to call Captain Biff.

He answered on the first ring. "Now what?"

"Need a favor," I said, explaining the concert situation.

"Boots on the ground?" he howled with laughter. "Tell that mall cop to pipe down. I'll send in some real officers. Manpower! Give me a break!"

Within a half hour, we had more cops than TD Garden for a Celtic playoff game. Captain Biff arrived to smooth the feathers of campus security.

I smiled at Captain Biff. "Thanks for saving the day."

"Don't mention it. Who's playing? Mick Jagger?"

"Gasoline Kisses."

"Never heard of them," he said, watching the band's dented van bounce across the parking lot. I thought I saw pot smoke plumes emitting out the windows. They backed into a parking spot that didn't exist and stumbled out of the van. Cheshire cat grins spread across their stoned faces.

"Good night, Irene!" said Captain Biff. "They can hardly walk, how are they going to play?"

"They're always like that."

Lydia smacked her tambourine like a gypsy queen while Kurt half-staggered, half-swayed behind her. I pointed them in the direction of the Goforth's coffee truck that Tanya had equipped for her last hurrah.

Tanya served them vats of coffee. She approached us and said, "They need ozone therapy in addition to the coffee. They're so stoned I don't know how they can see out the slits of their eyes."

"Don't worry, they'll rock once they get rolling."

Gasoline Kisses set up a booth to sell merch. I checked out their new cd with Thalia's fly girl splashed on the cover. I bought a cd and asked for a Sharpie at the coffee truck.

"Can you all sign this for me?" I asked.

They quickly autographed it. Jill — the self-appointed concert coordinator — whisked them toward the stage, filming their entrance. The students cheered when they plugged in.

"There's one more thing," said Captain Biff. "You're going to Rome for junior year."

"Since when?" I could barely catch my breath.

"The AOD will sponsor your year of study in Rome. It's only fair, considering Pilar made promises when she was a druid."

"That's awesome," I said, hugging him.

"We're preserving the Winter Hexagon Salon so that we can recruit the world's most promising architects. Thanks to your discovery, the AOD can learn from the early American architects. It also stopped Bauhaus from its demolition plans and spreading its wasteland. It's unbelievable how far Bauhaus was willing to go to find the salon."

"I can't wait to see future Winter Hexagon inspired buildings," I said.

"You will. But for now, send postcards," he said, flicking a half-chewed toothpick on the ground. "And call me when you need me. Anytime."

I ran off to find the Quadsters to tell them the news. Thalia was elated because we could continue with our plan to room together in Rome.

"Don't think you're escaping us," said Melissa, rolling a cooler toward us. "Every break we'll be on the red-eye."

She handed each of us a plastic cup with *holy grail* written on it with a Sharpie. Sheila poured the pre-mixed pink drink.

"Grail martinis," she said, dropping a maraschino cherry in each glass.

Gasoline Kisses started rocking, sounding better than ever. Axel draped his arm around my shoulder and pulled me in close for a kiss.

"You two lovebirds make me sick!" Melissa cackled, tossing her hair back.

I blushed. "I'm going to miss you next year."

Axel whispered, "I already spoke with Titus. He'll fly me there whenever we want. I don't want to lose you."

"That's the second-best news I heard today," I said, kissing him back.

We all clinked our grail martinis and group-hugged. "I couldn't have done it without you guys."

"Never doubted you for a second, Paigester," said Melissa, downing her martini.

Axel proposed a toast: "To Paige Moore — a woman for all seasons!"

# *Acknowledgements*

Soon after *The Eye in the Ceiling* was published in 2021, the writing of the sequel kicked into gear.

Every step of the way, my nephew **Brian Sampson** was on hand with his architectonic ideas, spreadsheets and inspiration gathered from his ongoing bike tour of the world. Naturally, pandemic restrictions set back his journey, but Brian returned to the road, tallying 42,000-plus miles throughout the United States and Canada. The camping aspect of Brian's trip turned his sights toward constellations, particularly the Winter Hexagon which became a significant detail in the sequel.

As we wrapped up the writing and editing of *The Winter Hexagon*, Brian had toured 49 states and 11 Canadian provinces as he continues his checklist from Patricia Shultz' book *1,000 Places to See Before You Die*. Implementing his specialized rating system, Lake O'Hara in Yoho National Park received the highest rating because of its mesmerizing blue lake, mountain peaks and glaciers. Follow Brian's bike tour — justfeltlikebiking.blogspot.com; Instagram @brian.sampson4.

# *Appreciation*

A heartfelt thank you to John Sampson who provided unwavering support throughout the process of writing this novel. I appreciate the reminders that nothing worthwhile is ever easy!

Troy Sampson and Sheila Sampson deserve special thanks for entertaining my *fiction head.*

A special thanks to Dan Pope, my writing sage, for professional guidance and precision diagnostics every step of the creative journey.

Great appreciation goes to brave beta readers: Professor Ted Benitt for his astronomy insights and extensive notes, as well as Robert Leader for his thorough and thoughtful response toward early drafts.

CPSIA information can be obtained
at www.ICGtesting.com
Printed in the USA
LVHW051458220123
737717LV00004B/89

9 781958 878026